A Historical Christmas Present

NEW YORK TIMES BESTSELLER
LISA KLEYPAS

"Through deft plotting and simple yet stylish prose,
Kleypas distinguishes herself as a master of her craft."
—*Publishers Weekly*

NEW YORK TIMES BESTSELLER
LYNSAY SANDS

"Lynsay Sands has just the right touch of humor to hold
you in her grasp."
—*RT BOOKreviews*

USA TODAY BESTSELLER
LEIGH GREENWOOD

"Every book is a gem and Leigh Greenwood polishes
every story until it shines! Brilliant writing and
characterization!"
—*Literary Times*

LISA KLEYPAS
LYNSAY SANDS
LEIGH GREENWOOD

A Historical Christmas Present

LOVE SPELL NEW YORK CITY

LOVE SPELL®

October 2008

Published by

Dorchester Publishing Co., Inc.
200 Madison Avenue
New York, NY 10016

ISBN 10: 0-505-52788-X
ISBN 13: 978-0-505-52788-2

Printed in the United States of America.

10 9 8 7 6 5 4 3 2 1

A Historical
Christmas Present

TABLE OF CONTENTS

I Will
    by Lisa Kleypas...1

Three French Hens
    by Lynsay Sands...107

Father Christmas
    by Leigh Greenwood....................................203

LISA KLEYPAS

I Will

CHAPTER ONE

London, 1833

It was not easy to ask a favor of a woman who despised him. But Andrew, Lord Drake, had always been beyond shame, and today was no exception. He needed a favor from a morally upright woman, and Miss Caroline Hargreaves was the only decent female he knew. She was proper and straitlaced to a fault . . . and he wasn't the only man to think so, judging by the fact that she was still unmarried at the age of twenty-six.

"Why are you here?" Caroline asked, her voice threaded with quiet hostility. She kept her gaze fastened on the large square frame propped by the settee, a wooden lace stretcher used to reshape curtains and tablecloths after they were washed. The task was a meticulous one, involving sticking a pin through each tiny loop of lace and affixing it to the edge of the frame until the cloth was drawn tight. Although Caroline's face was expressionless, her inner tension was betrayed by the stiffness of her fingers as she fumbled with a paper of pins.

"I need something from you," Andrew said, staring at her intently. It was probably the first time he had ever been completely sober around her, and now that he was free of his habitual alcoholic haze, he had noticed a few things about Miss Caroline Hargreaves that intrigued him.

She was far prettier than he had thought. Despite the little spectacles perched on her nose, and her frumpy manner of dressing, she possessed a subtle beauty that had escaped him before. Her figure was not at all spectacular—Caroline was small and slight, with practically no hips or breasts to speak of. Andrew preferred big, voluptuous women who were willing to engage in the vigorous bedroom romps he enjoyed. But Caroline had a lovely face, with velvety brown eyes and thick black lashes, surmounted by dark brows that arched with the precision of a hawk's wing. Her hair was a neatly pinned mass of sable silk, and her complexion was as fine and clear as a child's. And that mouth . . . why in God's name had he never noticed her mouth before? Delicate, expressive, the upper lip small and bow shaped, the lower curved with generous fullness.

Right now those tempting lips were pulled tight with displeasure, and her brow was furrowed in a perplexed expression. "I can't conceive of what you could possibly want from me, Lord Drake," Caroline said crisply. "However, I can assure you that you won't get it."

Andrew laughed suddenly. He threw a glance at his friend Cade—Caroline's younger brother—who had brought him to the parlor of the Hargreaves family home. Having predicted that Caroline would not be willing to help him in any way, Cade now looked both annoyed and resigned at his sister's stubbornness. "I told you," Cade murmured.

Not willing to give up so easily, Andrew returned his attention to the woman seated before him. He considered her thoughtfully, trying to decide what approach to use. No doubt she was going to make him crawl . . . not that he blamed her for that in the least.

Caroline had never made a secret of her dislike for him, and Andrew knew exactly why. For one thing, he was a bad influence on her younger brother Cade, a pleasant-natured fellow who was far too easily swayed by the opinions of his friends. Andrew had invited Cade along on far too many wild evenings of gambling, drinking, and debauchery, and returned him home in a sorry condition.

As Cade's father was dead, and his mother was a hopeless feather-wit, Caroline was the closest thing to a parent that Cade had. She tried her best to keep her twenty-four-year-old brother on the straight-and-narrow path, wanting him to assume his responsibilities as the man of the family. However, Cade naturally found it more tempting to emulate Andrew's profligate lifestyle, and the two of them had indulged in more than a few dissolute evenings.

The other reason that Caroline despised Andrew was the simple fact that they were complete opposites. She was pure. He was tarnished. She was honest. He tailored the truth to fit his own purposes. She was self-disciplined. He had never restrained himself in any regard. She was calm and serene. He had never known a moment's peace in his life. Andrew envied her, and so he had mocked her mercilessly on the few previous occasions when they had met.

Now Caroline hated him, and he had come to ask for a favor—a favor he desperately needed. Andrew found the situation so amusing that a wry smile cut through tension on his face.

Abruptly he decided to be blunt. Miss Caroline Hargreaves did not seem to be the kind of woman who would tolerate game playing and prevarication. "I'm here because my father is dying," he said.

The words caused her to accidentally prick her finger, and she jumped slightly. Her gaze lifted from the lace stretcher. "I am sorry," she murmured.

"I'm not."

Andrew saw from the widening of her eyes that she

was shocked by his coldness. He did not care. Nothing could make him feign sorrow at the passing of a man who had always been a poor excuse for a father. The earl had never given a damn about him, and Andrew had long ago given up trying to earn the love of a manipulative son of a bitch whose heart was as soft and warm as a block of granite. "The only thing I'm sorry about," Andrew continued calmly, "is that the earl has decided to disinherit me. You and he seem to share similar feelings about my sinful way of living. My father has accused me of being the most self-indulgent and debased creature he has ever encountered." A slight smile crossed his lips. "I can only hope that he is right."

Caroline seemed more than a little perturbed by his statement. "You sound proud of being such a disappointment to him," she said.

"Oh, I am," he assured her easily. "My goal was to become as great a disappointment to him as he has been to me. Not an easy task, you understand, but I proved myself equal to it. It has been the greatest success of my life."

He saw Caroline throw a troubled glance at Cade, who merely shrugged sheepishly and wandered to the window to contemplate the serene spring day outside.

The Hargreaves house was located on the west side of London. It was a pleasant Georgian-style manor house, pink-washed and framed by large beech trees, the kind of home that a solid English family should possess.

"And so," Andrew continued, "in an eleventh-hour effort to inspire me to reform, the earl has cut me out of his will."

"But surely he cannot do so entirely," Caroline said. "The titles, the property in town, and your family's country estate . . . I would have thought they were entailed."

"Yes, they are entailed." Andrew smiled bitterly. "I'll get

the titles and the property no matter what the earl does. He can't break the entailment any more than I can. But the money—the entire family fortune—that is *not* entailed. He can leave it to anyone he wishes. And so I'll likely find myself turning into one of those damned fortune-hunting aristocrats who has to marry some horse-faced heiress with a nice fat dowry."

"How terrible." Suddenly Caroline's eyes were lit with a challenging gleam. "For the heiress, I mean."

"Caro," came Cade's protesting voice.

"That's all right," Andrew said. "Any bride of mine would deserve a great deal of sympathy. I don't treat women well. I've never pretended to."

"What do you mean, you don't treat women well?" Caroline fumbled with a pin and stuck her finger again. "Are you abusive?"

"No." He scowled suddenly. "I would never physically harm a woman."

"You are merely disrespectful to them, then. And no doubt neglectful, and unreliable, and offensive and ungentlemanly." She paused and looked at him expectantly. When Andrew made no comment, she prompted with an edge to her tone, "Well?"

"Well, what?" he countered with a mocking smile. "Were you asking a question? I thought you were making a speech."

They regarded each other with narrowed eyes, and Caroline's pale complexion took on the rosy hue of anger. The atmosphere in the room changed, becoming strangely charged and hot, snapping with tension. Andrew wondered how in the hell a skinny little spinster could affect him like this. He, who had made it a lifetime's habit never to care about anything or anyone, including himself, was suddenly more troubled and aroused than he could ever recall being before. My God, he thought, *I must be one perverted bastard to desire Cade Hargreaves's sister.* But he did. His blood was pumping with heat and energy, and his nerves simmered relentlessly as he thought of the various ways he would like to put that delicate, innocent mouth to use.

It was a good thing that Cade was there. Otherwise Andrew was not certain he could have stopped himself from showing Miss Caroline Hargreaves exactly how depraved he was. In fact, standing up as he was, that fact was soon going to become all too obvious through the thin covering of his fashionably snug fawn-colored trousers. "May I have a seat?" he asked abruptly, gesturing to the chair near the settee she occupied.

Unworldly as she was, Caroline did not seem to notice his burgeoning arousal. "Please do. I can hardly wait to hear the details of this favor you intend to ask, especially in light of the charm and good manners you have displayed so far."

God, she made him want to laugh, even as he wanted to strangle her. "Thank you." He sat and leaned forward casually, bracing his forearms on his knees. "If I want to be reinstated in the earl's will, I have no choice but to indulge him," he said.

"You intend to change your ways?" Caroline asked skeptically. "To reform yourself?"

"Of course not. My cesspool of a life suits me quite well. I'm only going to *pretend* to reform until the old man meets his maker. Then I'll be on my way, with my rightful fortune intact."

"How nice for you." Distaste flickered in her dark eyes.

For some reason Andrew was stung by her reaction—he, who had never given a damn what anyone thought of him. He felt the need to justify himself to her, to explain somehow that he wasn't nearly as contemptible as he seemed. But he kept silent. He would be damned if he would try to explain anything about himself to her.

Her gaze continued to hold his. "What role am I supposed to play in your plans?"

"I need you to pretend an interest in me," he said flatly. "A romantic interest. I'm going to convince my father that I've given up drinking, gambling, and skirt chasing . . . and that I am courting a decent woman with the intention of marrying her."

Caroline shook her head, clearly startled. "You want a sham engagement?"

"It doesn't have to go that far," he replied. "All I am asking is that you allow me to escort you to a few social functions . . . share a few dances, a carriage ride or two . . . enough to start a few tongues wagging until the rumors reach my father."

She regarded him as if he belonged in Bedlam. "Why in heaven's name do you think anyone would believe such a ruse? You and I are worlds apart. I cannot conceive of a more ill-suited pair."

"It's not all that unbelievable. A woman your age . . ." Andrew hesitated, considering the most tactful way to express himself.

"You are trying to say that since I am twenty-six years old, it naturally follows that I must be desperate to marry. So desperate, in fact, that I would accept your advances no matter how repulsive I find you. That is what people will think."

"You have a sharp tongue, Miss Hargreaves," he commented softly.

She frowned at him from behind her glinting spectacles. "That is correct, Lord Drake. I am sharp-tongued, I am a bluestocking, and I have resigned myself to being an old maid. Why would anyone of good sense believe that you have a romantic interest in me?"

Well, that was a good question. Just a few minutes ago Andrew himself would have laughed at the very idea. But as he sat close to her, his knees not far from hers, the stirring of attraction ignited in a sudden burst of heat. He could smell her fragrance—warm female skin and some fresh out-of-doors scent, as if she had just walked in from the garden. Cade had confided that his sister spent a great deal of time in the garden and the hothouse, cultivating roses and experimenting with plants. Caroline seemed like a rose herself—exquisite, sweetly fragrant, more than a little prickly. Andrew could scarcely believe that he had never noticed her before.

He flashed a glance at Cade, who was shrugging to indicate that arguing with Caroline was a hopeless endeavor. "Hargreaves, leave us alone for a few minutes," he said curtly.

"Why?" Caroline asked suspiciously.

"I want to talk privately with you. Unless . . ." He gave her a taunting smile that was guaranteed to annoy. "Are you afraid to be alone with me, Miss Hargreaves?"

"Certainly not!" She threw her brother a commanding glance. "Leave, Cade, while I deal with your so-called friend."

"All right." Cade paused at the threshold of the doorway, his boyishly handsome face stamped with concern as he added, "Just give a shout if you need help."

"I will not need help," Caroline assured him firmly. "I am capable of handling Lord Drake by myself."

"I wasn't speaking to you," Cade replied ruefully. "I was speaking to Drake."

Andrew struggled to suppress a grin as he watched his friend leave the room. Returning his attention to Caroline, he moved beside her on the settee, placing their bodies into closer proximity.

"Don't sit there," she said sharply.

"Why?" He gave her a seductive look, the kind that had melted many a reluctant woman's resistance in the past. "Do I make you nervous?"

"No, I left a paper of pins there, and your backside is about to resemble a hedgehog's."

Andrew laughed suddenly, fishing for the packet until he located it beneath his left buttock. "Thanks for the warning," he said dryly. "You could have let me find out for myself."

"I was tempted," Caroline admitted.

Andrew was amazed by how pretty she was, with amusement glimmering in her brown eyes, and her cheeks still flushed pink. Her earlier question—why anyone would believe he would be interested in her—abruptly seemed ludicrous. Why would he *not* be interested in her? Vague fantasies drifted through his mind . . . he would like to lift that dainty body in his arms right now, settle her on his lap, and kiss her senseless. He wanted to reach under the skirts of her plain brown cambric gown and slide his hands over her legs. Most of all he wanted to pull down the top of her bodice and uncover her pert little breasts. He had never been so intrigued by a pair of breasts, which was odd when one considered that he had always been interested in well-endowed women.

He watched as she turned her attentions back to the wooden frame. Clearly she was distracted, for she fumbled with the pins and managed to prick her fingers yet again as she tried to fasten the lace properly. Suddenly exasperated, Andrew took the pins from her. "Allow me," he said. Expertly he stretched the lace with just the right amount of tension and secured it with a row of pins, each miniature loop fastened exactly on the edge of the frame.

Caroline did not bother to hide her amazement as she watched him. "How did you learn to do that?"

Andrew regarded the lace panel with a critical eye before setting it aside. "I grew up as the only child on a large estate, with few playmates. On rainy days I would help the housekeeper with her tasks." He gave her a self-mocking grin. "If you are impressed by my lace stretching, you should see me polish silver."

She did not return his smile, but stared at him with new curiosity. When she spoke, her tone had softened a few degrees. "No one would believe the charade you propose. I know what kind of women you pursue. I have talked with Cade, you see. And your reputation is well established. You would never take an interest in a woman like me."

"I could play the part convincingly," he said. "I've got a huge fortune at stake. For that I would court the devil himself. The question is, can you?"

"I suppose I could," she returned evenly. "You are not a bad-looking man. I suppose some might even regard you as handsome in a debauched, slovenly sort of way."

Andrew scowled at her. He was not vain, and rarely considered his own appearance other than to make certain he was clean and his clothes were decently tailored. But without conceit, he knew that he was tall and well proportioned, and that women often praised his long black hair and blue eyes. The problem was his way of life. He spent too much time indoors, too little time sleeping, and he drank too often and too long. More often that not, he woke up at midday with bloodshot, dark-circled eyes, his complexion pasty from a night of hard drinking. And he had never cared . . . until now. In comparison to the dainty creature before him, he felt like a huge, untidy mess.

"What incentive were you planning to offer me?" Caroline asked. It was clear that she would not consider his plan; she was merely interested to discover how he would have tried to entice her.

Unfortunately that was the weak aspect of his scheme. He had little to entice her with. No money, no social advantage, no possessions that would allure her. There was only one thing he had been able to come up with that might be sufficiently tempting.

"If you agree to help me," he said slowly, "I will leave your brother alone. You know what kind of influence I am on him. He is in debt up to his ears, and he is doing his best to keep pace with the pack of miscreants and degenerates I like to call friends. Before long Cade is going to end up exactly like me—rotten, cynical, and beyond all hope of redemption."

Caroline's expressive face revealed that this was exactly what she feared.

"How far in debt is he?" she asked stiffly.

He named a sum that astonished and sickened her. Reading the horror in her eyes, Andrew experienced a surge of predatory satisfaction. *Yes* . . . he had guessed correctly. She loved her younger brother enough to do anything to save him. Even pretend to fall in love with a man she despised.

"That is only the beginning," Andrew told her. "Before long Cade will be in a pit so deep that he'll never be able to climb out."

"And you would be willing to let that happen? You would simply stand by and let him ruin his life? And impoverish my mother and myself?"

Andrew responded with a casual shrug. "It is his life," he pointed out matter-of-factly. "I'm not his keeper."

"My God," she said unsteadily. "You don't care about anyone but yourself, do you?"

He kept his expression blank, and studied the scuffed, unpolished surface of his very expensive boot. "No, I don't give a damn who gets dragged down with me. But if you decide to help me, I'll take care of Cade. I'll make certain the others in our set don't invite him to their clubs or their favorite bawdy houses. I will ensure that all the list-makers I know—and believe me, that is a considerable number—will not extend him credit. He won't be allowed into any high-stakes games in London. Moreover, if I am reinstated in my father's will, I will assume all of Cade's financial obligations."

"Does Cade know about your plan?" Caroline was pale and intent as she stared at him.

"No. But it would prove his salvation."

"And if I refuse to accept your offer?"

A hard, somewhat cruel smile curved his lips. His father's smile, Andrew thought, with bitter self-awareness. "Then your brother is on the path to hell . . . right along-side me. And you will be left to pick up the pieces. I would hate to see your family's estate sold to pay off Cade's debts. Not a pleasant prospect for your mother, be-ing forced to live off the charity of relatives in her old age. Or you, for that matter." He gave her an insultingly thorough glance, his gaze lingering on her bosom. "What skills do you have that would earn enough to support a family?"

"You fiend," Caroline whispered, visibly trembling, though it was impossible to discern whether her emotion was fear or anger, or perhaps a mixture of both.

In the silence, Andrew was aware of a twisting sensa-tion somewhere in his chest, and suddenly he wanted to take it all back . . . reassure and soothe her . . . promise her that he would never allow a bit of harm to come to her family. He had a terrible feeling of tenderness that he struggled to thrust away, but it remained stubbornly lodged within him.

"What choice do I have?" Caroline asked angrily, forestalling any repentant words from him.

"Then you agree to my plan? You'll pretend to engage in a courtship with me?"

"Yes . . . I will." She sent him a simmering glare. "How long must this last? Weeks? Months?"

"Until the earl reinstates me in his will. If you and I are sufficiently convincing, it shouldn't take long."

"I don't know if I can bear it," she said, regarding him with patent loathing. "Exactly how far will this charade have to go? Words? Embraces? Kisses?" The prospect of kissing him seemed as enthralling as if she had been required to kiss a goat. "I warn you, I will not allow my reputation to be compromised, not even for Cade!"

"I haven't thought out the details yet." He kept his face unreadable, although relief shot through him in a piercing note. "I won't compromise you. All I want is the appearance of pleasant companionship."

Caroline sprang from the settee as if she had suddenly been released from the law of gravity. Agitation was evident in every line of her body. "This is intolerable," she muttered. "I cannot believe that through no fault of my own . . ." She whirled around to glare at Andrew. "When do we start? Let it be soon. I want this outrageous charade to be done with as quickly as possible."

"Your enthusiasm is gratifying," Andrew remarked, with a sudden flare of laughter in his eyes. "Let's begin in a fortnight. My half brother and his wife are giving a weekend party at their country estate. I will prevail on them to invite your family. With any luck, my father will attend as well."

"And then to all appearances, you and I will develop a sudden overwhelming attraction to each other," she said, rolling her eyes heavenward.

"Why not? Many a romantic liaison has begun that way. In the past, I've had more than a few—"

"*Please*," she interrupted fervently. "Please do not regale me with stories of your sordid affairs. I find you repulsive enough as it is."

"All right," he said agreeably. "From now on I'll leave the subjects of conversation to you. Your brother tells me that you enjoy gardening. No doubt we'll have enthralling discourses on the wonders of manure." He was satisfied to see her porcelain complexion turn mottled with fury.

"If I can manage to convince a single person that I am attracted to you," Caroline said through gritted teeth, "I vow to begin a career on the stage."

"That could be arranged," Andrew replied dryly. His half brother, Logan Scott, was the most celebrated actor of the day, as well as being the owner and manager of the Capital Theater. Although Andrew and Logan had been friends since childhood, they had only recently discovered that they were related. Logan was the by-blow of an affair the earl had conducted with a young actress long ago. Whereas Andrew had been raised in an atmosphere of luxury and privilege, Logan had grown up in a hovel, frequently starving and abused by the family that had taken him in. Andrew doubted that he would ever rid himself of the guilt of that, even though it hadn't been his fault.

Noticing that Caroline's spectacles were smudged, he approached her with a quiet murmur. "Hold still."

She froze as he reached out and plucked the steel-framed spectacles from her nose. "Wh-what are you doing? I . . . *stop*; give those back. . . ."

"In a minute," he said, using a fold of his soft linen shirt to polish the lenses until they gleamed brightly. He paused to examine them, and glanced at Caroline's face. Bereft of the spectacles, her eyes looked large and fathomless, her gaze slightly unfocused. How vulnerable she seemed. Again he experienced an odd surge of protectiveness. "How well can you see without them?" he asked, carefully replacing them on her small face.

"Not well at all," she admitted in a low voice, her composure seeming fractured. As soon as the spectacles were safely on her nose, she backed away from Andrew and sought to collect herself. "Now I suppose you are going to make some jest at my expense."

"Not at all. I like your spectacles."

"You do?" she asked with clear disbelief. "Why?"

"They make you look like a wise little owl."

Clearly she did not consider that a compliment, although Andrew meant it as one. He couldn't help imagining what she would look like wearing nothing *but* the spectacles, so prim and modest until he coaxed her into passionate abandonment, her small body writhing uncontrollably against his—

Abruptly aware that his erection was swelling again, Andrew shoved the images out of his mind. Damn, but he had never expected to be so fascinated by Hargreaves's spinster sister! He would have to make certain that she never realized it, or she would have even more contempt for him. The only way to keep her from guessing at his attraction to her was to keep her thoroughly annoyed and hostile. No problem there, he thought sardonically.

"You may leave now," Caroline said sharply. "I assume our business is concluded for the time being."

"It is," he agreed. "However, there is one last thing. Could you manage to dress with a bit more style during the weekend party? The guests—not to mention my father—would find it easier to accept my interest in you if you didn't wear something quite so . . ."

Now even the lobes of her ears were purple. "Quite so *what?*" she said in a hiss.

"Matronly."

Caroline was silent for a moment, obviously suppressing an urge to commit murder. "I will try," she finally said in a strangled voice. "And you, perhaps, might engage the services of a decent valet. Or if you already have one, replace him with someone else."

Now it was Andrew's turn to be offended. He felt a scowl twitching at the muscles of his face. "Why is that?"

"Because your hair is too long, and your boots need polish, and the way *you* dress reminds me of an unmade bed!"

"Does that mean you'd like to lie on top of me?" he asked.

He slipped around the door of the parlor and closed it just before she threw a vase.

The sound of shattering porcelain echoed through the house.

"Drake!" Cade strode toward him from the entrance hall, looking at him expectantly. "How did it go? Did you get her to agree?"

"She agreed," Andrew said.

The words caused a flashing grin to cross Cade's boyishly handsome face. "Well done! Now you'll get back in your father's good graces, and everything will go swimmingly for us, eh, old fellow? Gaming, drinking, carousing . . . oh, the times we're going to have!"

"Hargreaves, I have something to tell you," Andrew said carefully. "I don't think you're going to like it."

CHAPTER TWO

Caroline sat alone for a long time after Lord Drake left. She wondered uneasily what would become of her. Gossip would certainly abound once the news got out that she and Drake were courting. The unlikeliness of such a match would cause no end of jokes and snickers. Especially in light of the fact that she was notoriously particular in her choice of companionship.

Caroline had never been able to explain even to herself why she had never fallen in love. Certainly she was not a cold person—she had always had warm relationships with friends and relatives, and she knew herself to be a woman of very deep feeling. And she enjoyed dancing and talking and even flirting on occasion. But when she had tried to make herself feel something beyond casual liking for any one gentleman, her heart had remained stubbornly uninvolved.

"For heaven's sake, love is not a prerequisite for marriage," her mother had often exclaimed in exasperation. "You cannot *afford* to wait for love, Caro. You have neither the fortune nor the social position to be so fastidious!"

True, her father had been a viscount, but like the majority of viscounts, he did not possess a significant amount of land. A title and a small London estate were all the Hargreaves could boast of. It would have benefited the family tremendously if Caroline, the only daughter, could have married an earl or perhaps even a marquess. Unfortunately most of the available peers were either decrepit old men, or spoiled, selfish rakes such as Andrew, Lord Drake. Given such a choice, it was no wonder that Caroline had chosen to remain unwed.

Dwelling on the subject of Andrew, Caroline frowned pensively. Her reaction to him was troubling. Not only did he seem to have a remarkable ability to provoke her, but he seemed to do it intentionally, as if he delighted in stoking her temper. But somewhere in the midst of her annoyance, she had felt a strange sort of fascination for him.

It couldn't possibly be his looks. After all, she was not so shallow as to be undone by mere handsomeness. But she had found herself staring compulsively at the dark, ruined beauty of his face . . . the deep blue eyes shadowed from too little sleep, the cynical mouth . . . the slightly bloated look of a heavy drinker. Andrew possessed the face of a man who was determined to destroy himself. Oh, what terrible company he was for her brother Cade! Not to mention herself.

Her thoughts were interrupted by the arrival of her mother, Fanny, who had returned from a pleasant afternoon of visiting with friends. Strangers were often surprised to learn that the two were mother and daughter, for they did not resemble each other in any way except for their brown eyes. Caroline and Cade had inherited their late father's looks and temperament. Fanny, by contrast, was blond and plump, with the mercurial disposition of a child. It was always disconcerting to try to converse with Fanny, for she disliked serious subjects and did not choose to face unpleasant realities.

"Caro," Fanny exclaimed, coming into the parlor after

giving her frilly plumed hat and light summer wrap to the housekeeper. "You look rather displeased, dear. What has caused such a sour expression? Has our darling Cade been up to his usual pranks?"

"Our darling Cade is doing his best to ensure that you will spend your final years in a workhouse," Caroline replied dryly.

Her mother's face wrinkled in confusion. "I'm afraid I don't understand, dear. What do you mean?"

"Cade has been gambling," Caroline said. "He is going through all our money. Soon there will be nothing left. If he doesn't stop soon, we'll have to sell everything we own . . . and even *that* won't fully satisfy his debts."

"Oh, but you're teasing!" Fanny said with an anxious laugh. "Cade promised me that he would try to restrain himself at the hazard tables."

"Well, he hasn't," Caroline replied flatly. "And now we're all going to suffer for it."

Reading the truth in her daughter's eyes, Fanny sat down heavily on the pink brocade settee. In the grim silence that followed, she folded her hands in her lap like a punished child, her rosebud mouth forming an O of dismay. "It's all your fault!" she burst out suddenly.

"My fault?" Caroline gave her an incredulous stare. "Why on earth would you say that, Mother?"

"We wouldn't be in this predicament if you had married! A rich husband would have provided enough funds for Cade to indulge his little habits with his friends, and taken care of us as well. Now you've waited too long . . . your bloom has faded, and you're almost *twenty-seven*. . . ." Pausing, Fanny became a bit tearful at the thought of having an unmarried daughter of such an advanced age. Pulling a lace handkerchief from her sleeve, she dabbed delicately at her eyes. "Yes, your best years are behind you, and now the family will come to ruin. All because you refused to set your cap for a wealthy man."

Caroline opened her mouth to argue, then closed it with an exasperated sound. It was impossible to debate with someone so inured to the concept of logic. She had tried to argue with Fanny in the past, but it had served only to frustrate them both. "Mother," she said deliberately. "Mother, stop crying. I have some news that might cheer you. This afternoon I received a visit from one of Cade's friends—Lord Drake . . . do you remember him?"

"No, dear. Cade has so many acquaintances, I can never keep them all straight."

"Drake is the Earl of Rochester's only legitimate heir."

"Oh, that one." Fanny's expression brightened with interest, her tears vanishing instantly. "Yes, what a fortune he will come into! I do indeed remember him. A handsome man, I recollect, with long, dark hair and blue eyes—"

"And the manners of a swine," Caroline added.

"With an inheritance like that, Caro, one can overlook a few tiny breaches in etiquette. Do tell, what did Lord Drake say during his visit?"

"He . . ." Caroline hesitated, galled by the words she was about to say. She did not dare tell Fanny that the courtship between her and Drake would be only a charade. Her mother was a notorious gossip, and it would be only a matter of days—no, hours—before she let the truth slip to someone. "He expressed an interest in courting me," Caroline said, stone-faced. "Toward that end, you and I will allow him to escort us to a weekend party given by Mr. and Mrs. Logan Scott, to be held within a fortnight."

The news was almost too much for Fanny to digest at once. "Oh, Caro," she exclaimed. "An earl's son, interested in *you* . . . I can scarcely believe . . . Well, it's nothing less than a miracle! And if you can bring him to scratch . . . what a fortune you will have! What land, what jewels! You would certainly have your own carriage, and accounts at the finest shops. . . . Oh, this is the answer to all our problems!"

"So it would seem," Caroline said dryly. "But do not get your hopes too high, Mother. The courtship hasn't yet begun, and there is no guarantee that it will lead to marriage."

"Oh, but it will, it will!" Fanny practically danced around the room. Her blond curls fluttered and her well-rounded form jiggled with excitement. "I have a feeling in my bones. Now, Caro, you must heed my advice—I will tell you exactly how to set the hook and reel him in. You must be agreeable, and flatter his vanity, and give him admiring gazes . . . and you must never, never argue with him. And we must do something about your bosom."

"My bosom," Caroline repeated blankly.

"You will let me sew some quilted lining into the bodice of your chemise. You are a lovely girl, Caro, but you are in definite need of enhancement."

Assailed by a mixture of outrage and rueful laughter, Caro shook her head and smiled. "Quilted lining is not going to fool anyone. Especially not Lord Drake. But even if I did manage to deceive him, don't you think it would be a great disappointment on our wedding night to discover that my bosom was false?"

"By then it would be too late for him to do anything about it," her mother pointed out pragmatically. "And I would not call it a deception, Caro dear. After all, everyone must try to present herself or himself in the best light possible . . . that is what courtship is all about. The trick is to disguise all the unpleasant little faults that may put a man off, and maintain an air of mystery until you have finally landed him."

"No wonder I have never caught a husband," Caroline said with a faint smile. "I've always tried to be open and honest with men."

Her mother regarded her sadly. "I do not know where you have gotten these ideas, dear. Honesty has never fanned the flames of a man's ardor."

"I will try to remember that," Caroline replied gravely, fighting the temptation to laugh.

"The carriage is here," Fanny said with a squeal, staring out the parlor window at the vehicle moving along the front drive. "Oh, it is so fine! All that red lacquer and a Salisbury boot and crane neck, and what a fine large wrought-iron baggage rack. And no less than *four* outriders. Hurry, Caroline, do come and have a look."

"I had no idea you were so versed in the features of carriage construction, Mother," Caroline said dryly. She joined her mother at the window, and her stomach clenched with anxiety as she saw the Rochester coat of arms on the side of the carriage. It was time for the charade to begin. "Where is Cade?" she asked.

"In the library, I believe." Fanny continued to stare out the window, enthralled. "That dear, dear Lord Drake. Of all Cade's acquaintances, he has always been my favorite."

Amused despite her nervousness, Caroline laughed. "You didn't even remember who he was until I told you!"

"But then I recalled how much I liked him," Fanny countered.

Smiling wryly, Caroline wandered from the parlor to the small library, where her treasured collection of books was neatly stacked in the mahogany cases. Cade was at the sideboard, pouring a snifter of brandy from a crystal decanter.

"Are you ready to depart?" Caroline asked. "Lord Drake's carriage is here."

Cade turned with a glass in hand. His features, so like her own, were stamped with a scowl. "No, I am not ready," he said sourly. "Perhaps after I drink the rest of this bottle, I will be."

"Come, Cade," she chided. "One would think you were being sent to Newgate instead of attending a weekend party with friends."

"Drake is no friend of mine," Cade muttered. "He has seen to it that I am deprived of everything I enjoy. I'm not welcome at any hazard table in town, and I have not been invited to a single damned club for the past two weeks. I've been reduced to playing vingt-et-un for shillings. How will I ever earn enough to repay my debts?"

"Perhaps working?"

Cade snorted at what he perceived was a great insult. "No Hargreaves has occupied himself with trade or commerce for at least four generations."

"You should have thought of that before you gambled away everything Father left us. Then we wouldn't have to attend this dratted weekend party, and I would not have to pretend interest in a man I detest."

Suddenly shamefaced, Cade turned away from her. "I am sorry, Caro. But my luck was about to turn. I would have won back all the money, and more."

"Oh, Cade." She approached him and slid her arms around him, pressing her cheek against his stiff back. "Let us make the best of things," she said. "We'll go to the Scotts' estate, and I'll make calf eyes at Lord Drake, and you'll make yourself agreeable to everyone. And someday Lord Drake will be back in his father's will, and he will take care of your debts. And life will return to normal."

Suddenly they were interrupted by the housekeeper's voice. "Miss Hargreaves, Lord Drake has arrived. Shall I show him to the parlor?"

"Is my mother still in there?" Caroline asked.

"No, miss, she has gone upstairs to put on her traveling cloak and bonnet."

Wishing to avoid being alone with Drake, Caroline prodded her brother. "Cade, why don't you go welcome your friend?"

Evidently he was no more eager to see Drake than she. "No, I am going to show the footmen how I want our trunks and bags loaded on the carriage. You be the one to make small talk with him." Cade turned to glance at her, and a rueful grin spread across his face. "It is what you will be doing all weekend, sweet sister. You may as well practice now."

Giving him a damning look, Caroline left with an exasperated sigh and went to the parlor. She saw Andrew's tall form in the center of the room, his face partially concealed as he stared at a landscape that hung on the wall. "Good day, my lord," she said evenly. "I trust that you are . . ."

Her voice died away as he turned to face her. For a fraction of a second, she thought that the visitor was not Andrew, Lord Drake, but some other man. Stunned, she struggled silently to comprehend the changes that had taken place in him. The long, trailing locks of his dark hair had been cut in a new short style, cropped closely at the nape of his neck and the sides of his head. The alcoholic bloat of his face was gone, leaving behind a marvelously clean-lined jaw and hard-edged cheekbones. It seemed that he must have spent some time out-of-doors, for the paleness of his skin had been replaced by a light tan and the touch of windburn on the crests of his high cheekbones. And the eyes . . . oh, the eyes. No longer dark-circled and bloodshot, they were the clear, bright blue of sapphires. And they contained a flash of something—perhaps uncertainty?—that unraveled Caroline's composure. Andrew seemed so young, so vital, remarkably different from the man who had stood with her in this very parlor just a fortnight ago.

Then he spoke, and it became evident that although his outward appearance had changed, he was still the same insufferable rake. "Miss Hargreaves," he said evenly. "No doubt Cade has seen fit to tell you that I have upheld my part of the bargain. Now it is your turn. I hope you've been practicing your love-struck glances and flirtatious repartee."

Somehow Caroline recovered herself enough to reply. "I thought all you wanted was 'the appearance of pleasant companionship' . . . those were your exact words, were they not? I think 'love-struck' is a bit much to ask, don't you?"

"This past week I've gotten a complete accounting of Cade's debts," he returned grimly. "For what I'm going to have to pay, you owe me 'love-struck' and a damn sight more."

"You have yourself to blame for that. If you hadn't taken Cade along with you so many evenings—"

"It's not entirely my fault. But at this point I'm not inclined to quarrel. Gather your things, and let's be off."

Caroline nodded. However, she couldn't seem to make herself move. Her knees had locked, and she strongly suspected that if she took one step forward, she would fall flat on her face. She stared at him helplessly, while her heart thumped in a hard, uncontrollable rhythm, and her body flooded with heat. She had never experienced such a response to anyone in her life. Awareness of him pounded through her, and she realized how badly she wanted to touch him, draw her fingertips down the side of his lean cheek, kiss his firm, cynical mouth until it softened against hers in passion.

It can't be, she thought with a burst of panic. She could not feel such things for a man as immoral and depraved as Andrew, Lord Drake.

Something in her round-eyed gaze made him uncomfortable, for he shifted his weight from one leg to another, and shot her a baleful glance. "What are you staring at?"

"You," she said pertly. "I believe all your buttons have been fastened in the correct holes. Your hair appears to have been brushed. And for once you don't reek of spirits. I was merely reflecting on the surprising discovery that you can be made to look like a gentleman. Although it seems that your temper is as foul as ever."

"There is good reason for that," he informed her tersely. "It's been two weeks since I've had a drink or a wh—a female companion, and I've spent nearly every day at the family estate in the proximity of my father. I've visited with tenants and managers, and I've read account books until I've nearly gone blind. If I'm not fortunate enough to die of boredom soon, I'm going to shoot myself. And to top it all off, I have this damned weekend to look forward to."

"You poor man," she said pityingly. "It's terrible to be an aristocrat, isn't it?" He scowled at her, and she smiled. "You do look well, however," she said. "It appears that abstinence becomes you."

"I don't like it," he grumbled.

"That is hardly a surprise."

He stared down into her smiling face, and his expression softened. Before Caroline could react, he reached out and plucked her spectacles from her nose.

"My lord," she said, unsettled, "I wish you would stop doing that! Hand those back at once. I can't see."

Andrew extracted a folded handkerchief from his pocket and polished the lenses. "It's no wonder your eyes are weak, the way you go about with your spectacles smudged." Ignoring her protests, he polished them meticulously and held them up to the light from the window. Only when he was satisfied that they were perfectly clean did he replace them on her nose.

"I could see perfectly well," she said.

"There was a thumbprint in the middle of the right lens."

"From now on, I would appreciate it if you simply *told* me about a smudge, rather than ripping my spectacles off my face!" Caroline knew she was being ungrateful and thorny-tempered. Some part of her mind was appalled by her own bad manners. However, she had the suspicion that if she did not maintain a strategic animosity toward him, she might do something horribly embarrassing—such as throw herself against his tall, hard body and kiss him. He was so large and irascible and tempting, and the mere sight of him sent an inexplicable heat ripping through her.

She did not understand herself—she had always thought that one had to *like* a man before experiencing this dizzying swirl of attraction. But evidently her body was not reconciled with her emotions, for whether she liked him or not, she wanted him. To feel his big, warm hands on her skin. To feel his lips on her throat and breast.

A flaming blush swept all the way from her bodice to her hairline, and she knew his perceptive gaze did not miss the tide of betraying color.

Mercifully, he did not comment on it, but answered her earlier remark. "Very well," he said. "What do I care if you walk into walls or trip over paving stones when you can't see through your damn spectacles?"

It was the most peculiar carriage-ride Andrew had ever experienced. For three hours he suffered under Cade's disapproving glare—the lad regarded him as an utter Judas, and this in spite of the fact that Andrew was willing to pay all his debts in the not-too-distant future. Then there was the mother, Fanny, surely one of the most empty-headed matrons he had ever met in his life. She chattered in unending monologues and seemed never to require a reply other than the occasional grunt or nod. Every time he made the mistake of replying to one of her comments, it fueled a new round of inane babble. And then there was Caroline sitting opposite him, silent and outwardly serene as she focused on the ever-changing array of scenery outside the window.

Andrew stared at her openly, while she seemed completely oblivious to his perusal. She was wearing a blue dress with a white pelisse fastened over the top. The scooped neck of her bodice was modest, not revealing even a hint of cleavage—not that she had much cleavage to display. And yet he was unbearably stimulated by the little expanse of skin that she displayed, that exquisite hollow at the base of her throat, and the porcelain smoothness of her upper chest. She was tiny, almost doll-like, and yet he was spellbound by her, to the extent of being half-aroused despite the presence of her brother *and* mother.

"What are you looking at?" he asked after a while, irritated by her steadfast refusal to glance his way. "Find the sight of cows and hedges enthralling, do you?"

"I have to stare at the scenery," Caroline replied without moving her gaze. "The moment I try to focus on something inside the carriage, I start to feel ill, especially when the road is uneven. I've been this way since childhood."

Fanny interceded anxiously. "Caroline, you must try to cure yourself of that. How vexing it must be for a fine gentleman such as Lord Drake to have you staring constantly out the window rather than participating in our conversation."

Andrew grinned at hearing himself described as a "fine gentleman."

Cade spoke then. "She's not going to change, Mother. And I daresay that Drake would prefer Caro to stare at the scenery rather than cast her accounts all over his shoes."

"Cade, how vulgar!" Fanny exclaimed, frowning at him. "Apologize to Lord Drake at once."

"No need," Andrew said hastily.

Fanny beamed at him. "How magnanimous of you, my lord, to overlook my son's bad manners. As for my daughter's unfortunate condition, I am quite certain that it is not a defect that might be passed on to any sons or daughters."

"That is good news," Andrew said blandly. "But I rather enjoy Miss Hargreaves's charming habit. It affords me the privilege of viewing her lovely profile."

Caroline glanced at him then, quickly, rolling her eyes at the compliment before turning her attention back to the window. He saw her lips curve slightly, however, betraying her amusement at the flattery.

Eventually they arrived at the Scotts' estate, which featured a house that was reputed to be one of the most attractive residences in England. The great stone mansion was surrounded with magnificent expanses of green lawn and gardens, and an oak-filled park in the back. The row of eight stone pillars in front was topped by huge sparkling windows, making the facade of the building more glass than wall. It seemed that only royalty should live in such a place, which made it rather appropriate for the family of Logan Scott. He was royalty of a sort, albeit of the London stage.

Caroline had been fortunate enough to see Scott perform in a production at the Capital Theater, and like every other member of the audience, she had found Scott to be breathtaking in his ability and presence. It was said that his Hamlet surpassed even the legendary David Garrick's, and that people would someday read of him in history books.

"How interesting that a man like Mr. Scott is your half brother," Caroline murmured, staring at the great estate as Andrew assisted her from the carriage. "Is there much likeness between you?"

"Not a farthing's worth," Andrew said, his face expressionless. "Logan was given a damned poor start in life, and he climbed to the top of his profession armed with nothing but talent and determination. Whereas I was given every advantage, and I've accomplished nothing."

They spoke in quiet murmurs, too low to be heard by Cade and Fanny.

"Are you jealous of him?" Caroline could not help asking.

Surprise flickered across Andrew's face, and it was clear that few people ever spoke so openly to him. "No, how could I be? Logan has earned everything he's gotten. And he's tolerated a great deal from me. He's even forgiven me for the time I tried to kill him."

"What?" Caroline stumbled slightly, and stopped to look up at him in astonishment. "You didn't really, did you?"

A grin crossed his dark face. "I wouldn't have gone through with it. But I was drunk as a wheelbarrow at the time, and I had just discovered that he had known we were brothers and hadn't told me. So I cornered him in his theater, brandishing a pistol."

"My God." Caroline stared up at him uneasily. "That is the behavior of a madman."

"No, I wasn't mad. Just foxed." Amusement danced in his blue eyes. "Don't worry, sweetheart. I plan to stay sober for a while . . . and even if I weren't, I would be no danger to you."

The word *sweetheart*, spoken in that low, intimate voice, did something strange to her insides. Caroline began to reprove him for his familiarity, then realized that was their entire purpose for being here—to create the impression that they were indeed sweethearts.

They entered the two-story great hall, which was lined with dark wood paneling and rich tapestries, and were welcomed by Mr. Scott's wife, Madeline. The girl was absolutely lovely, her golden brown hair coiled atop her head, her hazel eyes sparkling as she greeted Andrew with youthful exuberance. It was clear that the two liked each other immensely.

"Lord Drake," Madeline exclaimed, clasping his hands in her own small ones, her cheek turned upward to receive his brotherly kiss. "How well you look! It has been at least a month since we've seen you. I am terribly vexed with you for remaining away so long."

Andrew smiled at his sister-in-law with a warmth that transformed his dark face, making Caroline's breath catch. "How is my niece?" he asked.

"You won't recognize her, I vow. She has grown at least two inches, and she has a tooth now!" Releasing

his hands, Madeline turned toward Cade, Fanny, and
Caroline, and curtsied gracefully. "Good morning, my
lord, and Lady Hargreaves, and Miss Hargreaves." Her
vivacious gaze locked with Caroline's. "My husband and
I are delighted that you will be joining us this weekend.
Any friends of Lord Drake's are always welcome at our
home."

"You always despise my friends," Andrew remarked
dryly, and Madeline gave him a quick frown.

"Your usual ones, yes. But friends like *these* are defi-
nitely welcome."

Caroline interceded then, smiling at Madeline. "Mrs.
Scott, I promise we will do our best to distinguish ourselves from Lord Drake's usual sort of companions."

"Thank you," came the girl's fervent reply, and they
shared a sudden laugh.

"Wait a minute," Andrew said, only half in jest. "I
didn't plan for the two of you to become friendly with
each other. You had better stay away from my sister-in-
law, Miss Hargreaves—she's an incurable gossip."

"Yes," Madeline confirmed, sending Caroline a con-
spiratorial smile. "And some of my best gossip is about
Lord Drake. You'll find it vastly entertaining."

Fanny, who had been so in awe of their grandiose surroundings as to be rendered speechless, suddenly recovered her voice. "Mrs. Scott, we are so looking forward to
meeting your esteemed husband. Such a celebrated man,
so talented, so remarkable—"

A new voice entered the conversation, a voice so deep
and distinctive that it could only belong to one man.
"Madam, you do me too much honor, I assure you."

Logan Scott had approached them from behind, as
large and handsome as he appeared on the stage, his tall

form impeccably dressed in gray trousers, a formfitting black coat, and a crisp white cravat tied in an elaborate knot.

Looking from Andrew to his half brother, Caroline could see a vague likeness between them. They were both tall, physically imposing men, with strong, even features. Their coloring was not the same, however. Andrew's hair was as black as jet, whereas Logan Scott's was fiery mahogany. And Andrew's skin had a golden cast, as opposed to Scott's ruddier hue.

Watching them stand together, Caroline reflected that the main difference between the two men was in their bearing. It was clear that Logan Scott was accustomed to the attention that his celebrity had earned—he was self-confident, a bit larger than life, his gestures relaxed and yet expansive. Andrew, however, was quieter, far more closed and private, his emotions ruthlessly buried deep below the surface.

"Brother," Logan Scott murmured, as they exchanged a hearty handshake. It was clear that there was deep affection between the two.

Andrew introduced Scott to the Hargreaves family, and Caroline was amused to see that the presence of this living legend had reduced her mother to speechlessness once more. Scott's penetrating gaze moved from one face to another, until he finally focused on Andrew. "Father is here," he said.

The brothers exchanged a look that was difficult to interpret, and it was obvious that the two shared an understanding of the man that no one else in the world did.

"How is he?" Andrew asked.

"Better today. He didn't need quite so much of his medicine during the night. At the moment he is conserving his strength for the ball tonight." Scott paused before adding. "He wanted to see you as soon as you arrived. Shall I take you to his room?"

Andrew nodded. "No doubt I have committed a hundred offenses he'll wish to upbraid me for. I should hate to deprive him of such entertainment."

"Good," Scott said sardonically. "Since I've already had to run through that particular gauntlet today, there is no reason that you should be spared."

Turning to Caroline, Andrew murmured, "Will you excuse me, Miss Hargreaves?"

"Of course." She found herself giving him a brief reassuring smile. "I hope it goes well, my lord."

As their gazes met, she saw his eyes change, the hard opaqueness softening to warm blue. "Later, then," he murmured, and bowed before leaving.

The intimacy of their shared gaze had caused warm flutters in the pit of her stomach, and a sensation of giddy lightness that floated all through her. Slightly bemused, Caroline reflected that Logan Scott was not the only man in the family with acting ability. Andrew was playing his part so convincingly that anyone would believe he had a real interest in her. She could almost believe it herself. Sternly she concentrated on the thought that it was all a pretense. Money, not courtship, was Andrew's ultimate goal.

Andrew and Logan entered the house and crossed through the marble hall, its plasterwork ceiling embellished with mythological scenes and a mask-and-ribbon motif. Approaching the grand staircase, which curved in a huge gentle spiral, the brothers made their way upward at a leisurely pace.

"Your Miss Hargreaves seems a charming girl," Logan remarked.

Andrew smiled sardonically. "She is not *my* Miss Hargreaves."

"She's a pretty sort," Logan said. "Delicate in appearance, but she seems to possess a certain liveliness of spirit."

"Spirit," Andrew repeated wryly. "Yes ... she has plenty of that."

"Interesting."

"What is interesting?" Andrew asked warily, disliking his half brother's speculative tone.

"To my knowledge, you've never courted a lady before."

"It's not a real courtship," Andrew informed him. "It's merely a ruse to fool Father."

"What?" Logan stopped on the stairs and stared at him in surprise. "Would you care to explain, Andrew?"

"As you know, I've been cut out of the will. To be reinstated I've got to convince Father that I've changed my wicked ways, or he'll die without leaving me a damned shilling." Andrew proceeded to explain his bargain with Caroline, and the terms they had struck.

Logan listened intently, finally giving a gruff laugh. "Well, if you wish to change Father's mind about his will, I suppose your involvement with a woman like Miss Hargreaves is a good idea."

"It's not an 'involvement,'" Andrew said, feeling unaccountably defensive. "As I told you, it's merely a charade."

Logan slid a speculative glance his way. "I have a suspicion, Andrew, that your relationship with Miss Hargreaves is something more than a charade, whether you are willing to admit it or not."

"It's all for Father's benefit," Andrew said swiftly. "I am telling you, Scott, I have no designs on her. And even if I did, believe me, I would be the last man on earth whom she would take an interest in."

CHAPTER THREE

"Not if he were the last man on earth," Caroline said, glaring at her brother. "I am telling you, Cade, I feel no sort of attraction whatsoever to that . . . that *libertine*. Don't be obtuse. You know quite well that it is all a pretense."

"I thought it was," Cade said reflectively, "until I watched the two of you during that deuced long carriage ride today. Now I'm not so certain. Drake stared at you like at cat after a mouse. He didn't take his eyes off you once."

Caroline sternly suppressed an unwanted twinge of pleasure at her brother's words. She turned toward the long looking glass, needlessly fluffing the short sleeves of her pale blue evening gown. "The only reason he may have glanced my way was to distract himself from Mother's babbling," she said crisply.

"And the way you smiled at him this afternoon, before he left to see his father," Cade continued. "You looked positively besotted."

"Besotted?" She let out a burst of disbelieving laughter. "Cade, that is the most ridiculous thing I've ever heard you say. Not only am I *not* besotted with Lord Drake, I can barely stand to be in the same room with him!"

"Then why the new gown and hairstyle?" he asked. "Are you certain you're not trying to attract him?"

Caroline surveyed her reflection critically. Her gown was simple but stylish, a thin white muslin underskirt overlaid with transparent blue silk. The bodice was low-cut and square, edged with a row of glinting silver bead-work. Her dark, glossy brown hair had been pulled to the crown of her head with blue ribbons, and left to hang down the back in a mass of ringlets. She knew that she had never looked better in her life. "I am wearing a new gown because I am tired of looking so matronly," she said. "Just because I am a spinster doesn't mean I have to appear a complete dowd."

"Caro," her brother said affectionately, coming up behind her and putting his hands on her upper arms, "you're a spinster only by choice. You've always been a lovely girl. The only reason you haven't landed a husband is because you haven't yet seen fit to set your cap for someone."

She turned to hug him, heedless of mussing her gown, and smiled at him warmly. "Thank you, Cade. And just to be quite clear, I have *not* set my cap for Lord Drake. As I have told you a dozen times, we are simply acting. As in a stage performance."

"All right," he said, drawing back to look at her skeptically. "But in my opinion, you are both throwing yourself into your roles with a bit more zeal than necessary."

The sounds of the ball drifted to Caroline's ears as they went down the grand staircase. The luminous, agile melody of a waltz swirled through the air, undercut by the flow of laughter and chatter as the guests moved through the circuit of rooms that branched off from the central hall. The atmosphere was heavily perfumed from huge arrangements of lilies and roses, while a garden breeze wafted gently through the rows of open windows.

Caroline's gloved fingertips slid easily over the carved marble balustrade as they descended. She gripped Cade's arm with her other hand. She was strangely nervous, wondering if her evening spent in Andrew's company would prove to be a delight or torture. Fanny chattered excitedly as she accompanied them, mentioning the names of several guests she had already seen at the estate, including peers of the realm, politicians, a celebrated artist, and a noted playwright.

As they reached the lower landing, Caroline saw Andrew waiting for them at the nadir of the staircase, his dark hair gleaming in the brilliant light shed by legions of candles. As if he sensed her approach, he turned and glanced upward. His white teeth flashed in a smile as he saw her, and Caroline's heartbeat hastened to a hard, driving rhythm.

Dressed in a formal, fashionable scheme of black and white, with a starched cravat and a formfitting gray waistcoat, Andrew was so handsome that it was almost unseemly. He was as polished and immaculate as any gentleman present, but his striking blue eyes gleamed with the devil's charm. When he looked at her like that, his gaze hot and interested, she did not feel as if this entire situation were an obligation. She did not feel as if it were a charade. The lamentable fact was, she felt excited, and glad, and thoroughly beguiled.

"Miss Hargreaves, you look ravishing," he murmured, after greeting Fanny and Cade. He offered her his arm and guided her toward the ballroom.

"Not matronly?" Caroline asked tartly.

"Not in the least." He smiled faintly. "You never did, actually. When I made that comment, I was just trying to annoy you."

"You succeeded," she said, and paused with a perplexed frown. "Why did you want to annoy me?"

"Because annoying you is safer than—" For some reason he broke off abruptly and clamped his mouth shut.

"Safer than what?" Caroline asked, intensely curious as he led her into the ballroom. "What? What?"

Ignoring her questions, Andrew swept her into a waltz so intoxicating and potent that its melody seemed to throb inside her veins. She was at best a competent dancer, but Andrew was exceptional, and there were few pleasures to equal dancing with a man who was truly accomplished at it. His arm was supportive, his hands gentle but authoritative as he guided her in smooth, sweeping circles.

Caroline was vaguely aware that people were staring at them. No doubt the crowd was amazed by the fact that the dissolute Lord Drake was waltzing with the proper Miss Hargreaves. They were an obvious mismatch . . . and yet, Caroline wondered, was it really so inconceivable that a rake and a spinster could find something alluring in each other?

"You are a wonderful dancer," she could not help exclaiming.

"Of course I am," he said. "I'm proficient at all the trivial activities in life. It's only the meaningful pursuits that present a problem."

"It doesn't have to be that way."

"Oh, it does," he assured her with a self-mocking smile.

An uncomfortable silence ensued until Caroline sought a way to break it. "Has your father come downstairs yet?" she asked. "Surely you will want him to see us dance together."

"I don't know where he is," Andrew returned. "And right now I don't give a damn if he sees us or not."

In the upper galleries that overlooked the ballroom, Logan Scott directed a pair of footmen to settle his father's fragile, tumor-ridden form onto a soft upholstered chaise longue. A maidservant settled into a nearby chair, ready to fetch anything that the earl might require. A light blanket was draped over Rochester's bony knees, and a goblet of rare Rhenish wine was placed in his claw-like fingers.

Logan watched the man for a moment, inwardly amazed that Rochester, a figure who had loomed over his entire life with such power and malevolence, should have come to this. The once-handsome face, with its hawklike perfection, had shrunk to a mask of skeletal paleness and delicacy. The vigorous, muscular body had deteriorated until he could barely walk without assistance. One might have thought that the imminent approach of death would have softened the cruel earl, and perhaps taught him some regret over the past. But Rochester, true to form, admitted to no shred of remorse.

Not for the first time, Logan felt an acute stab of sympathy for his half brother. Though Logan had been raised by a tenant farmer who had abused him physically, he had fared better than Andrew, whose father had abused his very soul. Surely no man in existence was colder and more unloving than the Earl of Rochester. It was a wonder that Andrew had survived such a childhood.

Tearing his thoughts away from the past, Logan glanced at the assemblage below. His gaze located the tall form of his brother, who was dancing with Miss Caroline Hargreaves. The petite woman seemed to have bewitched Andrew, who for once did not seem bored, bitter, or sullen. In fact, for the first time in his life, it appeared that Andrew was exactly where he wanted to be.

"There," Logan said, easily adjusting the heavy weight of the chaise longue so that his father could see better. "That is the woman Andrew brought here."

Rochester's mouth compressed into a parchment-thin line of disdain. "A girl of no consequence," he pronounced. "Her looks are adequate, I suppose. However, they say she is a bluestocking. Do not presume to tell me that your brother would have designs on such a creature."

Logan smiled slightly, long accustomed to the elderly man's caustic tongue. "Watch them together," he murmured. "See how he is with her."

"It's a ruse," Rochester said flatly. "I know all about my worthless son and his scheming ways. I could have predicted this from the moment I removed his name from the will. He seeks to deceive me into believing that he can change his ways." He let out a sour cackle. "Andrew can court a multitude of respectable spinsters if he wishes. But I will go to hell before I reinstate him."

Logan forbore to reply that such a scenario was quite likely, and bent to wedge a velvet-covered pillow behind the old man's frail back. Satisfied that his father had a comfortable place from which to view the activities down below, he stood and rested a hand on the carved mahogany railing. "Even if it were a ruse," he mused aloud, "wouldn't it be interesting if Andrew were caught in a snare of his own making?"

"What did you say?" The old man stared at him with rheumy, slitted eyes, and raised a goblet of wine to his lips. "What manner of snare is that, pray tell?"

"I mean it is possible that Andrew could fall in love with Miss Hargreaves."

The earl sneered into his cup. "It's not in him to love anyone other than himself."

"You're wrong, Father," Logan said quietly. "It's only that Andrew has had little acquaintance with that emotion—particularly to be on the receiving end of it."

Understanding the subtle criticism of the cold manner in which he had always treated his sons, the legitimate one and the bastard, Rochester gave him a disdainful smile. "You lay the blame for his selfishness at *my* door, of course. You've always made excuses for him. Take care, my superior fellow, or I will cut *you* out of my will as well."

To Rochester's obvious annoyance, Logan burst out laughing. "I don't give a damn," he said. "I don't need a shilling from you. But have a care when you speak about Andrew. He is the only reason you're here. For some reason that I'll never be able to comprehend, Andrew loves you. A miracle, that you could have produced a son who managed to survive your tender mercies and still have the capability to love. I freely admit that I would not."

"You are fond of making me out to be a monster," the earl remarked frostily. "When the truth is, I only give people what they deserve. If Andrew had ever done anything to merit my love, I would have accorded it to him. But he will have to earn it first."

"Good God, man, you're nearly on your deathbed," Logan muttered. "Don't you think you've waited long enough? Do you have any damned idea of what Andrew would do for one word of praise or affection from you?"

Rochester did not reply, his face stubbornly set as he drank from his goblet and watched the glittering, whirling mass of couples below.

The rule was that a gentleman should never dance more than three times with any one girl at a ball. Caroline did not know why such a rule had been invented, and she had never resented it as she did now. To her astonishment, she discovered that she liked dancing with Andrew, Lord Drake, and she was more than a little sorry when the waltz was over. She was further surprised to learn that Andrew could be an agreeable companion when he chose.

"I wouldn't have suspected you to be so well-informed on so many subjects," she told him, while servants filled their plates at the refreshment tables. "I assumed you

had spent most of your time drinking, and yet you are remarkably well-read."

"I can drink and hold a book at the same time," he
said.

She frowned at him. "Don't make light of it, when I
am trying to express that . . . you are not . . ."

"I am not what?" he prompted softly.

"You are not exactly what you seem."

He gave her a slightly crooked grin. "Is that a compliment, Miss Hargreaves?"

She was slightly dazed as she stared into the warm blue
intensity of his eyes. "I suppose it must be."

A woman's voice intruded on the moment, cutting
through the spell of intimacy with the exquisite precision
of a surgeon's blade. "Why, Cousin Caroline," the woman
exclaimed, "I am *astonished* to see how stylish you look. It is
a great pity that you cannot rid yourself of the spectacles,
dear, and then you would be the toast of the ball."

The speaker was Julianne, Lady Brenton, the most
beautiful and treacherous woman that Caroline had ever
known. Even the people who despised her—and there
were no end of those—had to concede that she was physically flawless. Julianne was slender, of medium height,
with perfectly curved hips and a lavishly endowed bosom.
Her features were positively angelic, her nose small and
narrow, her lips naturally hued a deep pink, her eyes blue
and heavily lashed. Crowning all of this perfection was a
heavy swirl of blond hair in a silvery shade that seemed to
have been distilled from moonlight. It was difficult, if not
impossible, to believe that Caroline and this radiant creature could be related in any way, and yet they were first
cousins on her father's side.

Caroline had grown up in awe of Julianne, who was
only a year older than herself. In adulthood, however, ad-

miration had gradually turned to disenchantment as she realized that her cousin's outward beauty concealed a heart that was monstrously selfish and calculating. When she was seventeen, Julianne had married a man forty years older than herself, a wealthy earl with a penchant for collecting fine objects. There had been frequent rumors that Julianne was unfaithful to her elderly spouse, but she was far too clever to have been caught. Three years ago her husband died in his bed, ostensibly of a weak heart. There were whispered suspicions that his death was not of natural causes, but no proof was ever discovered.

Julianne's blue eyes sparkled wickedly as she stood before Caroline. Her immaculate blondness was complemented by a shimmering white gown that draped so low in front that the upper halves of her breasts were exposed.

Sliding a flirtatious glance at Andrew, Julianne remarked, "My poor little cousin is quite blind without her spectacles . . . a pity, is it not?"

"She is lovely with or without them," Andrew replied coldly. "And Miss Hargreaves's considerable beauty is matched by her interior qualities. It is unfortunate that one cannot say the same of other women."

Julianne's entrancing smile dimmed, and she and Andrew regarded each other with cool challenge. Unspoken messages were exchanged between them. Caroline's pleasure in the evening evaporated as a few things became instantly clear. It was obvious that Julianne and Andrew were well acquainted. There seemed to be some remnant of intimacy, of sexual knowledge between them, that could have resulted only from a past affair.

Of course they had once been lovers, Caroline thought resentfully. Andrew would surely have been intrigued by a woman of such sensuous beauty . . . and there was no doubt that Julianne would have been more than willing to grant her favors to a man who was the heir to a great fortune.

"Lord Drake," Julianne said lightly, "you are more handsome than ever . . . why, you seem quite reinvigorated. To whom do we owe our gratitude for such a pleasing transformation?"

"My father," Andrew replied bluntly, with a smile that didn't reach his eyes. "He cut me out of his will—indeed a transforming experience."

"Yes, I had heard about that." Julianne's bow-shaped lips pursed in a little moue of disappointment. "Your inheritance was one of your most agreeable attributes, dear. A pity that you've lost it." She shot Caroline a snide smile before adding, "Clearly your prospects have dwindled considerably."

"Don't let us keep you, Julianne," Caroline said. "No doubt you have much to accomplish tonight, with so many wealthy men present."

Julianne's blue eyes narrowed at the veiled insult. "Very well. Good evening, Cousin Caroline. And pray do show Lord Drake more of your 'interior beauty'—it may be your only chance of retaining his attention." A catlike smile spread across her face as she murmured, "If you can manage to lure Drake to your bed, cousin, you will find him a most exciting and talented partner. I can give you my personal assurance on that point." Julianne departed with a luscious swaying of her hips that caused her skirts to swish silkily.

Scores of male gazes followed her movement across the room, but Andrew's was not one of them. Instead he focused on Caroline, who met his scowling gaze with an accusing glare. "Despite my cousin's subtlety and discretion,"

Caroline said coolly, "I managed to receive the impression that you and she were once lovers. Is that true?"

Until Lady Brenton's interruption, Andrew had actually been enjoying himself. He had always disliked attending balls and soirees, at which one was expected to make dull conversation with matrimonially minded girls and their even duller chaperones. But Caroline Hargreaves, with her quick wit and spirit, was surprisingly entertaining. For the last half hour he had felt a peculiar sense of well-being, a glow that had nothing to do with alcohol.

Then Julianne had appeared, reminding him of all his past debauchery, and the fragile sensation of happiness had abruptly vanished. Andrew had always tried to emulate his father in having no regrets over the past . . . but there it was, the unmistakable stab of rue, of embarrassment, over the affair with Julianne. And the hell of it was, the liaison hadn't even been worth the trouble. Julianne was like those elaborate French desserts that never tasted as good as they looked, and certainly never satisfied the palate.

Andrew forced himself to return Caroline's gaze as he answered her question. "It is true," he said gruffly. "We had an affair two years ago . . . brief and not worth remembering."

He resented the way Caroline stared at him, as if she were so flawless that she had never done anything worthy of regret. Damn her, he had never lied to her, or pretended to be anything other than what he was. She knew he was a scoundrel, a villain . . . for God's sake, he'd nearly resorted to blackmail to get her to attend the weekend party in the first place.

Grimly he wondered why the hell Logan and Madeline

had invited Julianne here in the first place. Well, he couldn't object to her presence here merely because he'd once had an affair with her. If he tried to get her booted off the estate for that reason, there were at least half a dozen other women present who would have to be thrown out on the same grounds.

As if she had followed the turn of his thoughts, Caroline scowled at him. "I am not surprised that you've slept with my cousin," she said. "No doubt you've slept with at least half the women here."

"What if I have? What difference does it make to you?"

"No difference at all. It only serves to confirm my low opinion of you. How inconvenient it must be to have all the self-control of a March hare."

"It's better than being an ice maiden," he said with a sneer.

Her brown eyes widened behind the spectacles, and a flush spread over her face. "What? What did you call me?"

The edge in her tone alerted a couple nearby to the fact that a quarrel was brewing, and Andrew became aware that they were the focus of a few speculative stares. "Outside," he ground out. "We'll continue this in the rose garden."

"By all means," Caroline agreed in a vengeful tone, struggling to keep her face impassive.

Ten minutes later they had each managed to slip outside.

The rose garden, referred to by Madeline Scott as her "rose room," was a southwest section of the garden delineated by posts and rope swags covered with climbing roses. White gravel covered the ground, and fragrant lavender hedges led to the arch at the entrance. There was a massive stone urn on a pedestal in the center of the rose room, surrounded by a velvety blue bed of catmint.

The exotic perfumed air did nothing to soothe Andrew's frustration. As he saw Caroline's slight figure enter the rustling garden, he could barely restrain himself from pouncing on her. He kept still and silent instead, his jaw set as he watched her approach.

She stopped within arm's length of him, her head tilted back so that she could meet his gaze directly. "I have only one thing to say, my lord." Agitation pulled her voice taut and high. "Unlike you, I have a high regard for the truth. And while I would never take exception to an honest remark, no matter how unflattering, I *do* resent what you said back there. Because it is not true! You are categorically wrong, and I will not go back inside that house until you admit it!"

"Wrong about what?" he asked. "That you're an ice maiden?"

For some reason the term had incensed her. He saw her chin quiver with indignation. "Yes, that," she said in a hiss.

He gave her a smile designed to heighten her fury. "I can prove it," he said in a matter-of-fact tone. "What is your age . . . twenty-six?"

"Yes."

"And despite the fact that you're far prettier than average, and you possess good blood and a respected family name, you've never accepted a proposal of marriage from any man."

"Correct," she said, looking briefly bemused at the compliment.

He paced around her, giving her an insultingly thorough inspection. "And you're a virgin . . . aren't you?"

It was obvious that the question affronted her. He could easily read the outrage in her expression, and her blush was evident even in the starlit darkness. No proper young woman should even think of answering such an inquiry. After a long, silent struggle, she gave a brief nod.

That small confirmation did something to his insides, made them tighten and throb with savage frustration. *Damn* her, he had never found a virgin desirable before. And yet he wanted her with volcanic intensity . . . he wanted to possess and kiss every inch of her innocent body . . . he wanted to make her cry and moan for him. He wanted the lazy minutes afterward when they would lie together, sweaty and peaceful in the aftermath of passion. The right to touch her intimately, however and whenever he wanted, seemed worth any price. And yet he would never have her. He had relinquished any chance of that long ago, before they had ever met. Perhaps if he had led his life in a completely different manner . . . But he could not escape the consequences of his past.

Covering his yearning with a mocking smile, Andrew gestured with his hands to indicate that the facts spoke for themselves. "Pretty, unmarried, twenty-six, and a virgin. That leads to only one conclusion . . . ice maiden."

"I am *not!* I have far more passion, more honest feeling, than you'll ever possess!" Her eyes narrowed as she saw his amusement. "Don't you dare laugh at me!" She launched herself at him, her hands raised as if to attack.

With a smothered laugh, Andrew grabbed her upper arms and held her at bay . . . until he realized that she was not trying to claw his face, but rather to put her hands around his neck. Startled, he loosened his hold, and she immediately seized his nape. She exerted as much pressure as she was able, using her full weight to try to pull his head down. He resisted her easily, staring into her small face with a baffled smile. He was so much larger than she that any attempt on her part to physically coerce him was laughable. "Caroline," he said, his voice unsteady with equal parts of amusement and desire, "are you by chance trying to *kiss* me?"

She continued to tug at him furiously, wrathful and determined. She was saying something beneath her breath, spitting like an irate kitten. ". . . show you . . . make you sorry . . . I am *not* made of ice, you arrogant, presumptuous *libertine* . . ."

Andrew could not stand it any longer. As he viewed the tiny, indignant female in his arms, he lost the capability of rational thought. All he could think of was how much he desired her, and how a few stolen moments in the rose garden would not matter in the great scheme of things. He was nearly mad with the need to taste her, to touch her, to drag her body full-length against his, and the rest of the world could go to hell. And so he let it happen. He relaxed his neck and lowered his head, and let her tug his mouth down to hers.

Something unexpected happened with that first sweet pressure of her lips—innocently closed lips because she did not know how to kiss properly. He felt a terrible aching pressure around his heart, squeezing and clenching until he felt the hard wall around it crack, and heat came rushing inside. She was so light and soft in his arms, the smell of her skin a hundred times more alluring than roses, the fragile line of her spine arching as she tried to press closer to him. The sensation came too hard, too fast, and he froze in sudden paralysis, not knowing where to put his hands, afraid that if he moved at all, he would crush her.

He fumbled with his gloves, ripped them off, and dropped them to the ground. Carefully he touched Caroline's back and slid his palm to her waist. His other hand shook as he gently grasped the nape of her neck. Oh, God, she was exquisite, a bundle of muslin and silk in his hands, too luscious to be real. His breath rushed from his lungs in hard bursts, and he fought to keep his movements gentle as he urged her closer against his fiercely aroused body. Increasing the pressure of the kiss, he coaxed her lips to part, touched his tongue to hers, found the intoxicating taste of her. She started slightly at the unfamiliar intimacy. He knew it was wrong to kiss a virgin that way, but he couldn't help himself. A soothing sound came from deep in his throat, and he licked deeper, searching the sweet, dark heat of her mouth. To his astonishment, Caroline moaned and relaxed in his arms, her lips parting, her tongue sliding hotly against his.

Andrew had not expected her to be so ardent, so receptive. She should have been repelled by him. But she yielded herself with a terrible trust that devastated him. He couldn't stop his hands from wandering over her hungrily, reaching over the curves of her buttocks to hitch her higher against his body. He pulled her upward, nestling her closer into the huge ridge of his sex until she fit exactly the way he wanted. The thin layers of her clothes—and his—did nothing to muffle the sensation. She gasped and wriggled deliciously, and tightened her arms around his neck until her toes nearly left the ground.

"Caroline," he said hoarsely, his mouth stealing down the tender line of her throat, "you're making me insane. We have to stop now. I shouldn't be doing this—"

"Yes. Yes." Her breath puffed in rapid, hot expulsions, and she twined herself around him, rubbing herself against the rock-hard protrusion of his loins. They kissed again, her mouth clinging to his with frantic sweetness, and Andrew made a quiet, despairing sound.

"Stop me," he muttered, clamping his hand over her

writhing bottom. "Tell me to let go of you. . . . Slap me. . . ."

She tilted her head back, purring like a kitten as he nuzzled the soft space beneath her ear. "Where should I slap you?" she asked throatily.

She was too innocent to fully comprehend the sexual connotations of her question. Even so, Andrew felt himself turn impossibly hard, and he suppressed a low groan of desire. "Caroline," he whispered harshly, "you win. I was wrong when I called you a . . . No, don't do that anymore; I can't bear it. You win." He eased her away from his aching body. "Now stay back," he added curtly, "or you're going to lose your virginity in this damned garden."

Recognizing the vehemence in his tone, Caroline prudently kept a few feet of distance between them. She wrapped her slender arms around herself, trembling. For a while there was no sound other than their labored breathing.

"We should go back," she finally said. "People will notice that we're both absent. I . . . I have no wish to be compromised . . . that is, my reputation . . ." Her voice trailed into an awkward silence, and she risked a glance at him. "Andrew," she confessed shakily, "I've never felt this way bef—"

"Don't say it," he interrupted. "For your sake, and mine, we are not going to let this happen again. We are going to keep to our bargain—I don't want complications."

"But don't you want to—"

"No," he said tersely. "I want only the pretense of a relationship with you, nothing more. If I truly became involved with you, I would have to transform my life completely. And it's too bloody late for that. I am beyond redemption, and no one, not even you, is worth changing my ways for."

She was quiet for a long moment, her dazed eyes focused on his set face. "I know someone who *is* worth it," she finally said.

"Who?"

"You." Her stare was direct and guileless. "You are worth saving, Andrew."

With just a few words, she demolished him. Andrew shook his head, unable to speak. He wanted to seize her in his arms again . . . worship her . . . ravish her. No woman had ever expressed the slightest hint of faith in him, in his worthless soul, and though he wanted to respond with utter scorn, he could not. One impossible wish consumed him in a great purifying blaze—that somehow he could become worthy of her. He yearned to tell her how he felt. Instead he averted his face and managed a few rasping words. "You go inside first."

For the rest of the weekend party, and for the next three months, Andrew was a perfect gentleman. He was attentive, thoughtful, and good-humored, prompting jokes from all who knew him that somehow the wicked Lord Drake had been abducted and replaced by an identical stranger. Those who were aware of the Earl of Rochester's poor health surmised that Andrew was making an effort to court his father's favor before the old man died and left him bereft of the family fortune. It was a transparent effort, the gossips snickered, and very much in character for the devious Lord Drake.

The strange thing was, the longer that Andrew's pretend reformation lasted, the more it seemed to Caroline that he was changing in reality. He met with the Rochester estate agents and developed a plan to improve the land in ways that would help the tenants immeasurably. Then to the perplexity of all who knew him, Andrew sold much of his personal property, including a prize string of thoroughbreds, in order to finance the improvements.

It was not in character for Andrew to take such a risk, especially when there was no guarantee that he would inherit the Rochester fortune. But when Caroline asked him why he seemed determined to help the Rochester tenants, he laughed and shrugged as if it were a matter of no consequence. "The changes would have to be made whether or not I get the earl's money," he said. "And I was tired of maintaining all those damned horses—too expensive by half."

"Then what about your properties in town?" Caroline asked. "I've heard that your father planned to evict some poor tenants from a slum in Whitefriars rather than repair it—and you are letting them stay, and are renovating the entire building besides."

Andrew's face was carefully expressionless as he replied. "Unlike my father, I have no desire to be known as a slum lord. But don't mistake my motives as altruistic—it is merely a business decision. Any money I spend on the property will increase its value."

Caroline smiled at him and leaned close as if to confide a secret. "I think, my lord, that you actually care about those people."

"I'm practically a saint," he agreed sardonically, with a derisive arch of his brow.

She continued to smile, however, realizing that Andrew was not nearly as blackhearted as he pretended to be.

Just why Andrew should have begun to care about the people whose existence he had never bothered to notice before was a mystery. Perhaps it had something to do with his father's imminent demise . . . perhaps it had finally dawned on Andrew that the weight of responsibility would soon be transferred to his own shoulders. But he could easily have let things go on just as they were, allowing his father's managers and estate agents to make the decisions. Instead he took the reins in his own hands, tentatively at first, then with increasing confidence.

In accordance with their bargain, Andrew took Caroline riding in the park, and escorted her to musical evenings and soirees and the theater. Since Fanny was required to act as chaperon, there were few occasions for Caroline to talk privately with Andrew. They were forced instead to discuss seemly subjects such as literature or gardening, and their physical contact was limited to the occasional brush of their fingertips, or the pressure of his shoulder against hers as they sat next to each other. And yet these fleeting moments of closeness—a wordless stare, a stolen caress of her arm or hand—were impossibly exciting.

Caroline's awareness of Andrew was so excruciating that she sometimes thought she would burst into flames. She could not stop thinking about their impassioned embrace in the Scotts' rose garden, the pleasure of Andrew's mouth on hers. But he was so unrelentingly courteous now that she began to wonder if the episode had perhaps been some torrid dream conjured by her own fevered imagination.

Andrew, Lord Drake, was a fascinating puzzle. It seemed to Caroline that he was two different men—the arrogant, self-indulgent libertine, and the attractive stranger who was stumbling uncertainly on his way to becoming a gentleman. The first man had not appealed to her in the least. The second one . . . well, he was a far different matter. She saw that he was struggling, torn between the easy pleasures of the past and the duties that loomed before him. He still had not resumed his drinking and skirt chasing—he would have admitted it to her freely if he had. And according to Cade, Andrew seldom visited their club these days. Instead he spent his time fencing, boxing, or riding until he nearly dropped from exhaustion. He lost weight, perhaps a stone, until his trousers hung unfashionably loose and had to be altered. Although Andrew had always been a well-formed man, his body was now lean and impossibly hard, the muscles of his arms and back straining the seams of his coat.

"Why do you keep so active?" Caroline could not resist asking one day, as she pruned a lush bed of purple penstemons in her garden. Andrew lounged nearby on a small bench as he watched her carefully snip the dried heads of each stem. "My brother says that you were at the Pugilistic Club almost every day last week."

When Andrew took too long in answering, Caroline paused in her gardening and glanced over her shoulder. It was a cool November day, and a breeze caught a lock of her sable hair that had escaped her bonnet, and blew it across her cheek. She used her gloved hand to push away the errant lock, inadvertently smudging her face with dirt. Her heart lurched in sudden anticipation as she saw the expression in Andrew's searching blue eyes.

"Keeping active serves to distract me from . . . things." Andrew stood and came to her slowly, pulling a handkerchief from his pocket. "Here, hold still." He gently wiped away the dirt streak, then reached for her spectacles to clean them in a gesture that had become habitual.

Deprived of the corrective lenses, Caroline stared up at his dark, blurred face with myopic attentiveness. "What things?" she asked, breathless at his nearness. "I presume that you must mean your drinking and gaming. . . ."

"No, it's not that." He replaced her spectacles with great care, and used a fingertip to stroke the silky tendril of hair behind her ear. "Can't you guess what is bothering me?" he asked softly. "What keeps me awake unless I exhaust myself before going to bed each night?"

He stood very close, his gaze holding hers intimately. Even though he was not touching her, Caroline felt surrounded by his virile presence. The shears dropped from her suddenly nerveless fingers, falling to the earth with a soft thud. "Oh, I . . ." She paused to moisten her dry lips. "I suppose you miss h-having a woman. But there is no reason that you could not . . . that is, with so many who would be willing . . ." Flushing, she caught her bottom lip with her teeth and floundered into silence.

"I've become too damned particular." He leaned closer, and his breath fell gently against her ear, sending a pleasurable thrill down her spine. "Caroline, look at me. There is something I have no right to ask . . . but . . ."

"Yes?" she whispered.

"I've been considering my situation," he said carefully. "Caroline . . . even if my father doesn't leave me a shilling, I could manage to provide a comfortable existence for someone. I have a few investments, as well as the estate. It wouldn't be a grand mode of living, but . . ."

"Yes?" Caroline managed to say, her heart hammering madly in her chest. "Go on."

"You see—"

"Caroline!" came her mother's shrill voice from the French doors that opened onto the garden from the parlor. "Caroline, I insist that you come inside and act as a proper hostess, rather than make poor Lord Drake stand outside and watch you dig holes in the dirt! I suspect you have offered him no manner of refreshment, and . . . Why, this wind is intolerable, you will cause him to catch his death of cold. Come in at once, I bid you both!"

"Yes, Mother," Caroline said grimly, filled with frustration. She glanced at Andrew, who had lost his serious intensity, and was regarding her with a sudden smile. "Before we go inside," she suggested, "you may finish what you were going to say—"

"Later," he said, bending to retrieve her fallen shears.

Her fists clenched, and she nearly stamped her foot in annoyance. She wanted to strangle her mother for breaking into what was undoubtedly the most supremely interesting moment of her life. What if Andrew had been trying to propose? Her heart turned over at the thought. Would she have decided to accept such a risk . . . would she be able to trust that he would remain the way he was now, instead of changing back into the rake he had always been?

Yes, she thought in a rush of giddy wonder. *Yes, I would take that chance.*

Because she had fallen in love with him, imperfect as he was. She loved every handsome, tarnished inch of him, inside and out. She wanted to help him in his quest to become a better man. And if a little bit of the scoundrel remained . . . An irresistible smile tugged at her lips. Well, she would enjoy that part of him too.

A fortnight later, at the beginning of December, Caroline received word that the Earl of Rochester was on his deathbed. The brief message from Andrew also included a surprising request. The earl wanted to see her, for reasons that he would explain to no one, not even Andrew. *I humbly ask for your indulgence in this matter*, Andrew had written, *as your presence may bring the earl some peace in his last hours. My carriage will convey you to the estate if you wish to come . . . and if you do not, I understand and respect your decision. Your servant.*

And he had signed his name *Andrew*, with a familiarity that was improper and yet touching, bespeaking his distracted turn of mind. Or perhaps it betrayed his feelings for her.

"Miss Hargreaves?" the liveried footman murmured, evidently having been informed of the possibility that she might return with them. "Shall we convey you to the Rochester estate?"

"Yes," Caroline said instantly. "I will need but a few minutes to be ready. I will bring a maidservant with me."

"Yes, miss."

Caroline was consumed with thoughts of Andrew as the carriage traveled to Rochester Hall in Buckinghamshire, where the earl had chosen to spend his last days. Although Caroline had never seen the place, Andrew had described it to her. The Rochesters owned fifteen hundred acres, including the local village, the woods surrounding it, and some of the most fertile farmland in England. It had been granted to the family by Henry II in the twelfth century, Andrew had said, and he had gone on to make a sarcastic comment about the fact that the family's proud and ancient heritage would soon pass to a complete reprobate. Caroline understood that Andrew did not feel at all worthy of the title and the responsibilities that he would inherit. She felt an aching need to comfort him, to somehow find a way to convince him that he was a much better man than he believed himself to be.

With her thoughts in turmoil, Caroline kept her gaze focused on the scenery outside the window, the land covered with woods and vineyards, the villages filled with cottages made of flint garnered from the Chiltern hills. Finally they came to the massive structure of Rochester Hall, constructed of honey yellow ironstone and gray sandstone, hewn with stalwart medieval masonry. A gate centered in the entrance gave the carriage access to an open courtyard.

Caroline was escorted by a footman to the central great hall, which was large, drafty, and ornamented with dull-colored tapestries. Rochester Hall had once been a fortress, its roof studded with parapets and crenellation, the windows long and narrow to allow archers to defend the building. Now it was merely a cold, vast home that seemed badly in need of a woman's hand to soften the place and make it more comfortable.

"Miss Hargreaves." Andrew's deep voice echoed against the polished sandstone walls as he approached her.

She felt a thrill of gladness as he came to her and took her hands. The heat of his fingers penetrated the barrier of her gloves as he held her hands in a secure clasp. "Caro," he said softly, and nodded to the footman to leave them.

She stared up at him with a searching gaze. His emotions were held in tight rein . . . it was impossible to read the thoughts behind the expressionless mask of his face. But somehow she sensed his hidden anguish, and she longed to put her arms around him and comfort him.

"How was the carriage ride?" he asked, still retaining her hands. "I hope it didn't make you too uncomfortable."

Caroline smiled slightly, realizing that he had remembered how the motion of a long carriage ride made her sick. "No, I was perfectly fine. I stared out the window the entire way."

"Thank you for coming," he muttered. "I wouldn't have blamed you if you had refused. God knows why Rochester asked for you—it's because of some whim that he won't explain—"

"I am glad to be here," she interrupted gently. "Not for his sake, but for yours. To be here as your friend, as your . . ." Her voice trailed away as she fumbled for an appropriate word.

Her consternation elicited a brief smile from Andrew, and his blue eyes were suddenly tender. "Darling little friend," he whispered, bringing her gloved hand to his mouth.

Emotion welled up inside her, a singular deep joy that seemed to fill her chest and throat with sweet warmth. The happiness of being needed by him, welcomed by him, was almost too much to be borne.

Caroline glanced at the heavy oak staircase that led to the second floor, its openwork balustrade casting long, jagged shadows across the great hall. What a cavernous, sterile place for a little boy to grow up in, she thought. Andrew had told her that his mother had died a few weeks after giving birth to him. He had spent his childhood here, at the mercy of a father whose heart was as warm and soft as a glacier. "Shall we go up to him?" she asked, referring to the earl.

"In a minute," Andrew replied. "Logan and his wife are with him now. The doctor says it is only a matter of hours before he—" He stopped, his throat seeming to close, and he gave her a look that was filled with baffled fury, most of it directed at himself. "My God, all the times that I've wished him dead. But now I feel . . ."

"Regret?" Caroline suggested softly, removing her glove and laying her fingers against the hard, smooth-shaven line of his cheek. The muscles of his jaw worked tensely against the delicate palm of her hand. "And perhaps sorrow," she said, "for all that could have been, and for all the disappointment you caused each other."

He could not bring himself to reply, only gave a short nod.

"And maybe just a little fear?" she asked, daring to caress his cheek softly. "Because soon *you* will be Lord Rochester . . . something you've hated and dreaded all your life."

Andrew began to breathe in deep surges, his eyes locked with hers as if his very survival depended on it. "If only I could stop it from happening," he said hoarsely.

"You are a better man than your father," she whispered. "You will take care of the people who depend on you. There is nothing to fear. I know that you will not fall back into your old ways. You are a good man, even if you don't believe it."

He was very still, giving her a look that burned all through her. Although he did not move to embrace her, she had the sense of being possessed, captured by his gaze and his potent will beyond any hope of release. "Caro," he finally said, his voice tightly controlled, "I can't ever be without you."

She smiled faintly. "You won't have to."

They were interrupted by the approach of a housemaid who had been dispatched from upstairs. "M'lord," the tall, rather ungainly girl murmured, bobbing in an awkward curtsy, "Mr. Scott sent me to ask if Miss Hargreaves is here, and if she would please attend the earl—"

"I will bring her to Rochester," Andrew replied grimly.

"Yes, m'lord." The maid hurried upstairs ahead of them, while Andrew carefully placed Caroline's small hand on his arm.

He looked down at her with concern. "You don't have to see him if you don't wish it."

"Of course I will see the earl," Caroline replied. "I am extremely curious about what he will say."

The Earl of Rochester was attended by two physicians, as well as Mr. Scott and his wife Madeline. The atmosphere in the bedroom was oppressively somber and stifling, with all the windows closed and the heavy velvet drapes pulled shut. A dismal end for an unhappy man, Caroline reflected silently. In her opinion the earl was extremely fortunate to have his two sons with him, considering the appalling way he had always treated them.

The earl was propped to a semireclining position with a pile of pillows behind his back. His head turned as Caroline entered the room, and his rheumy gaze fastened on her. "The Hargreaves chit," he said softly. It seemed to take great effort for him to speak. He addressed the other occupants of the room while still staring at Caroline. "Leave, all of you. I wish . . . to speak to Miss Hargreaves . . . in private."

They complied en masse except for Andrew, who lingered to stare into Caroline's face. She gave him a reassuring smile and motioned for him to leave the room. "I'll be waiting just outside," he murmured. "Call for me if you wish."

When the door closed, Caroline went to the chair by the bedside and sat, folding her hands in her lap. Her face was nearly level with the earl's, and she did not bother to conceal her curiosity as she stared at him. He must have been handsome at one time, she thought, although he wore the innate arrogance of a man who had always taken himself far too seriously.

"My lord," she said, "I have come, as you requested. May I ask why you wished to see me?"

Rochester ignored her question for a moment, his slitted gaze moving over her speculatively. "Attractive, but . . . hardly a great beauty," he observed. "What does . . . he see in you, I wonder?"

"Perhaps you should ask Lord Drake," Caroline suggested calmly.

"He will not discuss you," he replied with frowning contemplation. "I sent for you because . . . I want the answer to one question. When my son proposes . . . will you accept?"

Startled, Caroline stared at him without blinking. "He has not proposed marriage to me, my lord, nor has he given any indication that he is considering such a proposition—"

"He will," Rochester assured her, his face twisting with a spasm of pain. Fumbling, he reached for a small glass on the bedside table. Automatically Caroline moved to help him, catching the noxious fragrance of spirits mixed with medicinal tonic as she brought the edge of the glass to his withered lips. Reclining back on the pillows, the earl viewed her speculatively. "You appear to have wrought . . . a miracle, Miss Hargreaves. Somehow you . . . have drawn my son out of his remarkable self-absorption. I know him . . . quite well, you see. I suspect your liaison began as a plan to deceive me, yet . . . he seems to have changed. He seems to love you, although . . . one never would have believed him capable of it."

"Perhaps you do not know Lord Drake as well as you think you do," Caroline said, unable to keep the edge from her tone. "He only needs someone to believe in him, and to encourage him. He is a good man, a caring one—"

"Please," he murmured, lifting a gnarled hand in a gesture of self-defense. "Do not waste. . . . what little time I have left . . . with rapturous descriptions of my . . . good-for-naught progeny."

"Then I will answer your question," Caroline returned evenly. "Yes, my lord, if your son proposes to me, I will accept gladly. And if you do not leave him your fortune, I will not care one whit . . . and neither will he. Some things are more precious than money, although I am certain you will mock me for saying so."

Rochester surprised her by smiling thinly, relaxing more deeply against the pillows. "I will not mock you," he murmured, seeming exhausted but oddly serene. "I believe . . . you might be the saving of him. Go now, Miss Hargreaves . . . Tell Andrew to come."

"Yes, my lord."

She left the room quickly, her emotions in chaos, feeling chilly and anxious and wanting to feel the comfort of Andrew's arms around her.

CHAPTER FOUR

It had been two weeks since the Earl of Rochester had died, leaving Andrew the entirety of his fortune as well as the title and entailed properties. Two interminable weeks during which Caroline had received no word from Andrew. At first she had been patient, understanding that Andrew must be wading through a morass of funeral arrangements and business decisions. She knew that he would come to her as soon as possible. But as day followed day, and he did not send so much as a single written sentence, Caroline realized that something was very wrong. Consumed with worry, she considered writing to him, or even paying an unexpected visit to Rochester Hall, but it was unthinkable for any unmarried woman under the age of thirty to be so forward. She finally decided to send her brother Cade to find Andrew, bidding him to find out if Andrew was well, if he needed anything . . . if he was thinking of her.

While Cade went on his mission to locate the new Lord Rochester, Caroline sat alone in her chilly winter garden, gazing forlornly at her clipped-back plants and the bare branches of her prized Japanese maples. There were only two weeks until Christmas, she thought dully. For her family's sake, Caroline had decorated the house with boughs of evergreens and holly, and had adorned the doors with wreaths of fruit and ribbons. But she sensed that instead of a joyous holiday, she was about to experience heartbreak for the first time in her life, and the black misery that awaited her was too awful to contemplate.

Something was indeed wrong, or Andrew would have come to her by now. And yet she could not imagine what was keeping him away. She knew that he needed her, just as she needed him, and that nothing stood in the way of their being together, if he so desired. Why, then, had he not come?

Just as Caroline thought she would go insane from the unanswered questions that plagued her, Cade returned home. The expression on his face did not ease her worry.

"Your hands are like ice," he said, chafing her stiff fingers and guiding her into the parlor, where a warm fire blazed in the hearth. "You've been sitting outside too long—wait, I'll send for some tea."

"I don't want tea." Caroline sat rigidly on the settee, while her brother's large form lowered to the space beside her. "Cade, did you find him? How is he? Oh, tell me something or I'll go mad!"

"Yes, I found him." Cade scowled and took her hands again, warming her tense fingers with his. He let out a slow sigh. "Drake . . . that is, Rochester . . . has been drinking again, quite a lot. I'm afraid he is back to his old ways."

She regarded him with numb disbelief. "But that's not possible."

"That's not all of it," Cade said darkly. "To everyone's surprise, Rochester has suddenly gotten himself engaged—to none other than our own dear cousin Julianne. Now that he's got the family fortune in his possession, it seems that Julianne sees his charms in a new light. The banns will be read in church tomorrow. They'll be married when the new year starts."

"Cade, don't tease like this," Caroline said in raw whisper. "It's not true . . . not true—" She stopped, suddenly unable to breathe, while flurries of brilliant sparks danced madly across her vision. She heard her brother's exclamation as if from a great distance, and she felt the hard, urgent grip of his hands.

"My God"—his voice was overlaid with a strange hum that filled her ears—"here, put your head down . . . Caro, what in the hell is wrong?"

She struggled for air, for equilibrium, while her heart clattered in a painful broken measure. "He c-can't marry her," she said through chattering teeth.

"Caroline." Her brother was unexpectedly steady and strong, holding her against him in a tight grip. "Good Lord . . . I had no idea you felt this way. It was supposed to be a charade. Don't tell me you had the bad sense to fall in love with Rochester, who has to be the worst choice a woman like you could make—"

"Yes, I love him," she choked out. Tears slid down her cheeks in scalding trails. "And he loves me, Cade, he *does* . . . Oh, this doesn't make sense!"

"Has he encouraged you to think that he would marry you?" her brother asked softly. "Did he ever say that he loved you?"

"Not in those words," she said in a sob. "But the way he was with me . . . he made me believe . . ." She buried her head in her arms, weeping violently. "Why would he marry Julianne, of all people? She is *evil* . . . oh, there are things about her that you don't know . . . things that Father told me about her before he died. She will ruin Andrew!"

"She's already made a good start of it, from all appearances," Cade said grimly. He found a handkerchief in his pocket and swabbed her sodden face with it. "Rochester is as miserable as I've ever seen him. He won't explain anything, other than to say that Julianne is a fit mate for him, and everyone is better off this way. And Caro . . ." His voice turned very gentle. "Perhaps he is right. You and Andrew . . . it is not a good match."

"Leave me alone," Caroline whispered. Gently she extricated herself from his arms and made her way out of the parlor. She hobbled like an old woman as she sought the privacy of her bedroom, ignoring Cade's worried questions. She needed to be alone, to crawl into her bed and hide like a wounded animal. Perhaps there she would find some way to heal the terrible wounds inside.

For two days Caroline remained in her room, too devastated to cry or talk. She could not eat or sleep, as her tired mind combed relentlessly over every memory of Andrew. He had made no promises, had offered no pledge of love, had given her no token to indicate his feelings. She could not accuse him of betrayal. Still, her anguish was evolving into wounded rage. She wanted to confront him, to force him to admit his feelings, or at least to tell her what had been a lie and what had been the truth. Surely it was her right to have an explanation. But Andrew had abandoned her without a word, leaving her to wonder desperately what had gone wrong between them.

This had been his plan all along, she thought with increasing despair. He had only wanted her companionship until his father died and left him the Rochester fortune. Now that Andrew had gotten what he wanted, she was of no further consequence to him. But hadn't he come to care for her just a little? She knew she had not imagined the tenderness in his voice when he had said, *I can't ever be without you. . . .*

Why would he have said that, if he had not meant it?

To Caroline's weary amusement, her mother, Fanny,

had received the news of Andrew's impending nuptials with a great display of hysterics. She had taken to her bed at once, loudly insisting that the servants wait on her hand and foot until she recovered. The household centered around Fanny and her delicate nerves, mercifully leaving Caroline in peace.

The only person Caroline spoke to was Cade, who had become a surprisingly steady source of support.

"What can I do?" he asked softly, approaching Caroline as she sat before the window and stared blankly out at the garden. "There must be something that would make you feel better."

She turned toward her brother with a dismal smile. "I suspect I will feel better as time goes by, although right now I doubt that I will ever feel happy again."

"That bastard Rochester," Cade muttered, sinking to his haunches beside her. "Shall I go thrash him for you?"

A wan chuckle escaped her. "No, Cade. That would not satisfy me in the least. And I suspect Andrew has quite enough suffering in store, if he truly plans to go through with his plans to marry Julianne."

"True." Cade considered her thoughtfully. "There is something I should tell you, Caro, although you will probably disapprove. Rochester sent me a message yesterday, informing me that he has settled all my debts. I suppose I should return all the money to him—but I don't want to."

"Do as you like." Listlessly she leaned forward until her forehead was pressed against the cold, hard pane of the window.

"Well, now that I'm out of debt, and you are indirectly responsible for my good fortune . . . I want to do something for you. It's almost Christmas, after all. Let me buy you a pretty necklace, or a new gown . . . just tell me what you want."

"Cade," she returned dully, without opening her eyes, "the only thing I would like to have is Rochester trussed up like a yuletide goose, completely at my mercy. Since you cannot make that happen, I wish for nothing."

An extended silence greeted her statement, and then she felt a gentle pat on her shoulder. "All right, sweet sister."

The next day Caroline made a genuine effort to shake herself from her cloud of melancholy. She took a long, steaming bath and washed her hair, and donned a comfortable gown that was sadly out of style but had always been her favorite. The folds of frayed dull-green velvet draped gently over her body as she sat by the fire to dry her hair. It was cold and blustery outside, and she shivered as she caught a glimpse of the icy gray sky through the window of her bedroom.

Just as she contemplated the idea of sending for a tray of toast and tea, the closed door was attacked by an energetic fist. "Caro," came her brother's voice. "Caro, may I come in? I must speak with you." His fist pounded the wood panels again, as if he were about some urgent matter.

A faint quizzical smile came to her face. "Yes, come in," she said, "before you break the door down."

Cade burst into the room, wearing the strangest expression . . . his face tense and triumphant, while an air of wildness clung to him. His dark brown hair was disheveled, and his black silk cravat hung limply on either side of his neck.

"Cade," Caroline said in concern, "what in heaven's name has happened? Have you been fighting? What is the matter?"

A mixture of jubilation and defiance crossed his face, making him appear more boyish than his twenty-four years. When he spoke, he sounded slightly out of breath. "I've been rather busy today."

"Doing what?" she asked warily.

"I've gotten you a Christmas present. It required a bit of effort, let me tell you. I had to get a couple of the fellows to help me, and . . . Well, we shouldn't waste time talking. Get your traveling cloak."

Caroline stared at him in complete bewilderment. "Cade, is my present outside? Must I fetch it myself, and on such a chilly day? I would prefer to wait. You of all people know what I have been through recently, and—"

"This present won't keep for long," he replied, straight-faced. Reaching into his pocket, he extracted a very small key, with a frivolous red bow attached. "Here, take this." He pressed the key into her palm. "And never say that I don't go to trouble for you."

Stupefied, she stared at the key in her hand. "I've never seen a key like this. What does it belong to?"

Her brother responded with a maddening smile. "Get your cloak and go find out."

Caroline rolled her eyes. "I am not in the mood for one of your pranks," she said pertly. "And I don't wish to go outside. But I will oblige you. Only heed my words: if this present is anything less than a queen's ransom in jewels, I shall be very put out with you. Now, may I at least be granted a few minutes to pin up my hair?"

"Very well," he said impatiently. "But hurry."

Caroline could not help being amused by her brother's suppressed exuberance. He fairly danced around her like some puckish sprite as she followed him down the stairs a minute later. No doubt he thought that his mysterious gift would serve to distract her from her broken heart . . . and though his ploy was transparent, she appreciated the caring thoughts behind it.

Opening the door with a flourish, Cade gestured to the family carriage and a team of two chestnuts stamping and blowing impatiently as the wind gusted around them. The family footman and driver also awaited, wearing heavy overcoats and large hats to shield them from the cold. "Oh, Cade," Caroline said in a groan, turning back into the house, "I am not going anywhere in that carriage. I am tired, and hungry, and I want to have a peaceful evening at home."

Cade startled her by taking her small face in his hands, and staring down at her with dark, entreating eyes. "Please, Caro," he muttered. "For once, don't argue or cause problems. Just do as I ask. Get into that carriage, and take the deuced key with you."

She returned his steady gaze with a perplexed one of her own, shaking her head within the frame of his hands. A dark, strange suspicion blossomed inside her. "Cade," she whispered, "what have you done?"

He did not reply, only guided her to the carriage and helped her inside, while the footman gave her a lap blanket and moved the porcelain foot warmer directly beneath her soles.

"Where will the carriage take me?" Caroline asked, and Cade shrugged casually.

"A friend of mine, Sambrooke, has a family cottage right at the outskirts of London that he uses to meet his . . . Well, that doesn't matter. For today, the place is unoccupied, and at your disposal."

"Why couldn't you have brought my gift here?" She pinned him with a doubtful glare.

For some reason the question made him laugh shortly. "Because you need to view it in privacy." Leaning into the carriage, he brushed her cold cheek with a kiss. "Good luck," he murmured, and withdrew.

She stared blankly through the carriage window as the door closed with a firm snap. Panic shuffled her thoughts, turning them into an incoherent jumble. *Good luck?* What in God's name had he meant by that? Did this by chance have anything to do with Andrew? Oh, she would cheerfully murder her brother if it did!

The carriage brought her past Hyde Park to an area west of London where there were still large tracts of sparsely developed land. As the vehicle came to a stop, Caroline fought to contain her agitation. She wondered wildly what her brother had arranged, and why she had been such an idiot as to fall in with his plans. The footman opened the carriage door and placed a step on the ground. Caroline did not move, however. She remained inside the vehicle and stared at the modest white roughcast house, with its steeply pitched slate roof and gravel-covered courtyard in front.

"Peter," she said to the footman, an old and trusted family servant, "do you have any idea what this is about? You must tell me if you do."

He shook his head. "No, miss, I know nothing. Do you wish to return home?"

Caroline considered the idea and abandoned it almost immediately. She had ventured too far to turn back now. "No, I'll go inside," she said reluctantly. "Shall you wait for me here?"

"If you wish, miss. But Lord Hargreaves's instructions were to leave you here and return in precisely two hours."

"I have a few choice words for my brother." Straightening her shoulders, she gathered her cloak tightly about herself and hopped down from the carriage. Silently she began to plan a list of the ways in which she would punish Cade. "Very well, Peter. You and the driver will leave, as my brother instructed. One would hate to thwart his wishes, as he seems to have decided exactly what must be done."

Peter opened the door for her, and helped her off with her cloak before returning outside to the carriage. The vehicle rolled gently away, its heavy wheels crunching the ice-covered gravel of the front courtyard.

Cautiously Caroline gripped the key and ventured inside the cottage. The place was simply furnished, with some oak paneling, a few family portraits, a set of ladder-back chairs, a library corner filled with old leather-bound books. The air was cold, but a cheerful little fire had been lit in the main room. Had it been lit for her comfort, or for someone else's?

"Hello?" she called out hesitantly. "If anyone is here, I bid you answer. Hello?"

She heard a muffled shout from some distant corner of the house. The sound gave her an unpleasant start, producing a stinging sensation along the nerves of her shoulders and spine. Her breath issued in flat bursts, and she gripped the key until its ridges dug deeply into her sweating palm. She forced herself to move. One step, then another, until she was running through the cottage, searching for whomever had shouted.

"Hello, where are you?" she called repeatedly, making her way toward the back of the house. "Where—"

The flickering of hearth light issued from one of the rooms at the end of the hall. Grabbing up handfuls of her velvet skirts, Caroline rushed toward the room. She crossed the threshold in a flurry and stopped so suddenly that her hastily arranged hair pitched forward. Impatiently she pushed it back and stared in astonishment at the scene before her. It was a bedroom, so small that it allowed for only three pieces of furniture: a washstand, a night table, and a large carved rosewood bed. However, the other guest at this romantic rendezvous had not come as willingly as herself.

. . . the only thing I would like to have is Rochester trussed up like a yuletide goose, completely at my mercy, she had unthinkingly told her witless brother. And Cade, the insane ass, had somehow managed to accomplish it.

Andrew, the seventh Earl of Rochester, was stretched full-length on the bed, his arms tethered above his head with what seemed to be a pair of metal cuffs linked by a chain and lock. The chain had been passed through a pair of carved openings in the solid rosewood headboard, securely holding Andrew prisoner.

His dark head lifted from the pillow, and his eyes gleamed an unholy shade of blue in his flushed face. He yanked at the cuffs with a force that surely bruised his imprisoned wrists. "Get these the hell off of me," he said in a growl, his voice containing a level of ferocity that made her flinch. He was like some magnificent feral animal, the powerful muscles of his arms bulging against his shirt-sleeves, his taut body arching from the bed.

"I am so sorry," she said with a gasp, instinctively rushing forward to help him. "My God . . . it was Cade . . . I don't know what got into his head—"

"I'm going to kill him," Andrew muttered, continuing to tug savagely at his tethered wrists.

"Wait, you'll hurt yourself. I have the key. Just be still and let me—"

"Did you ask him to do this?" he asked with a snarl as she climbed onto the bed beside him.

"No," she said at once, then felt scarlet color flooding her cheeks. "Not exactly. I only said I wished—" She broke off and bit her lip. "He told me about your betrothal to Cousin Julianne, you see, and I—" Continuing to blush, she crawled over him to reach the lock of the handcuffs. The delicate shape of her breast brushed over his chest, and Andrew's entire body jerked as if he had been burned. To Caroline's dismay, the key dropped from her fingers and fell between the mattress and the headboard. "Do be still," she said, keeping her gaze from his face as she levered her body farther over his and fumbled for the key. It was not easy avoiding eye contact with him when their faces were so close. The brawny mass of his body was hard and unmoving beneath her. She heard his breathing change, turning deep and quick as she strained to retrieve the key.

Her fingertips curled around the key and pried it free of the mattress. "I've got it," she murmured, risking a glance at him.

Andrew's eyes were closed, his nose and mouth almost touching the curve of her breast. He seemed to be absorbing her scent, savoring it with peculiar intensity, as if he were a condemned man being offered his last meal.

"Andrew?" she whispered in painful confusion.

His expression became closed and hard, his blue eyes opaque. "Unlock these damned things!" He rattled the chain that linked the cuffs. The noise startled her, jangled across her raw nerves. She saw the deep gouges the chain links had left on the solid rosewood, but despite the relentless tugging and sawing, the wood had so far resisted the grating metal.

Her gaze dropped to the key in her hand. Instead of using it to unlock the handcuffs, she closed her fingers around it. Terrible, wicked thoughts formed in her mind. The right thing to do would be to set Andrew free as quickly as possible. But for the first time in her entire sedate, seemly life, she did not want to do what was right.

"Before I let you go," she said in a low voice that did not quite sound like her own, "I would like the answer to one question. Why did you throw me aside in favor of Julianne?"

He continued to look at her with that arctic gaze. "I'll be damned if I'll answer any questions while I'm chained to a bed."

"And if I set you free? Will you answer me then?"

"No."

She searched his eyes for any sign of the man she had come to love, the Andrew who had been amusing, self-mocking, tender. There was nothing but bitterness in the depths of frozen blue, as if he had lost all feeling for her, himself, and everything that mattered. It would take something catastrophic to reach inside this implacable stranger.

"Why Julianne?" she persisted. "You said the affair with her was not worth remembering. Was that a lie? Have you decided that she can offer you something more, something better, than I can?"

"She is a better match for me than you could ever be."

Suddenly it hurt to breathe. "Because she is more beautiful? More passionate?" she forced herself to ask.

Andrew tried to form the word *yes*, but it would not leave his lips. He settled for a single jerking nod.

That motion should have destroyed her, for it confirmed every self-doubt she had ever possessed. But the look on Andrew's face . . . the twitch of his jaw, the odd glaze of his eyes . . . for a split second he seemed to be caught in a moment of pure agony. And there could be only one reason why.

"You're lying," she whispered.

"No, I'm not."

All at once Caroline gave rein to the desperate impulses that swirled in her head. She was a woman with nothing to lose. "Then I will prove you wrong," she said unsteadily. "I will prove that I can give you a hundred times more satisfaction than Julianne."

"How?"

"I am going to make love to you," she said, sitting up beside him. Her trembling fingers went to the neck of her gown, and she began working the knotted silk loops that fastened the front of her bodice. "Right now, on this bed, while you are helpless to prevent it. And I won't stop until you admit that you are lying. I'll have an explanation out of you, my lord, one way or another."

Clearly she had surprised him. She knew that he had never expected such feminine aggression from a respectable spinster. "You wouldn't have the damn nerve," he said softly.

Well, that sealed his fate. She certainly could not back down after such a challenge. Resolutely Caroline continued on the silk fastenings until the front of her velvet gown gaped open to reveal her thin muslin chemise. A feeling of unreality settled over her as she pulled her arms from one sleeve, then the other. In all her adult life, she had never undressed in front of anyone. Goose bumps rose on her skin, and she rubbed her bare upper arms. The chemise provided so little covering that she might as well have been naked.

She would not have been surprised had Andrew decided to mock her, but he did not seem amused or angry at her display. He seemed . . . fascinated. His gaze slid over her body, lingered at the rose-tinted shadows of her nipples, then returned to her face. "That's enough," he muttered. "Much as I enjoy the view, there is no point to this."

"I disagree." She slid off the bed and pushed the heavy gown to the floor, where it lay in a soft heap. Standing in her chemise and drawers, she tried to still the chattering of her teeth. "I am going to make you talk to me, my lord, no matter what it takes. Before I'm through, I'll have you babbling like an idiot."

His breath caught with an incredulous laugh. The sound heartened her, for it seemed to make him more human and less a frozen stranger. "In the first place, I'm not worth the effort. Second, you don't know what the hell you're doing, which throws your plans very much in doubt."

"I know enough," she said with false bravado. "Sexual intercourse is merely a matter of mechanics . . . and even in my inexperience, I believe I can figure out what goes where."

"It is *not* merely a matter of mechanics." He tugged at the handcuffs with a new urgency, his face suddenly contorted with . . . fear? . . . concern? "Damn it, Caroline. I admire your determination, but you have to *stop this now*, do you understand? You're going to cause yourself nothing but pain and frustration. You deserve better than to have your first experience turn out badly. Let me go, you bloody stubborn witch!"

The flare of desperate fury pleased her. It meant that she was breaking through the walls he had tried to construct between them, leaving him vulnerable to further assault.

"You may scream all you like," she said. "There is no one to hear you."

She crawled onto the bed, while his entire body went rigid.

"You're a fool if you think that I'm going to cooperate," he said between clenched teeth.

"I think that before long you will cooperate with great enthusiasm." Caroline took perverse delight in becoming cooler and calmer as he became more irate. "After all, you haven't had a woman in . . . how many months? At least three. Even if I lack the appropriate skills, I will be able to do as I like with you."

"What about Julianne?" His arms bulged with heavy muscle as he pulled at the handcuffs. "I could have had her a hundred times by now, for all you know."

"You haven't," she said. "You aren't attracted to her—that was evident when I saw the two of you together."

She began on the tight binding of his cravat, unwinding the damp, starch-scented cloth that still contained the heat of his skin. When his long golden throat was revealed, she touched the triangular hollow at the base with a gentle fingertip. "That's better," she said softly. "Now you can breathe."

He was indeed breathing, with the force of a man who had just run ten miles without stopping. His gaze fixed on hers, no longer cold, but gleaming with fury. "Stop it. I warn you, Caroline, stop *now*."

"Or what? What could you possibly do to punish me that would be worse than what you've already done?" Her fingers went to the buttons of his waistcoat and shirt, and she released them in rapid succession. She spread the edges of his garments wide, baring a remarkably muscular torso. The sight of his body, all that ferocious power rendered helpless before her, was awe-inspiring.

"I never meant to hurt you," he said. "You knew from the beginning that our relationship was just a pretense."

"Yes. But it became something else, and you and I both know it." Gently she touched the thick curls that covered his chest, her fingertips delving to the burning skin beneath. He jumped at the brush of her cool hand, the breath hissing between his teeth. How often she had dreamed of doing this, exploring his body, caressing him. The surface of his stomach was laced with tight muscles, so different from the smooth softness of her own. She stroked the taut golden skin, so hard and silken beneath her hand. "Tell me why you would marry Julianne when you've fallen in love with me."

"I . . . haven't," he managed to choke out. "Can't you get it th-through your stubborn head—"

His words ended in a harsh groan as she straddled him in a decisive motion, their loins separated only by the layers of his trousers and her gossamer-thin drawers. Flushed and determined, Caroline sat atop him in a completely wanton posture. She felt the protrusion of his sex nestle into the cleft between her thighs. The lascivious pressure of him against that intimate part of her body caused a silken ripple of heat all through her. She shifted her weight until he nudged right against her most sensitive area, a little peak that throbbed frantically at his nearness.

"All right," he said in a gasp, holding completely still. "All right, I admit it . . . I love you, damned tormenting bitch—now get *off* of me!"

"Marry me," she insisted. "Promise that you'll break off the betrothal to my cousin."

"*No.*"

Caroline reached up to her hair, pulling the pins loose, letting the rippling brown locks cascade down to her waist. He had never seen her hair down before, and his imprisoned fingers twitched as if he ached to touch her.

"I love you," she said, stroking the furry expanse of his chest, flattening her palm over the thundering rhythm of his heart. The textures of his body—rough silk, hard muscle, bone, and sinew—fascinated her. She wanted to kiss and stroke him everywhere. "We belong together. There should be no obstacles between us, Andrew."

"Love doesn't make a damn bit of difference," he almost snarled. "Idealistic little fool—"

His breath snagged in his throat as she grasped the hem

of her chemise, pulled it over her head, and tossed the whisperthin garment aside. Her upper body was completely naked, the small, firm globes of her breasts bouncing delicately, pink tips contracting in the cool air. He stared at her breasts without blinking, and his eyes gleamed with wolfish hunger before he turned his face away.

"Would you like to kiss them?" Caroline whispered, hardly daring to believe her own brazenness. "I know that you've imagined this, Andrew, just as I have." She leaned over him, brushing her nipples against his chest, and he quivered at the shock of their flesh meeting. He kept his face turned away, his mouth taut, his breath coming in hard gusts. "Kiss me," she urged. "Kiss me just once, Andrew. Please. I need you . . . need to taste you . . . kiss me the way I've dreamed about for so long."

A deep groan vibrated within his chest. His mouth lifted, searching for hers. She pressed her lips over his, her tongue slipping daintily into his hot, sweet mouth. Ardently she molded her body against his, wrapped her arms around his head, kissed him again and again. She touched his shackled wrists, her fingertips brushing his palms. He muttered frantically against her throat, "Yes . . . yes . . . let me go, Caroline . . . the key . . ."

"No." She moved higher on his chest, dragging her feverish mouth over the salt-flavored skin of his throat. "Not yet."

His mouth searched the tender place where her neck met the curve of her shoulder, and she wriggled against him, wanting more, her body filled with a craving that she could not seem to satisfy. She levered herself higher, higher, until almost by accident her nipple brushed the edge of his jaw. He seized it immediately, his mouth opening over the tender crest and drawing it deep inside. His tongue circled the delicate peak and feathered it with rapid, tiny strokes. For a long time he sucked and licked, until Caroline moaned imploringly. His mouth released the rosy nipple, his tongue caressing it with one last swipe.

"Give me the other one," he said in a rasping whisper. "Put it in my mouth."

Trembling, she obeyed, guiding her breast to his lips. He feasted on her eagerly, and she gasped at the sensation of being captured by his mouth, held by its heat and urgency. Exquisite tension gathered between her wide-open thighs. She writhed, undulated, pressed as close to him as possible, but it was not close enough. She wanted to be filled by him, crushed and ravished and possessed. "Andrew," she said, her voice low and raw. "I want you . . . I want you so badly I could die of it. Let me . . . let me . . ." She took her breast from his mouth and kissed him again, and reached frantically down to the huge, bulging shape beneath the front of his trousers.

"No," she heard him say hoarsely, but she unfastened his trousers with unsteady fingers. Andrew swore and stared at the ceiling, seeming to will his body not to respond . . . but as her cool little hand slid inside his trousers, he groaned and flushed darkly.

Caroline brought out the hard, pulsing length of his sex, and clasped the thick shaft with trembling fingers. She was fascinated by the satiny feel of his skin, the nest of coarse curls at his groin, the heavy, surprisingly cool weight of his testicles down below. The thought of taking the entire potent length of him inside her own body was as shocking as it was exciting. Awkwardly she caressed him, and was startled by his immediate response, the instinctive upward surge of his hips, the stifled grunt of pleasure that came from his throat.

"Is this the right way?" she asked, her fingers sliding up to the large round head.

"Caroline . . ." His tormented gaze was riveted on her face. "Caroline, listen to me. I don't want this. It won't be good for you. There are things I haven't done for you . . . things your body needs . . . for God's sake—"

"I don't care. I want to make love to you."

She peeled off her drawers and garters and stockings, and returned to crouch over his groin, feeling clumsy and yet inflamed. "Tell me what to do," she begged, and pressed the head of his sex directly against the soft cove of her body. She lowered her weight experimentally, and froze at the intense pressure and pain that threatened. It seemed impossible to make their bodies fit together. Baffled and frustrated, she tried again, but she could not manage to push the stiff length of him through the tightly closed opening. She stared at Andrew's taut face, her gaze pleading. "Help me. Tell me what I'm doing wrong."

Even in this moment of crucial intimacy, he would not relent. "It's time to stop, Caroline."

The finality of his refusal was impossible to ignore.

She was swamped with a feeling of utter defeat. She took a long, shivering breath, and another, but nothing would relieve the burning ache in her lungs. "All right," she managed to whisper. "All right. I'm sorry." Tears stung her eyes, and she reached beneath her spectacles to wipe at them furiously. She had lost him again, this time permanently. Any man who could resist a woman at such a moment, while she begged to make love to him, could not truly be in love with her. Groping for the key, she continued to cry silently.

For some reason the sight of her tears drove him into a sort of contained frenzy, his body stiffening with the effort not to flail at his chains. "Caroline," he said in a shaking whisper. "Please open the damned lock. Please. God . . . don't. Just get the key. Yes. Let me go. Let me—"

As soon as she turned the tiny key in the lock, the world seemed to explode with movement. Andrew moved with the speed of a leaping tiger, freeing his wrists and pouncing on her. Too stunned to react, Caroline found herself being flipped over and pressed flat on her back. The half-naked weight of his body crushed her deep into the mattress, the startling thrust of his erection hard against her quivering stomach. He moved against her once, twice, three times, the pouch of his ballocks dragging tightly through her dark curls, and then he went still, holding her until she could hardly breathe. A groan escaped him, and a liquid wash of heat seeped between their bodies, sliding over her stomach.

Dazed, Caroline lay still and silent, her gaze darting over his taut features. Andrew let out a ragged sigh and opened his eyes, which had turned a brilliant shade of molten blue. "Don't move," he said softly. "Just lie still for a moment."

She had no other choice. Her limbs were weak and trembling . . . she burned as if from a fever. Miserably she watched as he left the bed, then glanced down at her stomach. She touched a fingertip to the glossy smear of liquid there, and she was puzzled and curious and woeful all at the same time. Andrew returned with a wet cloth, and joined her on the bed. Closing her eyes, Caroline flinched at the coldness of the cloth as he gently cleansed her body. She could not bear the sight of his impassive face, nor could she stand the thought of what he might say to her. No doubt he would berate her for her part in this humiliating escapade, and she certainly deserved it. She bit her lip and stiffened her limbs against the tremors that shook her . . . she was so hot everywhere, her hips lifting uncontrollably, a sob catching in her throat. "Leave me alone," she whispered, feeling as if she were going to fly into pieces.

The cloth was set aside, and Andrew's fingers carefully hooked under the sidepieces of her spectacles to lift them from her damp face. Her lashes lifted. He was leaning over her, so close that his features were only slightly blurred. His gaze traveled slowly down the length of her slender body. "My God, how I love you," he murmured, shocking her, while his hand cupped her breast and squeezed gently. His fingertips trailed downward in a lazy path, until they slipped into the plump cleft between her thighs.

Caroline arched wildly, completely helpless at his touch, while small, pleading cries came from her throat.

"Yes." His voice was like dark velvet, his tongue flicking the lobe of her ear. "I'll take care of you now. Just tell me what you want, sweetheart. Tell me, and I'll do it."

"Andrew . . ." She gasped as he separated the tender lips and stroked right between them. "Don't t-torture me, please. . . ."

Amusement threaded through his tone. "After what you've done to me, I think you deserve a few minutes of torture . . . don't you?" His fingertip glided in a small circle around the aching little tip of flesh where all sensation was gathering. "Would you like me to kiss you here?" he asked softly. "And touch it with my tongue?"

The questions jolted her—she had never imagined such a thing—and yet her entire body quivered in response.

"Tell me," he prompted gently.

Her lips were dry, and she had to wet them with her tongue before she could speak. To her utter shame, once the first words were out, she could not stop herself from begging shamelessly. "Yes, Andrew . . . kiss me there, use your tongue, I need you now, now *please*—"

Her voice dissolved into wild groans as he moved downward, his dark head dropping between her spread legs, his fingers smoothing the little dark curls and opening her pink lips even wider. His breath touched her first, a soft rush of steam, and then his tongue danced over her, gently prodding the burning little nub, flicking it with rapid strokes.

Caroline bit her lower lip sharply, struggling desperately to keep quiet despite the intense pleasure of his mouth on her. Andrew lifted his head as he heard the muffled sounds she made, and his eyes gleamed devilishly. "Scream all you like," he murmured. "There's no one to hear you."

His mouth returned to her, and she cried out, her bottom lifting eagerly from the mattress as she pushed herself toward him. He grunted with satisfaction and cradled her taut buttocks in his large, warm hands, while his mouth continued to feast on her. She felt the broad tip of his finger stroke against the tiny opening of her body, circling, teasing . . . entering with delicate skill.

"Feel how wet you are," he murmured against her slick flesh. "You're ready to be taken now. I could slide every inch of my cock inside you."

Then she understood why she had not been able to accommodate him before. "Please," she whispered, dying of need. "Please, Andrew."

His lips returned to her vulva, nuzzling the moist, sensitive folds. Gasping, Caroline went still as his finger slid deeply inside her, stroking in time to the sweet, rhythmic tug of his mouth. "My God," she said between frantic pants for breath, "I can't . . . oh, I can't bear it, please Andrew, my God—"

The world vanished in an explosion of fiery bliss. She sobbed and shivered, riding the current of pure ecstasy until she finally drifted in a tide of lethargy unlike anything she had ever experienced. Only then did his mouth and fingers leave her. Andrew tugged at the covers and linens, half lifting Caroline's body against his own, until they were wrapped in a cocoon of warm bedclothes. She lay beside him, her leg draped over his, her head pillowed on his hard shoulder. Shaken, exhausted, she relaxed in his arms, sharing the utter peace of aftermath, like the calm after a violent storm.

Andrew's hand smoothed over the wild ripples of her hair, spreading them over his own chest. After a long moment of bittersweet contentment, he spoke quietly, his lips brushing her temple.

"It was never a charade for me, Caroline. I fell in love with you from the moment we struck our infernal bargain. I loved your spirit, your strength, your beauty. . . . I realized at once how special you were. And I knew that I didn't deserve you. But I had the damned foolish idea that somehow I might be able to become worthy of you. I wanted to make a new beginning, with you by my side. I even stopped caring about my father's bloody fortune. But in my arrogance I didn't consider the fact that no one can escape his past. And I have a thousand things to atone for . . . things that will keep turning up to haunt me for the rest of my life. You don't want to be part of that ugliness, Caroline. No man who loves a woman would ask her to live with him, wondering every day when some wretched part of his past will reappear."

"I don't understand." She lifted herself onto his chest, staring into his grave, tender expression. "Tell me what Julianne has done to change everything."

He sighed and stroked back a lock of her hair. It was clear that he did not want to tell her, but he would no longer withhold the truth. "You know that Julianne and

I once had an affair. For a while afterward, we remained friends of a sort. We are remarkably similar, Julianne and I—both of us selfish and manipulative and cold-hearted—"

"No," Caroline said swiftly, placing her fingers on his mouth. "You're not like that, Andrew. At least not anymore."

A bleak smile curved his lips, and he kissed her fingers before continuing. "After the affair was over, Julianne and I amused ourselves by playing a game we had invented. We would each name a certain person—always a virtuous and well-respected one—whom the other had to seduce. The more difficult the target, the more irresistible the challenge. I named a high-ranking magistrate, the father of seven children, whom Julianne enticed into an affair."

"And whom did she select for you?" Caroline asked quietly, experiencing a strange mixture of revulsion and pity as she heard his sordid confession.

"One of her 'friends'—the wife of the Italian ambassador. Pretty, shy, and known for her modesty and God-fearing ways."

"You succeeded with her, I suppose."

He nodded without expression. "She was a good woman with a great deal to lose. She had a happy marriage, a loving husband, three healthy children. . . . God knew how I was able to persuade her into a dalliance. But I did. And afterward, the only way she could assuage her guilt was to convince herself that she had fallen in love with me. She wrote me a few love letters, highly incriminating ones that she soon came to regret. I wanted to burn them—I should have—but I returned them to her, thinking that it would ease her worry if she could destroy them herself. Then she would never have to fear that one of them would turn up and ruin her life. Instead the little fool kept them, and for some reason I'll never understand, she showed them to Julianne, who was posing as a concerned friend."

"And somehow Julianne gained possession of them," Caroline said softly.

"She's had them for almost five years. And the day after my father died, and it became known that he left me the Rochester fortune, Julianne paid me an unexpected visit. She has gone through her late husband's entire fortune. If she wishes to maintain her current lifestyle, she will have to marry a wealthy man. And it seems I have been given the dubious honor of being her chosen groom."

"She is blackmailing you with the letters?"

He nodded. "Unless I agreed to marry her, Julianne said she would make the damned things public, and ruin her so-called friend's life. And two things immediately became clear to me. I could never have you as my wife knowing that our marriage was based on the destruction of someone else's life. And with my past, it is only a matter of time until something else rears its ugly head. You would come to hate me, being constantly faced with new evidence of the sins I've committed." His mouth twisted bitterly. "Damned inconvenient thing, to develop a conscience. It was a hell of a lot easier before I had one."

Caroline was silent, staring down at his chest as her fingers stroked slowly through the dark curls. It was one thing to be told that a man had a wicked past, and certainly Andrew had never pretended otherwise. But the knowledge made far more of an impression on her now that she knew a few specifics about his former debauchery. The notion of his affair with Julianne, and the revolting games they had played with others' lives, sickened her. No one would blame her for rejecting Andrew, for agreeing that he was far too tarnished and corrupt. And yet . . . the fact that he had learned to feel regret, that he wished to protect the ambassador's wife even at the expense of his own happiness . . . that meant he had changed. It meant he was capable of becoming a far better man than he had been.

Besides, love was about caring for the whole man, including his flaws . . . and trusting that he felt the same about her. To her, that was worth any risk.

She smiled into Andrew's brooding face. "It is no surprise to me that you have a few imperfections." She climbed farther onto his chest, her small breasts pressing into the warm mat of hair. "Well, more than a few. You're a wicked scoundrel, and I fully expect that at some point in the future there will be more unpleasant surprises from your past. But you are *my* scoundrel, and I want to face all the unpleasant moments of life, and the wonderful ones, with no one but you."

His fingers slid into her hair, clasping her scalp, and he stared at her with fierce adoration. When he spoke his voice was slightly hoarse. "What if I decide that you deserve someone better?"

"It's too late now," she said reasonably. "You have to marry me after debauching me this afternoon."

Carefully he brought her forward and kissed her cheeks. "Precious love . . . I didn't debauch you. Not completely, at any rate. You're still a virgin."

"Not for long." She wriggled on his body, feeling his erection rising against the inside of her thigh. "Make love to me." She nuzzled against his throat and spread kisses along the firm line of his jaw. "All the way this time."

He lifted her from his chest as easily as if she were an exploring kitten, and stared at her with anguished yearning. "There's still the matter of Julianne and the ambassador's wife."

"Oh, that." She perched on him, with her hair streaming over her chest and back, and touched his small, dark nipples with her thumbs. "I will deal with my cousin Julianne," she informed him. "You'll have those letters back, Andrew. It will be my Christmas gift to you."

His gaze was patently doubtful. "How?"

"I don't wish to explain right now. What I want is—"

"I know what you want," he said dryly, rolling to pin her beneath him. "But you're not going to get it, Caroline. I won't take your virginity until I'm free to offer you marriage. Now explain to me why you're so confident that you can get the letters back."

She ran her hands over his muscular forearms. "Well . . . I've never told this to anyone, not even Cade, and especially not my mother. But soon after Julianne's rich old husband died—I suppose you've heard the rumors that his death was not of natural causes?"

"There was never any proof otherwise."

"Not that anyone knows of. But right after Lord Brenton passed on to his reward, his valet, Mr. Stevens, paid a visit to my father one night. My father was a well-respected and highly trustworthy man, and the valet had met him before. Stevens behaved oddly that night—he seemed terribly frightened, and he begged my father to help him. He suspected Julianne of having poisoned old Lord Brenton—she had recently been to the chemist's shop, and then Stevens had caught her pouring something into Brenton's medicine bottle the day before he died. But Stevens was afraid to confront Julianne with his suspicions. He thought that she might somehow falsely implicate him in the murder, or punish him in some other devious way. To protect himself, he collected evidence of Julianne's guilt, including the tainted medicine bottle. He begged my father to help him find new employment, and my father recommended him to a friend who was living abroad."

"Why did your father tell you about this?"

"He and I were very close—we were confidantes, and there were few secrets between us." She gave him a small, triumphant smile. "I know exactly where Stevens is located. And I also know where the evidence against Julianne is hidden. So unless my cousin wishes to face being accused and tried for her late husband's murder, she will give me those letters."

"Sweetheart . . ." He pressed a gentle kiss to her forehead. "You're not going to confront Julianne with this. She is a dangerous woman."

"She is no match for me," Caroline replied. "Because I am not going to let her or anyone else stand in the way of what I want."

"And what is that?" he asked.

"You." She slid her hands to his shoulders and lifted her knees to either side of his hips. "All of you . . . including every moment of your past, present, and future."

CHAPTER FIVE

The most difficult thing that Andrew, Lord Rochester, had ever done was to wait for the next three days. He paced and fretted alone at the family estate, alternately bored and anxious. He nearly went mad from the suspense. But Caroline had asked him to wait for word from her, and if it killed him, he would keep his promise. Try as he might, he could not summon much hope that she would actually retrieve the letters. Julianne was as sly and devious as Caroline was honest . . . and it was not the easiest trick in the world to blackmail a blackmailer. Moreover, the thought that Caroline was lowering herself in this way in an attempt to clean up a nasty mess that he had helped to create . . . it made him squirm. By now he should be accustomed to feeling the heat of shame, but he still suffered mightily at the thought of it. A man should protect the woman he loved—he should keep her safe and happy—and instead Caroline was having to rescue *him*. Groaning, he thought longingly of having a drink—but he would be damned if he would drown himself in the comforting oblivion of alcohol ever again. From now on he would face life without any convenient crutch. He would allow himself no more excuses, no place to hide.

And then, just a few days before Christmas, a footman dispatched from the Hargreaves residence came to the Rochester estate bearing a small wrapped package.

"Milord," the footman said, bowing respectfully. "Miss Hargreaves instructed me to deliver this into your hands, and no one else's."

Almost frantically Andrew tore open the sealed note attached to the package. His gaze skittered across the neatly written lines:

> My lord,
>   Please accept this early Christmas gift. Do with it what you will, and know that it comes with no obligations—save that you cancel your betrothal to my cousin. I believe she will soon be directing her romantic attentions toward some other unfortunate gentleman.
>
>   Yours,
>   Caroline

"Lord Rochester, shall I convey your reply to Miss Hargreaves?" the footman asked.

Andrew shook his head, while an odd feeling of lightness came over him. It was the first time in his life that he had ever felt so free, so full of anticipation. "No," he said, his voice slightly gravelly. "I will answer Miss Hargreaves in person. Tell her that I will come to call on Christmas Day."

"Yes, milord."

Caroline sat before the fire, enjoying the warmth of the yule log as it cast a wash of golden light over the family receiving room. The windows were adorned with glossy branches of holly, and festooned with red ribbons and sprays of berries. Wax tapers wreathed with greens burned on the mantel. After a pleasant morning of exchanging gifts with the family and servants, everyone had departed to pursue various amusements, for there were abundant parties and suppers to choose from. Cade was dutifully escorting Fanny to no less than three different events, and they would likely not return until after midnight. Caroline had resisted their entreaties to come along, and refused to answer their questions concerning her plans. "Is it Lord Rochester?" Fanny had demanded in mingled excitement and worry. "Do you expect him to call, dearest? If so, I must advise you on the right tone to take with him—"

"Mother," Cade had interrupted, flashing Caroline a rueful gaze, "if you do not wish to be late for the Danburys' party, we must be off."

"Yes, but I must tell Caroline—"

"Believe me," Cade said firmly, plopping a hat onto his mother's head and tugging her to the entrance hall, "if Rochester should decide to appear, Caroline will know exactly how to deal with him."

Thank you, Caroline had mouthed to him silently, and they exchanged a grin before he removed their inquisitive mother from the premises.

The servants had all been given the day off, and the house was quiet as Caroline waited. Sounds of Christmas drifted in from outside . . . passing troubadours, children caroling, groups of merry revelers traveling between houses.

Finally, as the clock struck one, a knock came at the door. Caroline felt her heart leap. She rushed to the door with unseemly haste and flung it open.

Andrew stood there, tall and handsome, his expression serious and a touch uncertain. They stared at each other, and although Caroline remained motionless, she felt her entire being reaching for him, her soul expanding with yearning. "You're here," she said, almost frightened of what would happen next. She wanted him to seize her in his arms and kiss her, but instead he removed his hat and spoke softly.

"May I come in?"

She welcomed him inside, helped him with his coat, and watched as he hung the hat on the hall stand. He turned to face her, his vivid blue eyes filled with a heat that caused her to tremble. "Merry Christmas," he said.

Caroline wrung her hands together nervously. "Merry Christmas. Shall we go into the parlor?"

He nodded, his gaze still on her. He didn't seem to care where they went as he followed her wordlessly into the parlor. "Are we alone?" he asked, having noticed the stillness of the house.

"Yes." Too agitated to sit, Caroline stood before the fire and stared up at his half-shadowed face. "Andrew," she said impulsively, "before you tell me anything, I want to make it clear . . . my gift to you . . . the letters . . . you are not obligated to give me anything in return. That is, you needn't feel as if you owe me—"

He touched her then, his large, gentle hands lightly framing the sides of her face, thumbs skimming over the blushing surface of her cheeks. The way he looked at her, tender and yet somehow devouring, caused her entire body to tingle in delight. "But I am obligated," he murmured, "by my heart, soul, and too many parts of my anatomy to name." A smile curved his lips. "Unfortunately the only thing I can offer you is a rather questionable gift . . . somewhat tarnished and damaged, and of very doubtful value. Myself." He reached for her small, slender hands and brought them to his mouth, pressing hot kisses to the backs of her fingers. "Will you have me, Caroline?"

Happiness rose inside her, making her throat tight. "I will. You are exactly what I want."

He laughed suddenly, and broke the fervent clasp of

their hands to fish for something in his pocket. "God help you, then." He extracted a glittering object and slipped it onto her fourth finger. The fit was just a little loose. Caroline balled her hand into a fist as she stared the ring. It was an ornately carved gold band adorned with a huge rose-cut diamond. The gem sparkled with heavenly brilliance in the light of the yule log, making her breath catch. "It belonged to my mother," Andrew said, watching her face closely. "She willed it to me, and hoped that I would someday give it to my wife."

"It is lovely," Caroline said, her eyes stinging. She lifted her mouth for his kiss, and felt the soft brush of his lips over hers.

"Here," he murmured, a smile coloring his voice, and he removed her spectacles to clean them. "You can't even see the damned thing, the way these are smudged." Replacing the polished spectacles, he took hold of her waist and pulled her body against his. His tone sobered as he spoke again. "Was it difficult to get the letters from Julianne?"

"Not at all." Caroline could not suppress a trace of smugness as she replied. "I enjoyed it, actually. Julianne was furious—I have no doubt she wanted to scratch my eyes out. And naturally she denied having had anything to do with Lord Brenton's death. But she gave me the letters all the same. I can assure you that she will never trouble us again."

Andrew hugged her tightly, his hands sliding repeatedly over her back. Then he spoke quietly in her hair, with a meaningful tone that made the hairs on the back of her neck prickle in excitement. "There is a matter I have yet to take care of. As I recall, I left you a virgin the last time we met."

"You did," Caroline replied with a wobbly smile. "Much to my displeasure."

His mouth covered hers, and he kissed her with a mixture of adoration and avid lust that caused her knees to weaken. She leaned heavily against him, her tongue sliding and curling against his. Excitement thumped inside her, and she arched against him in an effort to make the embrace closer, her body craving the weight and pressure of him.

"Then I'll do my best to oblige you this time," he said when their lips parted. "Take me to your bedroom."

"Now? Here?"

"Why not?" She felt him smile against her cheek. "Are you worried about propriety? You, who had me handcuffed to a bed—"

"That was Cade's doing, not mine," she said, blushing.

"Well, you didn't mind taking advantage of the situation, did you?"

"I was desperate!"

"Yes, I remember." Still smiling, he kissed the side of her neck and slid his hand to her breast, caressing the gentle curve until her nipple contracted into a hard point. "Would you rather wait until we marry?" he murmured.

She took his hand and pulled him out of the parlor, leading him upstairs to her bedroom. The walls were covered with flower-patterned paper that matched the pink-and-white embroidered counterpane on the bed. In such dainty surroundings, Andrew looked larger and more masculine than ever. Caroline watched in fascinated delight as he began to remove his clothes, discarding his coat, waistcoat, cravat, and shirt, draping the fine garments on a shield-backed chair. She unbuttoned her own gown and stepped out of it, leaving it in a crumpled heap on the floor. As she stood in her undergarments and stockings, Andrew came to her and pulled her against his naked body. The hard, thrusting ridge of his erection burned through the frail muslin of her drawers, and she let out a small gasp.

"Are you afraid?" he whispered, lifting her higher against him, until her toes almost left the ground.

She turned her face into his neck, breathing in the scent of his warm skin, lifting her hands to stroke the thick, cool silk of his hair. "Oh, no," she breathed. "Don't stop, Andrew. I want to be yours. I want to feel you inside me."

He set her on the bed and removed her clothes slowly, kissing every inch of her skin as it was uncovered, until she lay naked and open before him. Murmuring his love to her, he touched her breasts with his mouth, licked and teased until her nipples formed rosy, tight buds. Caroline arched up to him in ardent response, urging him to take her, until he pulled away with a breathless laugh. "Not so fast," he said, his hand descending to her stomach, stroking in soothing circles. "You're not ready for me yet."

"I am," she insisted, her body aching and feverish, her heart pounding.

He smiled and rolled her to her stomach, and she groaned as she felt his mouth trail down her spine, kissing and nibbling. His teeth nipped at her buttocks before his lips traveled to the fragile creases at the backs of her knees. "Andrew," she groaned, writhing in torment. "Please don't make me wait."

He turned her over once again, and his wicked mouth wandered up the inside of her thigh, higher and higher, and his strong hands carefully urged her thighs apart. Caroline whimpered as she felt him lick the damp, soft cleft between her legs. Another, deeper stroke of his tongue, and another, and then he found the excruciatingly tender bud and suckled, his tongue flicking her, until she shuddered and screamed, her ecstatic cries muffled in the folds of the embroidered counterpane.

Andrew kissed her lips and settled between her thighs. She moaned in encouragement as she felt the plum-shaped head of his sex wedge against the slick core of her body. He pushed gently, filling her . . . hesitating as she gasped with discomfort. "No," she said, clutching frantically at his hips, "don't stop . . . I need you . . . please, Andrew . . ."

He groaned and thrust forward, burying himself completely, while her flesh throbbed sweetly around him. "Sweetheart," he whispered, breathing hard, while his hips pushed forward in gentle nudges. His face was damp, suffused with perspiration and heat, his long, dark lashes spiky with moisture. Caroline was transfixed by the sight of him—he was such a beautiful man . . . and he was hers. He invaded her in a slow, patient rhythm, his muscles rigid, his forearms braced on either side of her head. Writhing in pleasure, she lifted her hips to take him more deeply. His mouth caught hers hungrily, his tongue searching and sliding.

"I love you," she whispered between kisses, her wet lips moving against his. "I love you, Andrew, love you. . . ."

The words seemed to break his self-control, and his thrusts became stronger, deeper, until he buried himself inside her and shuddered violently, his passion spending, his breath stopping in the midst of an agonizing burst of pleasure.

Long, lazy minutes later, while they were still tangled together, their heartbeats returning to a regular rhythm, Caroline kissed Andrew's shoulder.

"Darling," she said drowsily, "I want to ask something of you."

"Anything." His fingers played in her hair, sifting through the silken locks.

"Whatever comes, we'll face it together. Promise to trust me, and never to keep secrets from me again."

"I will." Andrew raised himself up on one elbow, staring down at her with a crooked smile. "Now I want to ask something of you. Could we forgo the large wedding, and instead have a small ceremony on New Year's Day?"

"Of course," Caroline said promptly. "I wouldn't have wanted a large wedding in any case. But why so soon?"

He lowered his mouth to hers, his lips warm and caressing. "Because I want my new beginning to coincide with the new year. And because I need you too badly to wait for you."

She smiled and shook her head in wonder, her eyes shining as she stared up at him. "Well, I need you even more."

"Show me," he whispered, and she did just that.

LYNSAY SANDS

Three French Hens

CHAPTER ONE

December 24

"Ye'd best set that aside and wipe yer hands, girl. Cook'll be wantin' ye in a minute."

"Hmm?" Brinna glanced up from the pot she had been scrubbing and frowned slightly at the old woman now setting to work beside her. "Why?"

"I was talkin' to Mabel ere I came back to the kitchen and she says one o' them guests His Lordship brought with him don't have no maid. Fell ill or something and they left her at court."

"So?"

"*So*, Lady Menton sent Christina in here to fetch a woman to replace her," she said dryly, and nodded toward the opposite end of the kitchen.

Following the gesture, Brinna saw that Aggie was right. Lady Christina was indeed in the kitchen speaking with Cook. A rare sight, that. You were more likely to find the daughter of the house with her nose buried in one of those musty old books she was forever dragging about than sniffing near anything domestic. It had been a bone of contention between her and her mother since the girl's return from the convent school.

"I still don't see what that's to do with me," Brinna muttered, turning to frown at the older woman again, and Aggie tut-tutted impatiently.

"I didn't raise ye to be a fool, girl. Just look about. Do you see any likely lady's maids 'sides yerself?"

Letting the pot she had been scrubbing slide down to rest on the table before her, Brinna glanced around the kitchen. Two boys ground herbs with a mortar and pestle in a corner, while another boy worked at the monotonous task of turning a pig on its spit over the fire. But other than Lady Christina and Cook, she and Aggie were the only women present at the moment. The others were all rushing about trying to finish preparations for the sudden influx of guests that Lord Menton had brought home with him. Aggie herself was just returning from one such task.

"From what I heard as I entered, they've settled on ye as the most likely lady's maid," Aggie murmured.

"Mayhap they'll send you now that yer back," Brinna murmured. "That would make a, nice change fer ye."

"Oh, aye," Aggie said dryly. "Me runnin' up an' down those stairs, chasin' after some spoilt little girl. A nice change, that. Here it comes," Aggie added with satisfaction as Lady Christina left and Cook turned toward them.

"Brinna!"

"See. Now, off with ye and make me proud."

Releasing her breath in a sigh, Brinna wiped her hands dry on her skirts and hurried to Cook's side as she returned to the table that she had been working at before Lady Christina's arrival. "Ma'am?"

"Lady Christina was just here," the older woman announced as she bent to open a bag squirming beneath the table.

"Aye, ma'am. I saw her."

"Hmm." She straightened from the bag, holding a frantically squawking and flapping chicken by its legs.

"Well, it seems one of the lady's maids fell ill and remained behind at court. A replacement is needed while the girl is here. You're that replacement."

"Oh. But, well, yer awful short-staffed at the moment and—"

"Aye. I said as much to Lady Christina," Cook interrupted dryly as she picked up a small hatchet with her free hand. "And she suggested I go down to the village in search of extra help . . . just as soon as I dispatch you to assist the lady in question."

"But—oh, nay, ma'am, I never could. Why I can't. I . . ."

"You could, you can, and you will," Cook declared, slamming the bird she held on the table with enough force to stun it, stilling it for the moment necessary for her to sever its head from its body with one smooth stroke of her ax. Pushing the twitching body aside, she wiped her hands on her apron, then removed it and set it aside before catching Brinna's elbow in her strong hand and directing her toward the door.

"Ye've been a scullery maid under me now for ten of yer twenty years, Brinna, and I've watched ye turn away one chance after another to advance up the ranks. And yet God has seen fit to send ye another, and if you think to turn this away for yer dear Aggie's sake—"

She paused and rolled her eyes skyward at Brinna's gasp of surprise. "Did ye think I was so dense that I'd believe ye actually enjoy washing pans all day every day? Or did ye think I was too blind to notice that ye start afore the others have risen and stay at it until well after they've quit for the night—all in an effort to cover the fact that Aggie has slowed down in her old age?" Sighing, the cook shook her head and continued forward, propelling Brinna along with her. "I know you are reluctant to leave Aggie. She raised ye from a babe, mothered ye through chills, colds, and childhood injuries. And I know too that ye've been the best daughter a woman could hope for, mothering and caring for her in return these last many years. Covering for her as age crept over her, making the job too hard for her old body. But ye needn't have bothered. I am not so cruel that I would throw an old woman out on her duff after years of faithful service because she can not work as she used to. She does her best, as do you, and that leaves me well satisfied.

"So . . ." Pausing, she eyed Brinna grimly. "If you don't accept this opportunity to prove yourself and maybe move up the ranks through it, I'll swat ye up the side o' the head with me favorite ladle. And don't think I won't. Now." Cook turned her abruptly, showing Brinna that while she had been distracted by the woman's words, Cook had marched her out to the great hall and to the foot of the stairs leading to the bedchambers. "Get upstairs and be the best lady's maid ye can be. It's Lady Joan Laythem, third room on the right. Get to it."

She gave her a little push, and Brinna stumbled up several steps before turning to glance down at the woman uncertainly. "Ye'll really keep Aggie on, despite her being a bit slower than she used to be?"

"I told you so, didn't I?"

Brinna nodded, then cocked her head. "Why're ye only telling me now and not sooner?"

Surprise crossed the other woman's face. "What? And lose the best scullion I've ever had? Why it will take two women to replace you. Speaking of which, I'd best get down to the village and find half a dozen or so girls to help out while the guests are here. You get on up there now and do your best."

Nodding, Brinna turned away and hurried up stairs, not slowing until she reached the door Cook had directed her to. Pausing then, she glanced down at her stained and threadbare skirt, brushed it a couple of times in the vain hope that some of the stains might be crumbs she could easily brush away, then gave up the task with a sigh and knocked at the door. Hearing a muffled murmur to enter, she pasted a bright smile on her lips, opened the door, and stepped inside the room.

"Oh, fustian!" The snarled words preceded the crash of a water basin hitting the floor as Lady Joan bumped it while peeling off her glove. Stomping her foot, the girl gave a moan of frustration. "Now look what I have done. My hands are so frozen they will not do what I want and—"

"I'll tend it, m'lady." Pushing the door closed, Brinna rushed around the bed toward the mess. "Why don't you cozy yerself by the fire for a bit and warm up."

Heaving a sigh, Lady Laythem moved away to stand by the fire as Brinna knelt to tend to the mess. She had set the basin back on the chest and gathered the worst of the soaked rushes up to take them below to discard, when the bedroom door burst open and a pretty brunette bustled into the room.

"What a relief to be spending the night within the walls of a castle again. I swear! One more night camping by the roadside and—" Spying Brinna's head poking up curiously over the side of the bed, the woman came to a halt, eyes round with amazement. "Joan! What on earth are you doing on the floor?"

"Whatever are you talking about, Sabrina? I am over here."

Whirling toward the fireplace, the newcomer gasped. "Joan! I thought—" She turned abruptly back toward Brinna as if suddenly doubting that she had seen what she thought she had. She shook her head in amazement as Brinna straightened slowly, the damp rushes in her hands "Good Lord," Sabrina breathed. "Who are you?"

"I-I was sent to replace Lady Laythem's maid," Brinna murmured uncertainly.

This news was accepted with silence; then the brunette glanced toward Lady Laythem, who was now staring at Brinna with a rather stunned expression as well. "It is not just me," the cousin said with relief. "You see it, too."

"Aye," Lady Joan murmured, moving slowly forward. "I did not really look at her when she entered, but there is a resemblance."

"A resemblance?" the brunette cried in amazement, her gaze sliding back to Brinna again. "She is almost a mirror image of you, Joan. Except for that hair, of course. Yours has never been so limp and dirty."

Brinna raised a hand self-consciously to her head, glancing around in dismay as she realized that the ratty old strip of cloth that usually covered her head was gone. Seeing it lying on the floor, she bent quickly to pick it up, dropping the rushes so that she could quickly replace it. The cloth kept the hair out of her face while she scrubbed pots in the steaming kitchen, and half-hid the length of time between baths during the winter when the cold made daily dips in the river impossible. She, like the rest of the servants, had to make do with pots of water and a quick scrub for most of the winter. The opportunity to actually wash her hair was rare during this season.

"She does look like me, does she not?" Lady Laythem murmured slowly now, and hearing her, Brinna shook her head. She herself didn't see a resemblance. Lady Joan's hair was as fine as flax and fell in waves around her fair face. Her eyes were green, while Brinna had always been told that her own were gray. She supposed their noses and lips were similar, but she wasn't really sure. She had only ever seen her reflection in the surface of water, and didn't believe she was anywhere near as lovely as Lady Laythem.

"Aye." The cousin circled Brinna, inspecting every inch of her. "She could almost be your twin. In fact, had she been wearing one of your dresses and not those pitiful rags, you could have fooled me into thinking she was you."

Lady Laythem seemed to suck in a shaky gasp at that, her body stilling briefly before a sudden smile split her face. "That is a brilliant idea, Sabrina."

"It is?" The brunette glanced at her with the beginnings of excitement, then frowned slightly. "What is?"

"That we dress her up as me and let her take my place during this horrid holiday."

"What?" Brinna and Sabrina gasped as one; then Sabrina rushed to her cousin's side anxiously. "Oh, Joan, what are you thinking of?"

"Just what I said." Smiling brightly, she moved to stand in front of Brinna. "It will be grand. You can wear my gowns, eat at the high table with the other nobles. Why, 'twill be a wonderful experience for you! Aye. I think it might actually even work. Of course, your speech needs a little work, and your hands—"

When the lady reached for her callused and chapped hands, Brinna put them quickly behind her back and out of reach as she began to shake her head frantically. "Oh, nay. 'Tis sorry I am, m'lady, but I couldn't be takin' yer place. Why, it's a punishable offense fer a free woman to pass herself off as a noble. Why they'd—well, I'm not sure what they'd do, but 'tis sure I am 'twould be horrible."

"Do you think so?" Lady Laythem glanced toward her cousin questioningly, but found no help there. Her cousin was gaping at them both as if they had sprouted a third head between them. Sighing, Joan turned back to beam at Brinna reassuringly. "Well, it does not matter. 'Twill not be a worry. If you are discovered, I shall simply say 'twas all my idea. That 'twas a jest."

"Aye, well . . ." Eyes wide and wary, Brinna began backing away. "I don't think—"

"I will pay you."

Pausing, she blinked at that. "Pay me?"

"Handsomely," Joan assured her, then mentioned a sum that made Brinna press a hand to her chest and drop onto the end of the bed to sit as her head spun. With that sum, Aggie could retire. She could while away the rest of her days in relative comfort and peace. Aggie deserved such a boon.

"Joan!" Dismay covering her face, Sabrina hurried forward now. "Whatever do you think you are doing? You can't have this—this *maid* impersonate you!"

"Of course I can. Don't you see? If she is me, I won't have to suffer the clumsy wooing of that backwoods oaf to whom my father is determined to marry me off. I may even find a way out of this mess."

"There is no way out of this mess—I mean, marriage. It was contracted when you were but a babe. It is—"

"There is always a way out of things," Joan insisted grimly. "And I will find it if I just have time to think. Having her pretend to be me will give me that time. I would already have figured a way out of it if Father had deigned to mention this betrothal ere he did. Why, when he sent for me from court, I thought, I thought—well, I certainly did not think it was simply to ship me here so that some country bumpkin could look me over for a marriage I did not even know about."

"I understand you are upset," Sabrina murmured gently. "But you have yet to even meet Royce of Thurleah. He may be a very nice man. He may be—"

"He is a lesser baron of Lord Menton's. He was the son of a wealthy land baron some fifteen years ago when my father made the betrothal, but his father ran the estate into the ground and left his son with a burdensome debt and a passel of trouble. He made a name for himself in battle while in service to the king, then retired to his estates where he is said to work as hard as his few vassals. He does not attend court, and does not travel much. In fact, he spends most of his time out there on his estate trying to wring some profit from his land."

Sabrina bit her lip guiltily. It was she herself who had gained all this information for Joan during the trip here from court. It had been easy enough to attain, a question here, a question there. Everyone seemed to know and respect the man. She pointed that out now, adding, "And he is succeeding at the task he has set for himself. He is slowly rebuilding the estate to its original glory."

"Oh, aye, with my dower, Thurleah shall no doubt be returned to its original wealth and grandeur . . . in about five, maybe ten years. But by the time that happens, I shall have died at childbirth or be too old to enjoy the benefits. Nay. I'll not marry him, cousin. This is the first time in my nineteen and a half years that I have even set foot outside of Laythem. I have dreamed my whole life that someday things would be different. That I would marry, leave Laythem, and visit court whenever I wish. I will not trade one prison for another and marry a man who stays on his estate all the time, a man who will expect me to work myself to death beside him."

"But—" Sabrina glanced between her cousin and Brinna with a frown. "Well, can you not simply go along with meeting and getting to know him until you come up with a plan to avoid the wedding? Why must you make the girl take your place?"

"Because 'twill give me more time to think. Besides, why should I suffer the wooing of a country bumpkin who probably does not even know what courtly love is? Let him woo the maid. His coarse words and ignorant manners will no doubt seem charming to her after the rough attentions she probably suffers daily as a serf."

"I am a free woman," Brinna said with quiet dignity. But neither woman seemed to hear, much less care about what she had to say, as Sabrina frowned, her eyes narrowing on Joan.

"I have never said anyone called Thurleah a country bumpkin or said that his manners were poor," Sabrina declared.

"Did you not?" Joan was suddenly avoiding her cousin's gaze. "Well, it does not matter. Someone did, and this maid can save me from all that by taking my place."

"Nay. She cannot," Sabrina said firmly. "It would not work. While you are similar in looks, you are not identical. She is even an inch or two taller than you."

"You are right, of course. If Father were here I would never dare try it, but it's almost providential that he fell ill and had to remain behind at court. But no one here has seen me before except for Lord Menton on the journey here, and then I was bundled up in my mantle and hood, with furs wrapped around me to keep warm. The only thing he saw was my nose poking out into the cold, and she has the same nose. The same is true of Lady Menton when we arrived. She greeted us on arrival, but 'twas only for a mere moment or two and I was still all bundled up."

"Mayhap, but what of the difference in height?"

Joan shrugged. "I was on my horse most of the journey and no doubt my mantle adds some height to me They will not notice. It will work."

"But she is a *peasant*, Joan. She does not know how to behave as a lady."

"We will teach her what she needs to know," Joan announced blithely.

"You expect to instill nineteen years' worth of training into her in a matter of hours?" Sabrina gasped in disbelief.

"Well . . ." The first signs of doubt played on Joan's face. "Perhaps not in hours. We can claim that I am weary from the journey and wish to rest in my room rather than join the others below for dinner tonight And I shall tutor her all evening." At Sabrina's doubtful look, she gestured impatiently. "It is not as if I must teach her to run a household or play the harp. She need only walk and talk like a lady, remember to say as little as possible, and not disgrace me. Besides she need only fool Lord Thurleah, and he could not possibly spend much time around proper ladies. He does not even go to court," she muttered with disgust. She turned to the maid.

"Girl?" Joan began, then frowned. "What is your name?"

"Brinna, m'lady."

"Well, Brinna, will you agree to be me?" When Brinna hesitated briefly, Joan moved quickly to a chest at the foot of the bed and tossed it open. Rifling through the contents, she found a small purse, opened it, and poured out several coins. "This is half of what I promised you. Agree and I will give them to you now. I shall give you the other half when 'tis over."

Brinna stared at those coins and swallowed as visions of Aggie resting in a chair by the fire in a cozy cottage filled her mind. The old woman had worked hard to feed and clothe Brinna and deserved to enjoy her last days so. With the coins from this chore, she could see that she did. And it wasn't as if it was dangerous. Lady Joan would explain that it was her idea if they got caught, she assured herself, then quickly nodded her head before she could lose her courage.

"Marvelous!" Grabbing her hand, Joan dropped the coins into her open palm, then folded her fingers closed over them and squeezed firmly. "Now, the first thing we must do is—"

The three of them froze, gazes shooting guiltily to the door, as a knock sounded. At Joan's muttered "Enter," the door opened and Lady Christina peered in.

"Mother sent me to see that all is well with your maid."

"Aye. She will do fine," Joan said quickly, a panicked look about her face. Brinna realized at once that the girl feared that seeing them together, Lady Christina might notice the similarity in their looks and somehow put paid to her plans. There was no way to reassure her that the other girl wasn't likely to notice such things. It was well known at Menton that Lady Christina paid little attention to the world around her unless it had something to do with her beloved books. Which was the reason Brinna was so startled when the girl suddenly tilted her head to the side, her deep blue eyes actually focusing for a moment as she gave a light laugh and murmured, "Look at the three of you. All huddled together with your heads cocked up. You look like three French hens at the arrival of the butcher. Except, of course, only two of you are from Normandy and therefore French. Still . . ."

Brinna felt Joan stiffen beside her as an odd expression crossed over Christina's face. But then it faded and her gaze slid around the room. "They have not brought your bath up yet? I shall see about that for you." Turning, she slid out of the room as quickly as she had entered, leaving the women sighing after her.

"Why ye've made me as beautiful as yerself," Brinna breathed in wonder as she was finally allowed to peer in the looking glass at herself.

It was dawn of the morning after Brinna had stepped through the door of Lady Joan's room as her temporary maid. The hours since then had been incredibly busy ones. While Sabrina had carried Joan's message that she was too tired to dine with the others to the dinner table, Brinna had reported to the kitchens, informing Cook that the lady required her to sleep on the floor in front of her door in her room as her own maid usually did: She had then grabbed a quick bite to eat from the kitchen and spared a moment to assure herself that all was well with Aggie before preparing a trencher and delivering it to the lady, only to find her in the bath Lady Christina had had sent up. After tending her in the bath, then helping her out, Brinna had found herself ordered into the now-chill water.

Ignoring her meal, Joan had seen to it that Brinna scrubbed herself from head to toe, then again, and yet again, until Brinna was sure that half of her skin had been taken off with the dirt. She had even insisted on scrubbing Brinna's long tresses and rinsing them three times before allowing her to get out of the water. Once out, however, she had not been allowed to redon her "filthy peasant's clothes," but had been given one of Joan's old shifts instead. They had dried their hair before the fire, brushing each other's tresses by turn.

The situation had become extremely odd for Brinna at that point as the boundary between lady and servant became blurred by Joan's asking her about her childhood and life in service, then volunteering information about her own life. To Brinna, the other girl's life had sounded poor indeed. For while she had had everything wealth and privilege could buy, it did seem that Joan had been terribly lonely. Her mother had died while she was still a child and her father seemed always away on court business. This had left the girl in the care and company of the servants. Brinna may not have had the lovely clothes and jewels the other girl had, but she'd had Aggie, had always known she was loved, had always had the woman to run to with scraped knees or for a hug. From Joan's descriptions of her childhood, she'd never had that. It seemed sad to Brinna. She actually felt sorry for the girl. . . . Until their hair was dry and the actual "lessons" began. Brinna quickly lost all sympathy for the little tyrant as the girl barked out orders, slapped her, smacked her, and prodded and poked her in an effort to get her to walk, talk, and hold her head "properly." It was obvious that she was determined that this should work. It was also equally obvious to Brinna that it would not. Lady Sabrina had not helped with her snide comments and dark predictions once she had returned to the room. By the time dawn had rolled around, Brinna was positive that this was the most foolish thing she had ever agreed to. . . .

Until she saw herself in that looking glass. She had thought, on first looking into the glass that Lady Joan held between them, that 'twas just an empty gilt frame and that 'twas Lady Joan herself she peered at. But then she realized that the eyes looking back at her were a soft blue gray, not the sharp green of the other girl's. Other than that, she did look almost exactly like Lady Joan. It was enough to boost her confidence.

"You see?" Joan laughed, lowering the mirror and moving away to set it on her chest before turning back to survey Brinna in the dark blue gown she had made her don.

"Aye. You will do," she decided with satisfaction. "Now, one more time. When you meet Lord Thurleah you . . . ?" She raised a brow questioningly and Brinna, still a little dazed by what she had seen in that glass, bobbed quickly and murmured, "Greetings, m'lord. I—"

"Nay, nay, nay." Joan snapped impatiently. "Why can you not remember? When you first greet him you must curtsy low, lower your eyes to the floor, then sweep them back up and say—"

"Greetings, my lord. I am honored to finally meet you," Brinna interrupted impatiently. "Aye. I remember now. I only forgot it for a moment because—"

"It doesn't matter why you forgot. You *must* remember, else you will shame me with your ignorance."

Brinna sighed, feeling all of the confidence that the glimpse of herself in the looking glass had briefly given her seep away like water out of a leaky pail. "Mayhap we'd best be fergettin' all about this tomfoolery."

"Mayhap we had best forget all about this foolishness," Joan corrected her automatically, then frowned. "You must remember to try to speak with—"

"Enough," Brinna interrupted impatiently. "Ye know ye can't be makin' a lady of me. 'Tis hopeless."

"Nay," Joan assured her quickly "You were doing wonderfully well. You are a quick study. 'Tis just that you are tired now."

"We are all tired now," Sabrina muttered wearily from where she sat slumped on the bed. "Why do you not give it up while you can?"

"She is right," Brinna admitted on a sigh. " 'Tisn't workin'. We should give it all up for the foolishness it is and—" A knock at the door made her pause. She moved automatically to open it, then stood blinking in amazement at the man before her.

He was a glorious vision. His hair was a nimbus of gold in the torchlight that lit the halls in the early morning gloom. His tall, strong body was encased in a fine amber-colored outfit. His skin glowed with the health and vitality of a man used to the outdoors, and his eyes shone down on her as true a blue as the northern English sky on a cloudless summer day. He was the most beautiful human Brinna had ever laid eyes on.

"Lady Joan? I am Lord Royce of Thurleah."

"Gor," Brinna breathed, her eyes wide. This was the backwoods oaf? The country bumpkin whose clumsy attentions they wanted her to suffer? She could die smiling while suffering such attentions. When his eyebrows flew up in surprise, and a pinch of her behind came from Joan, who was hiding out of sight behind the door, she realized what had slipped from her lips, and alarm entered her face briefly before she remembered to curtsy, performing the move flawlessly and glancing briefly at the floor before sweeping her eyes up to his face and smiling.

"My lord," she breathed, her smile widening as he took her hand to help her up, but that smile slipped when she saw his expression.

He was frowning, not looking the least pleased, and Brinna bit her lips uncertainly, wracking her brain for the reason behind it. Had she muffed the curtsy? Said the words wrong? What, she wondered with dismay, until he shifted impatiently.

"I arrived but a moment ago," he said.

Brinna's eyes dilated somewhat as she tried to think of what she should say to that.

"*I hope your journey was pleasant.*" She glanced around at those hissed words, her wide eyes blank as they took in Joan's impatient face peeking at her from behind the door. "*Say it. I hope your journey—*"

"Who are you talking to?"

Brinna turned back to him abruptly, stepping forward to block his entrance as he would have tried to peek around the door. The move stopped his advance, but also put them extremely close to each other, and Brinna felt a quiver go through her as she caught the musky outdoors scent of him. "Just a servant," she lied huskily, ignoring the indignant gasp from behind the door.

"Oh." Royce stared at the girl, his mind gone blank as he took in her features. She was not what he had expected. His cousin, Phillip of Radfurn, had spent several months in France in late fall, had traveled through Normandy on his way home, and had stopped a while at Laythem on his travels. He had then hied his way to Thurleah to regale Royce with his impressions of his betrothed. He had spoken a lot about her unpleasant nature, her snobbery, the airs she put on, the fact that she ran her father's home as similarly to court as she could manage. . . .

He had never once mentioned the impish, turned-up nose she had, the sweet bow-shaped lips, the large dewy eyes, or that her hair was like spun sunshine. Damn. He could have prepared a body and mentioned such things. Realizing that he had stood there for several moments merely gaping at the girl, Royce cleared his throat. "I came to escort you to Mass."

"Oh." She cast one uncertain glance back into the room, then seemed to make a decision and stepped into the hall. Pulling the door closed behind her, she rested her hand on the muscled arm he extended and smiled a bit uncertainly as he led her down the hallway.

"Well?"

Sabrina turned away from the door she had cracked

open to spy on the departing couple and glanced questioningly at Joan. "Well, what?"

"You are going with her, are you not? She will need help to carry this off."

Sabrina's eyes widened in surprise. "But I am your companion. I am not to leave you alone."

"Aye. And she is me just now. It will look odd if you leave her alone with him."

Sabrina opened her mouth to argue the point, then closed it with a sigh as she realized Joan was right. Sighing again, she hurried out the door after Royce and Brinna.

CHAPTER TWO

"The things I do for Joan."

Brinna sighed inwardly as Sabrina continued her tirade. The woman seemed to have a lot to say on the subject. Brinna just wished she wasn't the one to have to listen to it. Unfortunately, she was rather a captive audience, unable to escape the other girl. Sabrina attached herself to Brinna every time she left Lady Joan's room, and did not unattach herself until they returned.

It was the day after Christmas, the day after Lord Thurleah had arrived at Menton and come to Lady Joan's room to escort her to Holy Mass. And that was the last moment of peace Brinna had had. Mass had been longer than usual, it being Christmas Day, and Brinna had spent the entire time allowing the priest's words to flow over her as she had stared rather bemusedly at Lord Thurleah from beneath her lashes. He truly was a beautiful man, and Brinna could have continued to stare at him all day long, but of course, Mass had eventually come to an end and Lord Thurleah had turned to smile at her and ask if she would not like to take a walk to stretch their legs after the long ceremony.

Brinna had smiled back and opened her mouth to speak, only to snap it closed again as Sabrina had suddenly appeared beside her, declining the offer. Using the risk of getting a chill as an excuse, she had then grabbed Brinna's arm and dragged her from the chapel and back to the great hall, hissing at her to remember to keep her head down to hide her gray eyes, and to try to slouch a bit to hide the difference in height.

Brinna had spent the rest of that first day as Lady Joan, staring at her feet and keeping her shoulders hunched as Sabrina had led her in a game of what appeared to be musical chairs. She would insist they sit one place, spend several moments hissing about "the things I do for Joan," then suddenly leap up and drag her off to another spot should anyone dare to come near them or approach to speak to her. Eventually, of course, there had been nowhere left to hide in plain view, and Sabrina had stopped moving about, switching her tactics to simply blocking any communication with Brinna/ Joan by answering every single question addressed to Brinna as if she were a deaf mute. Most of those questions she answered had been addressed by Lord Thurleah, who had followed them around the great hall determinedly, then had seated himself beside Sabrina at dinner. He had tried to sit beside Brinna—who he thought was his betrothed Joan—but Sabrina had promptly stood and made Brinna switch seats on some lame pretext or other that Brinna hadn't even really caught. She had been too distracted by the frustration and anger that had flashed briefly on Lord Thurleah's face at Sabrina's antics to notice. It had been a great relief to her when the meal had been over and Sabrina had suggested, meaningfully and quite loudly, that she looked tired and might wish to retire early for the night.

Leaving Sabrina behind to beam obliviously at an obviously irate Lord Thurleah, Brinna had returned to Joan's room to find it empty of the lady who was supposed to occupy it. After a moment of uncertainty, Brinna had shrugged inwardly and set to work putting the room to rights, finding that she actually enjoyed the task. Working in the kitchen, and usually sleeping there as well on a bed of straw with the other kitchen help, made solitude a rare and valued commodity to Brinna. She had reveled in the silence and peace as she had puttered about the room, putting things away, then removing Lady Joan's fine gown and lying down to sleep on the pallet by the door in her shift. She had dozed off, only to awaken hours later when the door had cracked open to allow Joan to slip inside.

Brinna's eyes had widened in amazement as the dying embers from the fireplace had revealed her own worn clothes on the girl and that the strip of cloth she usually wore on her head was now hiding Joan's golden curls. But she had not said anything to let Joan know that she had seen her return dressed so when Joan had removed the tired old rags. It wasn't her place to question the lady as to her goings on. Besides, the stealthy way she had crept about and crawled into bed warned Brinna that her questions wouldn't be welcome. Pretending she hadn't seen her, Brinna had merely closed her eyes and drifted back to sleep.

Joan had still been sleeping when Lord Thurleah had arrived at the room that morning, but Brinna had been up and dressed and ready to continue the charade. Once again he had escorted her to Mass, and once again as they had prepared to leave the chapel, Sabrina had whisked her away into her game of musical chairs. Until the nooning meal, when Lady Menton had announced a need for more mistletoe. Christina had quickly arranged a party of the younger set to go out in search of the "kissing boughs." Most of the guests, Lord Royce included, were on horseback, but a wagon had been brought along to put the mistletoe in and Sabrina had managed to make some excuse to Lady Christina as to why she and "Joan" would rather ride in the wagon. So here Brinna sat, trapped in the back of a wagon with Sabrina, stuck listening to her rant about her cousin.

Who would have thought that being a lady could be so *boring*, she thought idly, her gaze slipping over the rest of the group traveling ahead of the wagon. Well, at least she was just bored and not miserable like that poor Lady Gibert, she thought wryly as her gaze settled on the other woman.

Eleanor was the girl's name. She had tried to introduce herself to Brinna/Joan the day before, and Sabrina had blocked her as she had everyone else. It was one of the few times that Brinna had been really angry at Joan's cousin and not just irritated. Eleanor was obviously terribly unhappy and in need of a friend, and Brinna felt Sabrina could have been a bit kinder about it.

Her gaze slid to the man who rode beside Lady Eleanor, and Brinna grimaced. James Glencairn. He was the girl's betrothed and also the one to blame for Eleanor's misery. The man had come to Menton as a boy, and had had a chip on his shoulders as wide as Menton's moat since arriving. Not surprising perhaps since, despite being treated well, he had been and still was a virtual hostage, kept and trained at Menton to ensure his father's good behavior in Scotland. Sadly, it appeared he was making the unfortunate Lady Eleanor just as miserable.

"You are not even listening to me," Sabrina hissed suddenly, elbowing Brinna in an effort to get her attention.

Taken by surprise by that blow to her stomach, Brinna swung back in her seat on the edge of the wagon, lost her balance, and tumbled backward out of the cart to Sabrina's distressed squeak. She landed on her back in the hard-packed snow of the lane and was left gasping for the breath that had been knocked out of her as Sabrina's assurances caroled in her ears. "Nay, nay, all is fine. Lady Joan and I have merely decided to walk. You keep on going."

"But—" the anxious driver's voice sounded before Sabrina cut him off.

"Go on now. Off with you."

Sighing as she was finally able to suck some small amount of air into her lungs, Brinna lifted her head slightly to see that the riders on horseback had not noticed her mishap and only the wagon driver was peering anxiously over his shoulder at her as he reluctantly urged his horses back into a walk. Sabrina was trudging back toward her through the snow, glaring daggers.

"What on earth are you trying to do? Kill me with embarrassment? Ruin Joan?"

"Me?" Brinna squealed in amazement.

"Aye, you. Ladies do not muck about in the snow, you know."

"I—"

"I do not want to hear your excuses," Sabrina interrupted sharply, perching her hands on her hips to mutter with disgust, "Peasants! Honestly! Get up off your—"

"Is everything all right, ladies?"

Sabrina's mouth snapped closed on whatever she had been about to say, her eyes widening in horror as Lord Thurleah's voice sounded behind her. They had both been too distracted to realize that he and his man had taken note of their predicament and ridden back to assist. Forcing a wide, obviously strained smile to her lips, Sabrina whirled to face both men as they dismounted. "Oh, my, yes. Everything is fine. Why ever would you think otherwise?"

Brinna rolled her eyes at the panicky sound to the other

girl's voice and the way her hands slid down to clutch at her skirts, tugging them to the side as if she thought she might hide Brinna's undignified position in the snow. By craning her neck, Brinna could just see Lord Thurleah's face as he arched one eyebrow, his lips appearing to struggle to hold back an amused smile. "Mayhap because Lady Joan has fallen in the snow?"

"Fallen?" Lady Sabrina's genuine horror seemed to suggest ladies simply did not *do* anything as embarrassing as fall off the back of the wagon into the snow. . . . And if they did, gentlemen shouldn't deign to notice or mention it. Sabrina's fingers twitched briefly where they held her skirts, then suddenly tugged them out wider as she gasped, "Oh, nay. You must be mistaken, my lord. Why, Lady Joan would never have fallen. She is the epitome of grace and beauty. She is as nimble as a fawn, as graceful as a swan. She is—"

"Presently lying in the snow," Lord Thurleah pointed out dryly.

Sabrina whirled around at that, feigning surprise as she peered at Brinna. "Oh, dear! However did that happen? It must have been the driver's fault. Oh, do get up, dear." Leaning forward, she clasped Brinna's arm and began a useless tugging even as Lord Thurleah bent to catch Brinna under the arms and lift her to her feet, then quickly helped Sabrina brush down her skirts before straightening to smile at Brinna gently. "Better?"

"Oh, yes, that is much better," Sabrina assured him, cutting off any reply Brinna might have given. "Thank you for your aid, my lord. Lady Joan is usually—"

"The epitome of grace," Royce murmured wryly.

"Aye. Exactly." She beamed at him as if he were a student who had just figured out a difficult sum. "Why, she has been trained in dance."

"Has she?" he asked politely, turning to smile down at Brinna.

"Aye. And that is not all," Sabrina assured him, stepping between him and Brinna to block his view of the girl. Apparently eager to convince him that this little mishap was an aberration, she began to rattle off Lady Joan's abilities. "She speaks French, Latin, and German. Knows her herbs and medicinals like the back of her hand. Is meticulous in the running of the household. Is trained in the harp and lute—"

"The harp?" Lord Thurleah interrupted, leaning sideways to peer around the brunette at Brinna.

"Oh, aye. She plays it like a dream," Sabrina assured him, shifting to block his vision again.

"Really?" Straightening, he smiled at Brinna. "Then mayhap you could be persuaded to play for us tonight after our meal? 'Twould make a nice break from that minstrel who attempted to sing for us last night."

"Aye, it would, would it not?" Sabrina laughed gaily.

Brinna's mouth dropped open in horror as the brunette continued. "Why, he was absolutely horrid. Joan would be much more pleasant to listen to." She glanced to the side then, as if to look proudly at Brinna, then frowned as she caught the girl's expression. "What are you—" she began anxiously, turning toward her fully. Then her own eyes rounded as she suddenly grasped the reason for Brinna's abject horror. Her own face suddenly mirroring it, she whirled back toward Lord Thurleah, shaking her head frantically. "Oh, nay. Nay! She couldn't possibly play. Why she . . . er . . . she . . ."

When Sabrina peered at her wild-eyed, Brinna sighed and moved forward, murmuring, "I am afraid I injured my hand quite recently. I would be no good at the harp just now. Mayhap later on during the holidays."

"Aye," Sabrina gasped with relief, and turned to beam at Royce. "She hurt her hand." Realizing that she looked far too pleased as she said that, Sabrina managed a frown. "Terrible, really. Awful accident. Sad. Horribly painful. She almost lost full use of her hand."

Brinna rolled her eyes as the girl raved on, not terribly surprised when her comments made Lord Thurleah lean forward to glance down at the hands she was presently hiding within Lady Joan's cloak "It sounds awful. Whatever happened?" he asked.

"Happened?" Sabrina blinked at the question, her face going blank briefly, then filling with desperation. "She . . . er . . . she . . . er . . . pricked her finger doing embroidery!" she finished triumphantly, and Brinna nearly groaned aloud as what sounded suspiciously like a snort of laughter burst from Lord Thurleah, before he could cover his mouth with his hand. Turning away, he made a great show of coughing violently, then cleared his throat several times before turning a solemn face back to them.

"Aye. Well, that *is* tragic." His voice broke on the last word, and he had to turn away again for a few more chortling coughs. By the time he turned back, Brinna was biting her upper lip to keep from laughing herself at the ridiculous story. Unaware that her eyes were sparkling with merriment as she met his gaze, that her cheeks were pink with health, and that she seemed almost to glow with vitality, she blinked in confusion when he suddenly gasped and stilled.

Frowning now, Sabrina glanced at the man, her mouth working briefly before she assured him, "Aye, well, it may not sound like much, but 'twas an awful prick."

Royce blinked at that, seeming startled out of his reverie. For a moment, Brinna thought he might have to turn away for another coughing fit, but he managed to restrain himself and murmur, "Aye, well, then we must not let her play the harp. Mayhap something less strenuous on her *pricked* finger. Chess perhaps?"

"I am sorry, my lord," Sabrina answered. "I fear chess is out of the question as well. Joan has . . . a . . . er . . . tendency to suffer the . . . er . . . aching head." At his startled glance, she nodded solemnly. "They come on any time she thinks too hard."

Brinna closed her eyes and groaned at that one. She couldn't help it. Really! It was hard to imagine that the girl was supposed to be on Lady Joan's side.

"So, thinking is out of the question?" she heard Lord Thurleah murmur with unmistakable amusement.

"I am afraid so."

"Aye. Well, it must be a family trait."

Brinna's eyes popped open at that. She was hardly able to believe that he had said that. To her it sounded as if he had just insulted Sabrina. Surely he hadn't meant it that way, she thought, but when she glanced at his face, he gave her a wink that assured her that she was brighter than Lady Sabrina would have him believe. He had just insulted the girl. Fortunately, Sabrina obviously hadn't caught on to the insult. Making a sad grimace with her lips, she nodded solemnly and murmured, "Aye, I believe the aching head does run in the family."

"Ah," Lord Thurleah murmured, then gestured up the path to where the others were now disappearing around a curve in the lane. "Mayhap we should catch up to the others?"

"Oh, dear." Sabrina frowned. "They *have* left us quite far behind, have they not?"

"Aye, but my man and I can take the two of you on our horses and catch up rather quickly, I am sure," he said gently, taking Sabrina's arm and leading her the few steps to where his man waited by the horses. Brinna followed more slowly, her gaze dropping of its own accord over his wide strong back, his firm buttocks, and muscled legs as he assisted Lady Sabrina onto his mount.

At least she had assumed it was his mount. Sabrina apparently had, too, Brinna realized as he suddenly stepped out of the way to allow his man to mount behind the girl and the brunette gasped anxiously. "Oh, but—"

"Lady Joan and I will be right behind you," Lord Thurleah said gaily over her protests, nodding to his man, then slapping the horse on the derriere so that it took off with a burst of speed, carrying away the suddenly struggling and protesting Lady Sabrina. She was squawking and flapping her arms not unlike the chicken Cook had held by the legs while talking to her the other day, and Brinna bit her lip to keep from laughing aloud at the wicked comparison. Lord Thurleah turned to face her.

"Now," he began, then paused, his thoughts arrested as he took in her amused expression.

"My lord?" she questioned gently after an uncomfortable moment had passed.

"I have heard people speak of eyes that twinkle merrily, but never really knew what it meant until today," he said quietly "Your eyes sparkle with life and laughter when you are amused. Did you know that?"

Brinna swallowed and shook her head. This must be the rough wooing Joan had spoken of, she realized, but for the life of her could find no fault with it. His voice and even his words seemed as smooth as the softest down to her.

"They do," he assured her solemnly, reaching out to brush a feather-light tress away from her cheek. "And your hair . . . It's as soft as a duckling's down, and seems to reflect the sun's light with a thousand different shades of gold. It's, quite simply, beautiful."

"Gor—" Brinna murmured faintly enough that he could not have caught the word, then paused uncertainly and swallowed as his eyes turned their focus on her mouth.

"And your lips. All I can think of when I peer at them is what it would feel like to kiss you."

"Oh," she breathed shakily, a blush suffusing her face even as her chest seemed to constrict somewhat and make it harder to breathe.

"Aye, you might very well blush did you know my thoughts. How I imagine covering your mouth with my own, nibbling at the edges, sucking your lower lip into my mouth, then slipping my tongue—"

"Oh, Mother," Brinna gasped, beginning to fan her suddenly heated face as if it were a hot summer day instead of a frigid winter one. His voice and what he was saying were having an amazing affect on her body, making it tingle in spots, and sending bursts of warm gushy feelings to others. Maybe she was coming down with something, she thought with a bit of distress as his face began to lower toward hers.

"Joan! Oh, Joan!"

Royce and Brinna both straightened abruptly and turned to see Lady Sabrina walking determinedly toward them, Lord Thurleah's mounted man following behind, an apologetic expression on his face as he met his lord's glance.

"Your cousin appears to be most persistent," Royce muttered dryly, and Brinna sighed.

"Aye. She's rather like a dog with a bone, isn't she?"

"The group has stopped just beyond that bend," Sabrina announced triumphantly as she neared. "It seems the spot is just crawling with mistletoe. Even as I speak, servants are climbing and shimmying up trees to bring down some of the vines."

Reaching them, Sabrina hooked her arm firmly through Brinna's and turned to lead her determinedly in the direction from which she had come, trilling, "It is fortunate, is it not? Else you may have gotten separated from the group and not caught up at all. Then you would have missed all the fun. Imagine that."

"Aye, just imagine." Royce sighed as he watched the brunette march his betrothed off around the bend.

"He is—"

"Aye, I know," Joan interrupted Brinna dryly. "He is a very nice man. You have said so at least ten times since returning to this room."

"Well, he is," Brinna insisted determinedly. They had arrived back at Menton nearly an hour ago. Sabrina had rushed her upstairs, then insisted Brinna wait in the hall while she went in and spoke to Joan alone. Brinna had stood there, alternately worrying over what was being said inside the room and fretting over how she would explain why she was loitering about in the hall should anyone happen upon her. Fortunately, no one had come along before Sabrina had reappeared. Stepping into the hall, she had gestured for Brinna to enter the room, then walked off, leaving her staring after.

A moment later, Brinna had straightened her shoulders and slid into the room to find Joan seated in the chair by the fire awaiting her. Brinna had not hesitated then, but had walked determinedly toward her. After rejoining the group, she had spent the better part of that afternoon considering everything she had learned to date. And it had seemed to her that, while Lady Joan was reluctant to marry Royce, it was due to some obvious misconceptions. Someone had misled her. Lord Thurleah was neither a backward oaf nor a country bumpkin given to rough wooing. He was just as polite and polished as any of the other lords. And it seemed to Brinna that she was in a position to correct this situation. All she had to do was tell Lady Joan the truth about Lord Thurleah's nature and the girl would resign herself to being his bride. Lady Joan, however, did not appear to wish to hear what she was trying to tell her. Still, she'd decided she had to try. "He isn't what you said. He doesn't woo roughly. He—"

"Brinna, please." Joan laughed, digging through her chest for Lord knows what as she went on gently. "My dear girl, you are hardly in a position to judge that. It is not as if you have spent a great deal of time around nobility."

"Aye, but, he-he spoke real pretty. He—"

"You mean he was very complimentary?" Joan asked, pausing to frown at her as Brinna nodded quickly. "Well, then, say that. Ladies do not say things like 'he spoke real pretty.' And do try to slow your speech somewhat. That is when you make the most mistakes."

Brinna sighed in frustration, then took a moment to calm herself before continuing in the modulated tones Joan had spent that first night trying to hammer into her head. "You are correct, of course," she enunciated grimly. "I apologize. But he truly is not the way you think he is. He was very *complimentary*. He said your eyes twinkled, your hair was as soft as down, and your lips—"

"It doesn't matter. I am not marrying him," Joan declared firmly, then closed the lid of the chest with a sigh and turned to face her. "Now, Sabrina told me about the little incident of your falling out of the wagon."

Brinna felt herself flush and sighed unhappily. "Aye. She nudged me and—"

"It doesn't matter. All I wanted to say was to be more careful in future. And try to remember that you are a lady while pretending to be me and should comport yourself accordingly."

"Aye, my lady," she murmured.

"So, you'd best change quickly and make your way down to the meal."

Brinna's eyes widened at that. "Should I not go below and fetch you something to eat first?"

Joan arched an eyebrow at that "That would look odd, do you not think? A lady fetching a meal for her servant?"

"Nay, I meant that I could change into my own dress and—"

"That will not be necessary. I have already eaten."

Brinna stilled at that news, confusion on her face as she considered how that could have come about. One look at Lady Joan's closed expression told her that she was not to dare ask. Sighing, she shook her head. "Still, I should at least go down to the kitchens for a minute. They will wonder if they don't see me every once in a while."

"They saw you today." When Brinna blinked at that news, the other girl smiled wryly and admitted, "I donned your dress and the cloth you wore over your hair in case anyone came looking for you while you were out on the mistletoe hunt as me. Someone did. I think it was your Aggie. At least she seemed a lot like the old woman you described to me."

"What happened?" Brinna gasped.

Joan shrugged. "Nothing. She said Cook had said 'twas all right for her to bring you something to eat and check on you. I told her that 'Lady Joan' had left a whole list of chores to do while she was gone and thanked her for the food. They won't expect to see you again today. That is why I told you to inform them that I wanted you to sleep in my room. So they wouldn't expect to see much of you."

"And she didn't suspect that you were not me?" Brinna asked with disbelief.

"Who else would she have thought I was?" Joan laughed dryly. "No one would suspect that a lady of nobility would willingly don the clothes of the servant class."

"Nay, I suppose not," Brinna agreed slowly, but felt an odd pinch somewhere in the vicinity of her chest. Aggie had raised her. Watched her grow into womanhood. Surely the woman could tell the difference between her own daughter and an impostor?

"Come now." Joan clapped her hands together. "Change and get downstairs, else you will be late for the meal."

"Aye, my lady."

CHAPTER THREE

"Riding? On that great beast?"

Brinna stared at the mount before her with nothing short of terror. This was the fourth day of her escapade, but it was the first day that she did not have Sabrina dragging her about, lecturing her as she avoided the rest of the guests while a frustrated Lord Thurleah trailed them, doing his best to be charming and friendly to the back of Brinna's head. Brinna had actually begun to feel sorry for the poor man as he'd tried to shower attendance on her while Sabrina blocked his every advance. His Lordship was not finding this courting easy. Or at least he hadn't been until this morning, for this morning Sabrina was bundled up in bed, attempting to fight off the same chills and nausea that had kept Lady Joan's maid and father from accompanying the others to Menton for Christmas.

Sabrina had started coming down ill the day before, and it had shown. She had lacked her usual bulldog-like promptness in blocking any speech between Brinna and the others, to the point that Brinna had actually had the opportunity to murmur, "Aye, my lord," twice. Brinna had also made their excuses when, after sitting down to sup with the others, Sabrina had stared at the food before them, her face turning several shades of an interesting green before she had suddenly clawed at Brinna's arm, gasping that they had to leave the table . . . at once!

Recognizing the urgency to her tone, Brinna had risen quickly and escorted Joan's cousin upstairs, where thee girl had made brief friends with the chamber pot before collapsing onto the bed clutching the stomach she had just emptied, proclaiming that she was surely dying. And if she wasn't, she wished she were.

She hadn't looked much better this morning. If anything she had seemed weaker, which was hardly surprising since she had spent the better part of the night with her head hanging over the chamber pot until there had simply been nothing left for her stomach to toss into it. Perhaps it was due to that weakness that she had not fought too hard to convince Joan to keep Brinna from impersonating her that day and to send a message that they were both ill. Whatever the case, she had not argued too vigorously, and Joan had decided that Brinna should go ahead, saying that Brinna had had several days in the company of the other nobles and would most likely be fine. Joan had merely reminded Brinna to try to say as little as possible, keep her head bowed, and not allow herself to be alone with Lord Thurleah.

Trying to tamp down the excitement whirling inside her, Brinna had nodded solemnly, then gone to the door to greet Lord Thurleah as he had arrived to escort her to Mass. If she had felt a secret pleasure at the idea of spending the day alone with Lord Thurleah, well, as alone as one could be in the company of the rest of the Menton guests, he had looked decidedly pleased by the news that Sabrina was too ill to accompany them that day.

Smiling charmingly, he had clasped her hand on his arm and escorted her to Mass as usual, but afterward, rather than steer her toward the great hall as he had every other morning, he instead had led her here to the stables, explaining that he had planned a surprise for her and

Sabrina that morning. He had thought that a ride might be a nice change and had sent word to the stables to prepare their horses. Which was how she found herself standing before the three great beasts now eyeing her suspiciously, her heart stuck somewhere in the vicinity of her throat as she contemplated dying trampled beneath their hooves. For surely that was what would happen should she attempt to ride one of the saddled animals before her. Lord Thurleah might think that a ride would be a nice change, but Brinna could not help but disagree with him. Scullery maids did not have reason to be around the beasts much, and certainly didn't get the chance to ride them.

"Did I make a mistake, m'lady? This is your mount, isn't it?" the stable boy asked anxiously. Brinna cleared her throat and forced a smile.

"Aye. 'Tis my horse. I. . . . I just thought. . . . Well, 'twas a long journey here. Mayhap 'twould be better if she was allowed to rest," she finished lamely, and wasn't surprised when the stable lad and Royce exchanged slightly amused smiles before Royce murmured, "I was told you arrived at noon the day before I did. If so, then your mount has had four days to rest, my lady. No doubt she would enjoy a bit of exercise about now."

"Oh, aye," she murmured reluctantly, and wondered what to do. Lady Joan had not prepared her for a situation like this. Though she probably would have had she had a horse handy in her room at the time, Brinna thought wryly. She blinked suddenly as a thought came to her. Mayhap the girl had prepared her. Managing a grimace of disappointment, she turned to face Royce and the stable boy.

"What a lovely surprise, and it would have made a nice change too," she said, careful to enunciate clearly as Joan had taught her. "But as Sabrina is too ill to accompany us, and it isn't proper for a lady to be alone with a man who isn't her husband, well . . ." She paused to add a dramatic little sigh before finishing with, "I fear the ride shall have to be put off until Sabrina can accompany us."

"Aye, you are right, of course." Frowning thoughtfully, Royce turned to pace several steps away, and Brinna was just beginning to relax when he suddenly snapped his fingers and whirled back. "My man can accompany us."

"What?" she cried in alarm.

"My man Cedric can accompany us. He will make a fine chaperon. Unsaddle Lady Sabrina's mount, lad, and prepare Cedric's instead," he instructed as Brinna's eyes widened in horror.

"Oh, but—" she began, panic stealing any sensible argument she might have come up with. She was left gaping after him as he strode out of the stables determinedly.

"Bloody hell," she breathed as he disappeared, then turned back to eye the mount that would be hers as the stable boy led Sabrina's horse off. Joan's mare didn't look any happier at this turn of events than she felt. The beast was eyeing her rather suspiciously, and Brinna couldn't help thinking the horse knew that she wasn't Joan and was wondering what had become of the girl. Brinna was so sure of what the look in the beast's eyes meant that she shifted uncomfortably and murmured, "I haven't harmed 'er. Yer lady's alive and well." Noting that the horse didn't look particularly convinced, Brinna frowned. "It's true. 'Sides, this is all her doin'. She—"

"Who are you talking to?"

Brinna gave a start at that question, and glanced over her shoulder to find that Royce had returned and now towered over her shoulder. He was big. Very big. Why, she imagined if they stood in the sun side by side, he would cast a fine patch of shade for her to stand in. "My mare," she murmured absently, trying to judge how much wider he was. Probably twice as wide as she, she decided a bit breathlessly, not noticing the way he shook his head before sharing an amused glance with the older man who now accompanied him.

"This is my man Cedric. You may remember him from the mistletoe hunt?"

"Oh, aye. Greetings, my lord," Brinna murmured, and recalling her lessons on greeting people, started to sweep into a graceful curtsy that Lord Thurleah halted by catching her elbow. "He is a knight, not a lord," Thurleah explained gently, and Brinna felt herself flush.

"Oh, well." She hesitated, unsure how to greet the man now, then merely nodded and offered a smile, which was gently returned.

"Here you are, m'lord. I returned the lady's horse to its stall and prepared Sir Cedric's." The stable lad led the new horse forward to join the other two.

"Ah. Very good. Fast work, boy," Giving him an approving nod, Royce turned Brinna toward the door and led her out of the stables, offering her a smile as he went. Swallowing, Brinna managed a weak smile in return, but her attention was on the three horses Sir Cedric was now leading out behind them.

"I . . ." Brinna began faintly as he brought the horses to a halt beside them, but whatever she would have said died in her throat and she nearly bit her tongue off as Royce suddenly turned, caught her at the waist, and lifted her up onto the animal that was Lady Joan's. Once he had set her down on the sidesaddle, he paused to eye her solemnly, his eyebrows rising slightly.

"Are you all right, Lady Joan? You have gone white as a clean linen."

"Fine," Brinna squeaked.

"You are not afraid of horses, are you?"

"Nay, nay," she gasped.

"Nay, of course not," he murmured to himself "You rode here on this beast."

"Ahhhaye." The lie came out as a moan.

Royce nodded almost to himself, then cleared his throat and murmured, "Then, if you are not afraid, my lady, why is it you are clutching me so tightly?"

Brinna blinked at the question, then shot her eyes to her hands. They had tangled themselves in the material of his golden tunic and now clawed into it with all the determination of someone who was positive that should he release her, she would surely fall to her death. Lady Joan would not do that, of course, she told herself firmly. Forcing a smile that felt as stiff as wood, she forced her hands to release their death grip and smoothed the material down. "'Tis fair soft material, my lord. Quite good quality."

"Ah." Looking unsure as to what to make of her behavior, he released his hold on her waist and started to move away, only to step quickly back and catch her once more as she immediately started to slip off the sidesaddle. "I am sorry, I thought you had already braced your feet," he muttered, easing her back onto the saddle again.

Swallowing, Brinna dug about the animal's side with her feet under her skirts in search of whatever it was he thought would be there to brace her feet. She found it after a moment, an inch or so higher than her feet fell. Of course, Lady Joan was a couple of inches shorter than her, and of course that would have been the perfect height for *her.* For Brinna it meant bending her legs more than she should have had to and resting at a most awkward position. This time when he released her, she managed to keep her seat, and even summoned a wobbly smile as she accepted the reins he handed her.

As he turned to mount his own horse, Brinna wrapped the reins desperately around her hands to be sure she did not lose them. Only then did she risk a glance toward the ground. As she had feared, it appeared to be a mile or more away. Aye, the ground was a long, long way down, and she could actually almost see it rushing toward her as if she were already falling off the beast. Shutting her eyes, she sat perfectly still, afraid to even breathe as she frantically wondered what the order was to make the animal move when the time came to do so. She needn't have worried. The moment Royce urged his own mount forward, and his man Cedric followed, the mare fell into line behind them.

They started at a sedate pace, but even that was enough to make Brinna wobble precariously in her seat and tighten her grasp on the reins desperately as they moved through the bailey. She was positive she would not make it out of the gates, but much to her amazement she did, and even began to relax a bit. But then they crossed the bridge and reached the land surrounding the castle and Royce suddenly urged his mount into a canter.

Brinna's horse followed suit at once, and she began to bounce around on the animal's back like a sack of turnips in the back of a cart on a rutted path. Every bone in her body was soon aching from the jarring they were taking. Still, she held on, her teeth gritting together, as she told herself that it would soon be over. It seemed to her that they had been riding for hours when Royce and his man suddenly turned to glance back at her. Forcing her lips into a tight smile, she freed a hand to wave at them in what she hoped was a careless manner. They had barely turned forward again when her foot slipped off the bar brace and she slid off the horse. All would have been well had she not wrapped the reins around her hands as she had. She would have tumbled from the horse into a nice pile of snow and that would have been that. Unfortunately, the reins were wrapped around her hand and she didn't at first have the presence of mind to unwrap them. She hung down the side of the mount, shrieking in terror as her feet and lower legs were dragged through the snow. Her shrieks, of course, just managed to terrify her mount and urge it into a faster run, which made her scream all the louder.

Royce glanced over his shoulder toward Lady Laythem, saw her wave, and glanced back the way he was heading. He had decided on this ride in an effort to get her alone. He had heard a great deal about her being spoiled and snobbish from his cousin, but so far the woman had not quite fit that description. While it was true she was silent most of the time, which could be mistaken for snobbery, he was beginning to think it merely shyness. Truly, the girl seemed to shrink within herself when in the company of others. Of course, that cousin of hers didn't help any. Sabrina answered every question he addressed to the girl in an effort to draw her out, and usually positioned herself between the two of them. It was most annoying. He was hoping that once alone Lady Laythem would shed some of that shyness and show her true nature.

"She's not much of a rider," Cedric commented, drawing Royce from his thoughts and making him nod in silent agreement. "When do you want me to drop back and give you some privacy?" Cedric asked, having been apprised of his lord's wishes when he had fetched him.

Before Royce could respond, a sudden shrieking made them both turn back again. They were just in time to see the lady's mount come flying up and pass them, dragging the lady herself behind, kicking and screaming like a madwoman.

"My God." They both gaped after the fleeing horse briefly, until Brinna finally managed to regain her scattered wits and untangle her hand from the reins. She slid free of the mount, disappearing into the deep snow alongside the trail as the mare raced wildly off into the woods.

"I shall fetch the mare," Cedric choked out around what sounded suspiciously like laughter before urging his horse into a gallop and chasing off into the woods after the beast.

Shaking his head, Royce bit his lip in his own amusement and urged his mount forward along the trail until he reached the spot where Lady Joan had disappeared. It was easy enough to find; she had left a trail as she had been dragged along through the snow. Where the trail ended was where she must have slid off the horse. But as he stopped his mount, Royce couldn't see any evidence of her presence. His amusement replaced by concern, Royce slid off of his horse and waded into the snow calling her name, shocked to find himself waist-deep in snow as fluffy as a newborn lamb's wool. Stumbling forward, he nearly tripped over her body, then bent quickly, shoveling some of the top snow away with his bare hands before reaching into the icy fluff to find her and drag her upward, turning her at the same time until he had her head resting against his bent knee.

"Joan?" he murmured worriedly, taking in her closed eyes and the icy pallor of her cheeks. Brinna opened one eye to peer at him, then closed it again on a groan. "Are you all right? Is anything broken?"

"Only me pride," she muttered, then opened both eyes

to admit wryly. "I was rather hoping ye'd just leave me here to die in shame alone."

Royce blinked at that, then felt his mouth stretch into a slow smile before he asked again, "Were you hurt? Is anything broken?"

"Nay." She sighed wryly. "But the snow went up me skirts so far me arse is a block of ice." When his eyes widened incredulously at that and a choked sound slid from his throat, Brinna stiffened anxiously She supposed ladies wouldn't refer to their behinds as arses. Or mayhap they wouldn't mention them at all. Arses or what they were called had not come up during Lady Joan's lessons. Still, from Lord Thurleah's reaction, she was pretty sure that she hadn't chosen the right word to use. The poor man looked as if he were choking on a stone.

Sitting up in his arms, she reached around to pat his back solicitously. The next moment, she clutched at his shirt with both hands under his mantle as he suddenly lunged to his feet, dragging her with him until they both stood in the small clearing he had made in the snow while digging her out. Once she was standing, he immediately began brushing down her skirts, but Brinna couldn't help noticing the way he avoided looking at her and the fact that his face was terribly red. She was trying to decide if this was from anger or embarrassment when he straightened and cleared his throat.

"Better?"

Brinna hesitated, gave her skirts a shake, then wiggled her bottom about a bit beneath them to allow the snow underneath to fall back out before allowing her skirts to drop back around her legs. Then she gave a wry shrug. "'Tis as good as 'tis likely to get 'til I can change, my lord."

"Aye." He sighed as he saw his plans to get her alone being dashed. "We had best head right back to see to that."

Taking her arm, he led her to his horse, mounted, then bent to the side and down, grasped her beneath her arms, and lifted her onto the horse before him. Settling her there with one arm around her waist to anchor her, he reached with the other for the reins.

Clutching his arm nervously, Brinna tried to relax and get her mind off the fact that she was actually on a horse again. It was as he started to turn his mount back the way that they had come when she realized that one of the sounds that she was hearing didn't quite belong. "What is that?"

Royce paused and glanced at her, then glanced around as he too became aware of the muffled sounds she had noticed just moments earlier. It sounded like someone cursing up a blue streak. After a brief hesitation, Royce turned his horse away from the castle again and urged his mount forward until they turned the bend and came upon a loaded-down wagon stopped at the side of the path. At first it looked abandoned, but then a man straightened up from the rear, shaking his head and muttering under his breath with disgust.

"A problem?" Royce asked, drawing the man's startled gaze to them and bringing him around the wagon.

"I'm sorry, m'lord. Is my wagon in yer way?"

"Nay. There's more than enough room to get by you should I wish to," Royce assured him. "Are you stuck?"

"Aye." He glanced back to his wagon with a sigh. "I was trying to stay to the side of the path to be sure there was room fer others to pass, but it seems I strayed too far. The wagon slid off to the side and now she won't budge."

Royce shifted behind her, and she glanced up just as a decision entered his eyes. "Wait here, my lady. I won't be a moment," he murmured, then slid from the mount.

Brinna hesitated, clutched the pommel of his mount

as the animal shifted restlessly beneath her, then slid from the saddle and followed to where the two men examined the situation. "Can I help?"

Both men glanced up with surprise at her question, but it was Royce who answered with a surprised smile. "Nay, Lady Joan, just stand you over there out of the way. We shall have this fellow out and on his way in a moment."

Biting her lip, Brinna nodded and moved aside, aware that ladies wouldn't trouble themselves with such problems. She stayed there as the men decided on a course of action, and even managed to restrain herself when Royce put his shoulder to the cart while the wagon driver moved to the horse's head to urge the animal forward. The wagon moved forward a bare inch or so, but then Royce's foot slid on the icy path and the wagon promptly slid back into its rut. When they paused long enough for Royce to reposition himself, Brinna couldn't restrain herself further. She wasn't used to standing on the sidelines twiddling her thumbs when there was work to be done. Giving up her ladylike pose, she hurried forward, positioning herself beside Royce to add her weight and strength to the task at hand. Royce straightened at once, alarm on his face.

"Oh, nay, Joan. Wait you over there. This is no job for a lady."

"He's right, m'lady. 'Tis kind of ye to wish to assist, but yer more like to be a hindrance than a help. You might get hurt."

Brinna rolled her eyes at that. A decade working in the kitchens carting heavy pots and vats around had made her quite strong. Of course they could hardly know that, and she could hardly tell them as much, so she merely lifted her chin stubbornly and murmured, "I am stronger than I look, sirs. And while I may not be of much help, it would seem to me you could use any little help you can get at the moment." On that note, she put her shoulder to the cart once more and arched a brow at first one man, then the other. "Are we ready? On the count of three, then."

After exchanging a glance, the two men shrugged and gave up trying to dissuade her from helping. Instead, they waited as she counted off, then applied their energies to shifting the wagon when she reached three. Brinna dug her heels into the icy ground and put all of her slight weight behind the cart, straining muscles that had been lax these last several days, grunting along with the men under the effort as the cart finally shifted, at first just an inch, then another, and another, until it suddenly began to roll smoothly forward and right back onto the path. She nearly tumbled to the ground then as the cart pulled away, but Royce reached out, catching her arm to steady her as he straightened.

"Whew." Brinna laughed, grinning at him widely before turning to the wagon driver as he hurried back to them.

"Thank ye, m'lord, and you too, m'lady," he gushed gratefully. "Thank ye so much. I didn't know how I was going to get out of that one."

"You are welcome." Royce assured him. "Just stick to the center of the path the rest of the way to the castle."

"Aye, m'lord. Aye." Tugging off his hat, the fellow made a quick bow to them both, then hurried back around the wagon to mount the driver's bench again and set off.

"Well—" Brinna straightened as the cart disappeared around the bend in the path, the clip-clop of the horse's hooves fading to silence. "That was fun."

"Fun?" Royce peered at her doubtfully.

"Well, perhaps not fun," she admitted uncertainly. "But there's a certain feeling of satisfaction when you get a job done well."

He nodded solemn agreement, then frowned as his gaze slid over her. "Your dress is ruined."

Brinna glanced down with disinterest, noting that aside from being soaked, it was now mud-splattered. "'Tis but mud. 'Twill wash out," she said lightly, then glanced back up, her eyebrows rising at his expression.

"You are a surprise, Lady Laythem," he murmured, then explained. "When you fell off the horse and were soaked, you did not cry that your gown was ruined, coif destroyed, or curse all four-legged beasts. You picked yourself up, dried yourself off, and said 'twas the best to be done until you could change."

"Actually, you picked me up," Brinna pointed out teasingly and he smiled, but continued.

"Then, when we came across the farmer with his wagon stuck in the snow, you did not whine that I would stop to help him before seeing you safely back to the castle, changed, and ensconced before the fire. Nay. You put your own shoulder to the man's wagon in an effort to help free it."

"Ah," Brinna murmured on a sigh as she considered just how out of character her actions must seem for a lady of nobility. "I suppose most ladies wouldn't have behaved so . . . um . . . hoydenishly." She murmured the last word uncertainly, for while Aggie had often called her a hoyden as a child, Brinna wasn't sure if "hoydenishly" was a word.

"Hoydenishly?" Royce murmured with a laugh that had Brinna convinced that it wasn't a word until he added, "'Twas not hoydenish behavior. 'Twas unselfish and thoughtful, and completely opposed to the behavior I expected from a woman who was described as a snobbish little brat to me."

"Who called me that?" Brinna demanded before she

could recall that it wasn't herself that had been described that way, but Joan.

"My cousin. Phillip of Radfurn." When she peered at him blankly, he added, "He visited Laythem some weeks ago."

"Oh. Of course."

"Aye, well, I fear he took your shyness and reticence as signs of snobbery and a . . . er, slightly spoilt nature. He had me quite convinced you were a terror."

"Really?" she asked curiously. "Then why did you come to Menton?" Her eyes widened. "Did you come here to cancel the betrothal?" That would be a fine thing, wouldn't it? If he had come to cancel it and she had put paid to his intentions with her actions.

"Oh, nay I could never cancel it. My people are counting on your dower." The last word was followed by silence as his eyes widened in alarm. "I mean—"

"'Tis all right," Brinna assured him gently when he began to look rather guilty. "I already knew that you needed the dower."

He sighed unhappily, looking not the least reassured. "Aye, well, without it I fear my people will not fare well through this spring."

"And you will do your best to provide them with what they need? Whether you want to or not?"

"Well . . ." Taking her arm, he turned to lead her back toward his horse. "It is the responsibility we have as members of the nobility, is it not? Tending to our people, fulfilling their needs to the best of our ability."

"Some of the nobility do not see it that way," she pointed out gently, and he grimaced.

"Aye. Well, some of them have no more honor than a gnat."

"But you are different."

When he gave a start at the certainty in her tone, she shrugged. "Most *lords* would not have troubled themselves to offer aid to a poor farmer either."

He smiled wryly. "I suppose not."

"But then from what I have heard, you are not like other lords. I was told that you are trying to correct neglect and damage done by those who came before you."

He remained silent, but grimaced, and she went on. "I was also told that you work very hard, even side by side with your vassals, in an effort to better things?"

His gaze turned wary, but he nodded. "I do what must be done and am not ashamed to work hard." He hesitated. "I realize that some ladies would be upset to have their husbands work side by side with the servants, but—"

"I think it is admirable," Brinna interrupted quickly, wishing to remove the worry from his face. It wasn't until she saw his tension ease that she recalled that Lady Joan had not seemed to be at all impressed by it. Before she could worry overly much about that, Royce turned to face her, taking her hands in his own.

"I need the dower. My people need it desperately. And to be honest, I would have married you for it whether you were hag, brat, whore, or simpleton—just to see my people fed and safe." He grimaced as her eyes widened incredulously at his words, then went on. "But you are none of those. You have proven to be giving and to be willing to do whatever is necessary when the need arises to help those less fortunate around you. And I want you to know that, the dower aside, I am beginning to see that I and my people will be fortunate to have you as their lady, Joan. I think we shall deal well together."

Joan. Brinna felt the name prick at her like the sharp end of a sword. She too was beginning to think that they would have dealt well together. Unfortunately, she wasn't the one he was going to marry. It was Joan. Her thoughts died abruptly as his face suddenly lowered, blocking the winter sun as his lips covered her own.

Heat. That was the first thing Brinna noticed. While her lips were chill and even seemed a bit stiff with cold, his were warm and soft as they slid across hers. They were also incredibly skilled, she realized with a sigh as he urged her own lips open and his tongue slid in to invade and conquer.

The kiss could have lasted mere moments or hours for all Brinna knew. Time seemed to have no meaning as she was overwhelmed with purely tactile sensations. She was lost in the musky scent of him, the taste and feel of him. She wanted the kiss to go on forever, and released an unabashed sigh of disappointment when it ended. When she finally opened her eyes, it was to find him eyeing her with a bit of bemusement as he caressed her cheek with his chill fingers.

"You are not at all what I expected, Joan Laythem. You are as lovely as a newly bloomed rose. Sweet. Unselfish . . . I never thought to meet a woman like you, let alone be lucky enough to marry her." With that he drew her into his arms again, kissing her with a passion that fairly stole her breath, made her dizzy, and left her clutching weakly at his tunic when he lifted his head and smiled at her. "We had best return. Else they will wonder what became of us."

"Aye." Brinna murmured, following docilely when he led her by the hand back to his mount. She would have followed him to the ends of the earth at that moment.

"Good Lord!"

Brinna turned from closing the bedroom door to spy Joan pushing herself from the seat by the fireplace and rushing toward her. She was wearing Brinna's own dress. The fact that Joan was there took Brinna a bit by surprise. The other girl had usually been absent until late at night, when she'd crept in like a thief and slid silently into bed to awake the next morning and act as if nothing were amiss. But then, Sabrina wasn't usually around this room either, and that was the cause. Brinna supposed it was possible Joan had stuck around to keep an eye on the ailing girl. On the other hand, it was equally possible that she had stuck around to avoid having the fact discovered that she usually slipped out as soon as they were gone. The lady was up to something.

"Look at you!" Joan cried now, clasping her hands and taking in her sodden clothes with a frown. "You are soaked through. What did he do to you?"

"He didn't do anything," Brinna assured her quickly. "I fell off your horse and—"

"Fell off my horse!" Joan screeched, interrupting her. "You don't ride. Do you?" she asked uncertainly.

"Nay. That is why I fell off," Brinna said dryly, and pulled away to move to the chest at the end of the bed.

Joan took a moment to digest that, then her eyes narrowed. "You didn't go out with him alone, did you?"

"Nay. Of course not. His man accompanied us," Brinna assured her as she sifted through the gowns in the chest. Picking one, she straightened and turned to face Joan unhappily. "Mayhap you should play you from now on."

Joan blinked at that. "Whatever for?"

"Well . . ." Brinna turned away and began to remove the gown she wore. "You are to be married. You really should get to know him."

Joan grimaced at that. "Not bloody likely. I'll not marry him. I shall join a convent before consenting to marry an oaf like that."

"He's not an oaf," Brinna got out from between gritted teeth as she flung the dress on the bed. She turned to face Joan grimly. "He's a very nice man. You could do worse than marry him."

Joan's eyes widened at her ferocious expression and attitude, then rounded in amazement. "Why, you are sweet on him."

"I am not," Brinna snapped stiffly.

"Aye, you are," she insisted with amusement, then tilted her head to the side and eyed Brinna consideringly. "Your color seems a bit high and you had a dreamy expression on your face when you came into the room. Are you falling in love with him?"

Brinna turned away, her mind running rife with memories of his body pressed close to hers, his lips soft on her own. Aye, she had most likely looked dreamy-eyed when she had entered. She had certainly felt dreamy-eyed until Joan had started screeching. And she would even admit to herself that she might very well be falling in love with him. It was hard not to. He was as handsome as sin, with a voice like Scottish whisky, and kisses just as intoxicating. But even worse, he was a good man. She had been told as much of course, or if not exactly told, she had heard Lady Joan and her cousin discussing what they considered to be his flaws. Which to her were recommendations of his character. The fact that he worked so hard to help his people, that he was determined to better things for them . . . He put their needs before his own, even in matters of marriage. How could one not admire that?

Aside from that, he had been nothing but gentleness itself in all his dealings with her. He was no backward oaf or country idiot. Or at least, if he was, Brinna couldn't tell. Nay, he had treated her sweetly and well, staying near her side during Mass and throughout every day since

Christmas morning. Despite Sabrina's interference, she had felt protected. And he had not taken advantage of her reaction to those kisses in the woods, though the Good Lord knows he could have. Brinna suspected that had he wished it, she would have let the man throw her skirts up and have her right there at the side of the path, and all it would have taken was a couple more kisses. She suspected he had known as much too, but he hadn't taken advantage of that fact. Nay, he was a good man. A man she could easily love with her whole heart. But if she gave her heart to him, it would be lost forever, for he was engaged to Joan, and he had to marry her, else he would lose the dower that his people needed so desperately.

He couldn't do that. She knew it. He wouldn't do it. She had not known him long, but she knew already that he was a man who took his responsibilities seriously. His people needed that dower, so he would marry to attain it and Brinna had no hope of having him. She couldn't go on with this charade. Couldn't risk her heart so. Not even for Aggie and the possibility of seeing her comfortable. She would not do this anymore. She had to convince Joan to resign herself to this marriage, but to do that, she had to convince her that he wasn't the backwards oaf someone had led her to believe he was.

"Who is it that told you that Lord Thurleah was a country bumpkin and oaf?" Brinna asked determinedly, and Joan got a wary look about her suddenly.

"Who?" she echoed faintly, then shrugged. "It must have been Sabrina. She questioned people on the journey here to find out more about him for me."

Brinna's gaze narrowed suspiciously. "But didn't she say the day I became your maid that she hadn't said that he was an oaf—just that he worked hard to improve his lot in life?"

Joan shrugged, avoiding her eyes. "Then someone else must have mentioned it."

"Could it have been Phillip of Radfurn?" Brinna asked carefully, feeling triumph steal up within her as the other girl gave a guilty start, her eyes wide with shock. "It *was* him, wasn't it? He is deliberately making trouble between the two of you. He visited you at Laythem, told you that Royce was a backward oaf, with no social graces, then went on to his cousin's to tell him that you were a—"

When she cut herself off abruptly, Joan's gaze narrowed. "To tell him that I was what?"

"Oh, well . . ." Now it was Brinna's turn to avoid eye contact. "I don't really recall exactly."

"You are lying," Joan accused grimly. "What did he say?"

Brinna hesitated, then decided to follow one of Aggie's maxims. The one that went, *If yer in a spot and don't know what to do or say, honesty is yer best option.* "He told Lord Thurleah that you were a selfish, spoilt brat."

"What?" The blood rushed out of Joan's face, leaving her looking slightly gray for a moment, then poured back in to color her red with rage. "Why, that—" Her eyes, cold and flinty, jerked to Brinna. "Change and return below," she ordered coldly, moving to the door. "And no more riding or anything else alone with Lord Thurleah. His man is not a suitable chaperon." Then she slid out of the room, pulling the door closed with a snap.

CHAPTER FOUR

"I think you are improving."

"Oh, aye." Brinna laughed dryly as she clutched at the hands Royce held at her waist to steady her as they skimmed along on the lake's frozen surface on the narrow-edged bones he had insisted she try. Royce called them skates, and claimed that what they were doing was skating. It was something he had picked up while on his travels in the Nordic countries. Brinna called it foolish, for a body was sure to fall and break something trying to balance on the sharp edge of the bones that he had strapped to her soft leather boots and his own.

He had been trying for days to convince her to try skating. Ever since the afternoon they had gone for the ride. The day Sabrina had felt under the weather. But it wasn't until today that she had given in and agreed, and that was only because she had wanted to please him. She caught herself doing that more and more often these days; doing things to try to please him. It was worrisome when she thought about it, so she tried not to.

"Nay, he is right, you are improving," Sabina called. Having overheard his comment and Brinna's answer as they had skated past where she stood on the edge of the frozen lake, Sabrina had called out the words cheerfully. "At least you have stopped screaming."

Brinna laughed good-naturedly at the taunt. Sabrina

had relaxed somewhat during the past several days. She had recovered quickly from her illness and returned to her chore as chaperone the morning after the ride. But she had taken a different approach on her return. She still accompanied Brinna everywhere, but no longer bothered to try to keep her from talking to everyone, Royce included. She had also stopped forcing herself between the two of them when they walked about or sat for a bit. Brinna supposed she had decided it wasn't worth the trouble when they had already spent a day together without her interference.

"You are starting to shiver," Royce murmured by her ear. "We have been out here quite a while. Mayhap we should head back to the castle to warm up."

"Aye," Brinna agreed as he steered them both back toward Sabrina. "Mayhap we should. 'Tis almost time to sup anyway."

Sabrina seemed to greet the decision to return with relief. She herself had refused to be persuaded to try the "sharp bones" as she called them, so she had stood on the side, watching Brinna's antics instead. While it had been amusing, her lack of activity meant that she was a bit chill and so was eager to return to the warmth of the castle. She waited a bit impatiently as they removed the bones from their feet, then accompanied them back to the castle, teasing "Lady Joan" gently about her ineptitude on the ice.

As it turned out, it was later than any of them had realized, and the others were already seated at table when Brinna, Royce, and Sabrina entered. They were laughing over Brinna's less-than-stellar performance on skates that afternoon, but fell silent as they realized that they were late. Not that most people noticed their entrance—the great hall was abuzz with excited chatter and laughter— but Lady Menton spotted them arriving.

Casting apologetic glances toward their hostess, the

three of them hurried to the nearest spot with an opening and managed to squeeze themselves in. It meant they ended up seated among the knights and villeins at the low tables, but such things couldn't be helped—besides, the high table seemed quite full even without them.

"It looks like a celebratory feast," Brinna murmured as the kitchen doors opened and six women filed out, each bearing a tray holding a succulent roast goose on it.

"Aye," Sabrina agreed with surprise. "I don't recall Lady Menton saying anything this morning about—"

Brinna glanced at the brunette sharply when her unfinished sentence was interrupted by a gasp. Spotting the alarm on Sabrina's face and the way she had blanched, Brinna frowned and touched her hand gently. "What is it? Are you not feeling well again?"

Sabrina's turned to her, mouth working but nothing coming out.

"Joan? My lady?"

Brinna glanced distractedly at Royce when he touched her arm. "Aye?"

"Is that not your father?"

"My father?" she asked blankly, but followed his gesture to the head table. Her gaze slid over the people seated there, and she suddenly understood why the table was full even without them. William of Menton and an older man now helped fill it. Her gaze fixed on the older man. He was handsome with blond hair graying at the temples, strong features, and a nice smile. Brinna would have recognized him anywhere. He was Lord Edmund Laythem, a good friend of Lord Menton's and a frequent visitor at Menton. He was also Joan's father.

Brinna's gaze was drawn to Lady Menton as the woman leaned toward her husband to murmur something. Whatever it was made the two men glance across the room toward Brinna. For a moment she felt frozen, pinned to her seat like a bug stuck in sticky syrup as her heart began to hammer in panic and her breathing became fast and shallow. What if he stood and came to greet her? He would know. They would all know. But he didn't rise. Edmund Laythem merely smiled slightly and nodded a greeting.

It took an elbow in her side from Sabrina to make Brinna nod back and force what she hoped was a smile to her own lips.

"Mayhap we should go greet him," Royce murmured beside her and started to rise, but Brinna clawed at his arm at once.

"Oh, nay! Nay. I—there is no sense disrupting Lady Menton's feast. Time enough to greet him afterward."

Royce hesitated, then settled in his seat reluctantly. "As you say, my lady," he murmured, then smiled wryly. "Well, now we know the reason behind the feast. Lady Menton must have put it on to welcome your father and her son."

"Aye," Brinna murmured faintly, then tore her eyes away from the high table and swiveled abruptly toward Sabrina.

"What are we going to do?" Sabrina asked in a panic before she could say a word, and Brinna's heart sank as she realized the brunette would be of little help.

"Are you not going to eat?"

Forcing a smile, Brinna turned to face forward at Royce's question. "Of course. Aye. We shall eat," she murmured, casting Sabrina a meaningful sideways glance.

Nodding, Sabrina set to her meal, but there was a frown between her eyes as she did, and she was still as tense as the strings on a harp as she cast nervous glances toward the head table. Brinna was aware of of her actions, but avoided looking at the head table at all costs herself. She

kept her head bowed, eyes fastened on her meal as she
ate, and slowly began to shrink in her seat.

It was the most excruciating meal Brinna had ever sat
through. Worse even than her first night as Joan's, fill-in.
She wasn't even sure what she ate. It all tasted like dust in
her mouth as her mind raced about in circles like a dog
chasing its tail, desperately searching for a way out of this
mess. An excuse to hurry up stairs right after the meal and
avoid Lord Laythem was needed, but her mind seemed
consumed with the fact that this was the end of the road
for her. She had thought she had a couple more days at
least to bask in the warmth of Lord Thurleah's attention,
but this was it. The end. These were her last moments
with him. If only—

She cut the wish off abruptly. It was no good. She could
not have Royce. He was a lord and she just a scullery
maid. He needed a large dower such as Joan could provide.
She had nothing but the ragged clothes presently on Lady
Joan's back. Still, he had come to her on Christmas Day
like a gift from God that had brightened her life and made
her experience things she had never thought to feel. It
broke her heart that he was a gift meant for someone else
and that she could not keep him.

"Are you done?" Royce asked after finishing off the last
of his ale. The meal was coming to a close. Several people
at the lower tables around them had already risen to return to their chores, or to find a place to relax and listen
to the minstrel, who was even now preparing to torture
them some more with his version of music. Even Brinna
had finished off what Royce had served her with, though
she couldn't recall actually eating a thing. "Shall we go
greet your father now?"

"Oh, I-I should . . . er . . ."

"Aye, we should," Royce agreed, misunderstanding her stammering and taking her arm as he rose to his feet.

Brinna remained silent, following reluctantly as he led her toward the head table where most of the guests still sat chatting over their ales, her mind still squirming about in search of escape. Luck lent a hand as the others began to rise in groups now to leave the tables, slowing them down and making Royce and Brinna proceed in single file as they weaved through the crowd. Royce let go of her hand then, and Brinna walked behind him for a couple of steps, then simply turned on her heel and made a beeline for the steps that led upstairs.

She had to get to Joan's room. She had to find Joan, and the only place she could think to look was the room. Not that she would normally be there at this hour. Joan didn't even sleep in her own room anymore. She had fallen into the pattern of leaving as soon as Brinna departed with Royce for Mass, then not returning until just ere dawn on the next morning. She had been doing so since the day Brinna had told her what Royce's cousin, Phillip of Radfurn, had said. The girl had stormed out in a fury, been absent through the night, then returned just moments before Royce had arrived to escort the woman he thought was Lady Joan to Mass. The fact that Lady Joan had been out all night had been worrisome enough to Brinna, but the fact that she had returned in a fabulous mood, and had actually glowed with satisfaction and happiness as she had insisted that they continue with the charade, had made Brinna fear that whatever was going on did not bode well for Royce.

Now, Brinna just hoped that the girl, wherever she normally spent her time, had heard about her father's arrival and had returned to the room, prepared to take over her role as a member of nobility.

Royce stepped onto the dais directly behind Lord Laythem and tapped the man on the shoulder, offering a polite smile when he turned on his seat to glance at him.

"Royce. Greetings, son." The older man stood at once, as did Lord Menton and his son William. "I hope you are having a good Christmas here with Robert and his family? I am sorry I haven't been here from the beginning, but I fear the ague and chills felled me where many men have failed."

Royce smiled at his wry words and nodded reassuringly. "I was told that you were ill. I hope you are recovered now?"

"Aye, aye. I'm still regaining my strength and I've a stone or two to put back on, but I feel much better."

"I'm glad to hear it. Your daughter and I—" He turned slightly to gesture Joan forward as he spoke, then paused, blinking in surprise as he saw that she was no longer with him. "Where did she—" he began in bewilderment, and Lord Laythem clapped a hand on his shoulder and smiled wryly.

"I think she slipped away when you moved through that one group halfway up the room," Edmund Laythem told him dryly, revealing that he had watched their approach.

Royce's eyes widened at this news. "Why would she—"

"She was none too pleased with me when last we met," the older man confessed, then shrugged. "I fear I handled things badly. I never really bothered to mention the betrothal agreement until she arrived at court on her way here. It was all a great surprise to her and she was understandably upset by my neglect."

"I see," Royce murmured thoughtfully.

"Aye, well, I am sorry if she has caused you any trouble because of it?" It was a question as well as an apology, and Royce reassured him quickly.

"Oh, nay. She has been delightful. Of course, Lady Sabrina was another matter at first. She would not even let me talk to Joan for the first few days."

Lord Laythem's eyebrows rose at that, but he shrugged. "Sabrina can be a bit overeager when a task is set to her. No doubt that is all that was." He smiled wryly, his gaze moving to the brunette, who still sat in her seat at the table, watching them anxiously. "Actually, I must have a word with her. Her father was at court over the holidays and arranged a marriage for her. He sent some men with me to retrieve her back to prepare for it. If you will excuse me?"

"Of course." Royce stepped aside to allow the man past him, then took a moment to greet William of Menton and compliment Lord and Lady Menton on the feast he had just enjoyed before turning to survey the room in search of Joan. Catching a glimpse of her disappearing up the stairs, he excused himself and hurried after her.

Brinna opened the door to enter Joan's room, and found herself pushed back out by a hand on her chest.

"I just have to check on something," Joan trilled gaily before allowing her body to follow her arm out of the room.

"What—" Brinna began in confusion as the girl pulled the door closed, but Joan waved her to silence, then glanced quickly up and down the hall before dragging her to the shadows near the top of the stairs to keep an eye on the people below.

"My father arrived today," Joan said.

"Aye, I know. 'Tis why I came up here. To avoid him."

Joan nodded at that, but frowned as she rubbed her forehead. "This complicates things."

"Complicates things?" Brinna goggled at her, but Joan didn't notice.

"Aye. My maid came with him. That is who I was talking to in our room."

"Your room," Brinna said firmly. "And to my mind this doesn't complicate things. It ends them. You shall have to go back to being you. 'Tis for the best anyway."

Joan did not appear to see the sense behind the suggestion as she shook her head grimly. "Nay. I cannot I need to—" Her expression closed as she caught herself, then said more calmly, "There is no need to end it now. I shall insist my maid rest for the remainder of my stay to recover from her recent illness and the journey here. That way you will not be expected to return to the kitchens, she will not get in the way, and we can continue with our agreement."

"What of your father?"

"Oh, damn, here comes Lord Thurleah."

Brinna glanced down the stairs at Joan's anxious tones, her heart skipping a beat as she saw him start up the stairs toward them. Her gaze returned to the other girl in a panic. They were both dressed as Lady Joan at the moment. It would not do to be seen together. "What—"

Joan cut her off by giving her a shove toward the stairs. "Get him out of here. He must not see us together."

"But your father!" Brinna cried in dismay, resisting her push.

"Just avoid him," Joan snapped impatiently. "Now, get going."

The shove she gave her this time nearly sent Brinna tumbling down the stairs. Catching herself at the last moment, she cast a glare back toward the shadows that hid Joan, then hurried down the stairs to meet Royce.

"Where did you go?" were his first words. "One moment you were behind me and the next you were gone."

"Oh . . . I . . . I went to my room to greet my maid," she lied lamely, not surprised when Royce arched one eyebrow doubtfully.

"Before greeting your father?"

"Well, she was very ill when I left her at court."

"As was your father," he pointed out dryly, and Brinna grimaced.

"Aye, but—"

"Your father told me that you were angered with him for keeping the news of our betrothal to himself and not giving you warning," he interrupted before she could say something else stupid.

"Aye, well . . ."

"And while he should have perhaps given you more warning, he seems to regret the rift between you."

"Yes, well—"

"Besides, you do not mind so much, do you? About marrying me, I mean?"

"Nay, of course not," she assured him quickly.

"There you are then. 'Tis only polite to greet him. Now, where has he got to?" Pausing halfway up the stairs, he peered about until he spotted Lord Laythem below talking to Sabrina. "Oh. He is still with your cousin. He is passing on a message from her father, your uncle." Hesitating, he glanced back at Brinna, smiling wryly. "Mayhap we should leave them in peace until they finish. Would you care for a beverage while we wait?"

"Aye," she murmured, then continued down the stairs with him until they reached the bottom and she spied a knight and one of the kitchen girls slipping outside. An idea springing to mind, Brinna stopped abruptly, tugging on his hand. "Nay."

He turned to her in surprise. "Nay?"

"Nay." She paled slightly as her gaze slid past him to see that Lord Laythem had finished speaking to Sabrina and was now rising, his gaze on where she and Royce stood. "I-I need . . . air."

Frowning with concern, Royce clasped her lightly by the arms. "Are you all right? You've gone quite pale."

Brinna dragged her gaze away from the approaching Lord Laythem and focused on Royce. "Nay," she said firmly. "I am not all right. 'Tis the heat. Do I not get out into the fresh air this minute, I'm sure to faint."

It was all she had to say. She barely had time for one more glance over his shoulder at Lord Laythem as he weaved his way toward them; then Royce had whirled her toward the great hall's doors and propelled her to and through them.

"Better?" he asked solicitously as the doors closed behind them.

Her arms moving automatically to hug herself against the cold winter night, Brinna glanced uncertainly about the courtyard. Lord Laythem had been close enough to see where they had gone to, and she very much feared his following them. Standing on the steps, handy for him to find on exiting the hall, hardly seemed the wisest thing to do.

"Perhaps the stables," she murmured thoughtfully. Surely Lord Laythem would never look for them there? Certainly it was the last place Brinna would have chosen to go were she not desperate to hide.

"The stables?"

"What a wonderful idea." Brinna beamed at him as if it had been his idea. "No doubt the stables shall make me feel better." Taking his arm, she attempted to move him down the steps. It was like trying to shift a centuries-old tree. The man was immovable. Certainly too damn big for her slight weight. "My lord? Will you not come with me to the stables? Tis warmer there," she coaxed, tugging at his arm.

Heaving a sigh, he started forward down the stairs. "I thought you said that the castle was too hot and you needed to be outside else you might faint. Now you wish to go to the stables because 'tis warmer?"

"Aye, well, the castle is too warm, and the night too cold. The stables shall be just right, I am sure," she muttered, dragging at his arm in an effort to speed him up. "Do you not think we might walk faster?"

"You were faint a moment ago," he protested.

"Aye, but the exercise will do me good."

Muttering under his breath, he picked up his pace a bit, hurrying across the courtyard behind her as she began a jog toward the stables.

"I am not sure this is a good idea," Royce complained as they reached the stables.

Ignoring him, Brinna tugged the stable doors open and slid inside. Turning to glance back the way they had come as he slid in behind her, she spied a dark shape that could have been Lord Laythem standing on the stairs staring after them, and felt her heart skip a beat. Whirling away as he closed the door, she eyed the stables almost desperately, searching for somewhere to hide lest Joan's father follow them. Then she started down the row of stalls determinedly.

"What are you doing?" Royce asked curiously, following her the length of the building until they reached the last stall.

"I thought to check on my mare," she lied grimly.

"She was back near the door," he pointed out dryly, and Brinna rolled her eyes at that bit of news, then for want of any other thought of what to do, whirled, caught him by the tunic, and reached up onto her tiptoes to plaster her lips on his. It was the only thing she could think to do. His kisses made her thought processes fuzzy and scattered and made her willing to follow him anywhere unquestioningly. She could only hope they had the same effect on him and would stop his questions. Unfortunately, it did seem to her that he was better at this. While their earlier kisses had been fiery and passionate, now, without his participation, it did seem to be a wasted exercise. Brinna was about to pull away when he suddenly relaxed and kissed her back.

Sighing in relief, Brinna leaned into him and let her arms creep up about his neck. She had the curious urge to arch and stretch against him like a cat, but he pulled away before she could, a question in his eyes.

"How do you feel now?"

"Wonderful," Brinna purred, leaning her head on his chest with a small sigh, only to stiffen at his next words.

"Then mayhap we should head back."

"Oh, nay," she gasped anxiously.

"We shouldn't be here alone. It isn't proper, Joan."

Joan. She stared at him silently. He was Joan's. But for just this moment in time, she wanted to pretend he was hers. Joan wouldn't care. She didn't want him. But Brinna did. She wanted to hold him close for one night. Then hold those memories close for all the days of her future as she worked in her little cottage.

"Joan?"

"Mayhap I don't feel proper," she whispered huskily, and Royce's eyes widened incredulously. For a moment they stood frozen in silence. Then he suddenly groaned and pulled her back into his arms, his mouth lowering to cover hers in a kiss that made her legs weak. This time there was no restraint. Nothing held back. He gave her all his passion, overwhelming her with it as his hands closed over her breasts through her gown.

Pressing her back against the stall, he broke the kiss and turned his attention briefly to undo the lacings of her dress. Brinna gasped as the neckline slid apart and he tugged the collar of her shift down, revealing her naked breasts. Cold winter air chilled them briefly before Royce covered them with his hands. Growling deep in his throat, he cupped them, his thumbs running over her erect nipples as he pressed another hard, fast kiss to her lips. Then he made a trail down her throat, across her collarbone, and down to the erect tip of one breast, which he sucked into his mouth hungrily.

Brinna shuddered. Her hands clenched in his hair, then dragged his face back up for a kiss, and she thrust her own tongue into his mouth as he had done to her. Releasing his head, she dropped her hands down to slide her fingers beneath his tunic, fanning them over his hard flat stomach, then running them up over his ribs to his chest.

She felt the cool breeze creep its way up her left leg with some peripheral part of her mind, but really didn't realize what it meant until his hand brushed against her hip. Before she could register surprise, his hand had slid around between her legs and up the inside of her thigh, a warm caress. Brinna gasped into his mouth, jerking in his arms as his hand covered her womanhood, cupping it briefly before he slid a finger between her folds to investigate her warmth and heat as he urged her legs further apart with a knee between her own.

She heard the keening whimpers for quite a while before she realized that they were coming from her own throat. Suddenly embarrassed, she tugged her mouth away and turned her head until she found his shoulder. Pressing her mouth against it, she retrieved her hands from beneath his shirt, then wasn't sure what to do with them. When Royce caught one of her hands and drew it down to the front of his braies, pressing it against the solid hardness that had grown there, she froze, raising fear-filled eyes to him. He met her gaze, read her fear, and paused, his hand stilling between her legs. She saw uncertainty burst to life in his eyes, and would have kicked herself had she been able to.

"You are afraid. Mayhap we should stop and—" he began, his voice dying, eyes widening in shock as she suddenly moved the hand that clasped him through his braies, and slid it down the front of his braies to touch his bare flesh.

"Move to the straw," she suggested huskily, giving him a gentle squeeze.

Uncertainty fleeing under passion, Royce caught her by the backs of her thighs and lifted her up. Brinna wrapped her legs around his hips, and caught them at the ankles to help hold them up as he turned to walk to the back corner of the stables where several bales of hay rested. He set her on one that would keep her at the same height, then reached up to tug her gown and shift off her shoulders as she released her legs and flattened them against the front of the bale she sat on. Once the cloth lay in a pool around her waist, Brinna leaned back, tilting her head back as she arched her breasts upward for his attention.

He did not disappoint her. His hands and mouth paid homage, touching, caressing, licking, nibbling, and sucking at her goose-bumped flesh until she moaned aloud with her desire for him. It wasn't until then that he caught at the hem of her skirt again. Sliding his hands beneath it, he clasped her ankles, then ran his hands up the flesh of her calves to her thighs, pushing the material before him, urging her legs apart as he did. His mouth moved to cover her gasps as she shuddered beneath his touch, and she drank of him deeply, then bit his lower lip as his hands met at her center. He caressed her, then slid one finger smoothly into her, and Brinna arched into the invasion, her hands shifting to his shoulders and clutching him desperately as she wriggled into the caress.

Tearing her mouth away then, she shook her head desperately and gasped as he slid his finger out, then back in. Reaching down into his braies again, she grasped him almost roughly, trying to tell him what she wanted as she bit into his shoulder to prevent crying out. She felt the cloth loosen around her hand, then felt it no longer as he sprang free in her hand. Brinna ran her hand the length of his shaft, then pressed her feet against the bale, sliding her behind to the edge of it in search of him.

Chuckling roughly at her eagerness, Royce gave in to her request and edged closer, brushing her hand away to grasp his manhood himself and steer it on the course it needed to follow. She felt him rub against her, caressing her as his hand had done a moment ago, and wiggled impatiently, but still he did not enter her, but teased and caressed and rubbed until Brinna thought she would go mad. It was at that point that the tension that had been building inside of her suddenly broke. Taken by surprise, Brinna cried out, her legs snapping closed on either side of his hips as she arched backward.

Covering her mouth with his own, Royce chose that moment to thrust into her. A sudden sharp pain flared briefly where they joined, and Brinna stiffened against it, then gasped and relaxed somewhat as it passed. When he began to draw himself out then, Brinna's eyes popped open, dismay covering her face as she clutched at his buttocks to keep him inside her.

"Nay," she gasped in protest, then blinked in surprise as he drove into her again. "Oh," she breathed, arching automatically and returning his smile a bit distractedly as she felt the tension begin to build again. "Oh."

"Aye," Royce murmured, slipping his hands beneath her buttocks and lifting her into his thrusts.

"Joan?"

Brinna blinked her eyes open with a sigh, sorry to see her stolen moment pass so swiftly. They had just finished the ride she had started. Royce had spilled his seed with a triumphant cry that had made the horses shift and whinny nervously in their stalls in response. Brinna had followed him quickly, biting into the cloth of his tunic as her body spasmed and twitched around him. Then he had slumped against her slightly, holding her even as she held him. Now it was over, it seemed, and he had brought reality back with that one name. *Joan.*

"Joan?" Straightening, he smiled down at her with a combination of uncertainty and gentleness. "Are you all right? I did not hurt—"

"Joan?"

They both stiffened at that shout from out of the darkness.

Brinna peered anxiously over Royce's shoulder even as he cast a glance that way himself. They both saw that the stable door was open and someone was walking up the shadowed aisle toward them. Cursing, Royce pulled out of her and quickly tugged her skirt down into place. Replacing himself inside his braies, he turned away, hiding her with his back as he faced the approaching man.

"Who goes there?" he asked tensely, reaching for his sword.

"Lord Laythem."

Brinna heard the breath whoosh out of Royce at that announcement, and bit her lip as she clasped Joan's gown to her breasts and ducked fully behind him. There was a moment of tense silence as the man approached, then the crunch of straw under his feet ended and there was a weary sigh.

"Well, it would seem I waited too long to see if you would return to the hall," he murmured, then added wryly, "Or perhaps not long enough."

"I am sorry, my lord," Royce began grimly. "I—"

"Do not be sorry, lad. I was young once myself. Besides, this makes me feel better. At least now I won't have to feel that I forced Joan into something."

Brinna saw Royce's hands unclench as he relaxed. Then Lord Laythem cleared his throat and murmured, "Though it may be a good idea to move the wedding date forward a bit."

"Aye. Of course," Royce agreed promptly. "Tomorrow?"

"Eager, are you?" Lord Laythem laughed. "I shall talk to Robert, but I do not think tomorrow is likely. We crown the Lord of Misrule tomorrow," he reminded him. "I'll see what I can arrange and let you know."

"As you wish, my lord." Brinna could hear the grin in Royce's voice and knew he was pleased. Her own heart seemed suddenly leaden. But then, she wasn't the one he would be marrying.

"Aye. Well, you had best collect yourselves and return to the hall. I would not want anyone else to catch the two of you so."

"Aye, my lord."

"Good." There was a rustle as he turned to leave, then

he paused. "Joan, I want to talk to you ere Mass on the morrow . . . Joan?"

"Aye," Brinna whispered, afraid to speak lest he notice that her voice differed from his daughter's. Not apparently noticing anything amiss, he wished them good night and left.

Royce whirled to face her as soon as Lord Laythem was gone. He was jubilant as he helped her redon Joan's gown, talking excitedly about how this was a wonderful thing. How the arrival of the dower early would aid his people. They would leave the day after the wedding. They would travel to Thurleah, purchase this, repair that, and spend every spare moment in bed. Brinna listened to all this, forcing herself to smile and nod, and doing her best to hide the fact that her heart was breaking.

CHAPTER FIVE

"Here, put this on."

Brinna turned from straightening the bed linens as Lady Joan slammed into the room. "My lady?"

"Put this on," Joan repeated grimly, stripping her gown even as she spoke. "And give me your dress."

"But—"

"Now, Brinna. There is no time."

Brinna started to undress, responding automatically to the authority in Joan's voice, then halted. "Nay We can not do this. I cannot. Your father is here now. He will—"

"Today they appoint the Lord of Misrule. All will be chaos all day. 'Sides, he will not bother with me—*you*. He will be drinking and carousing with Lord Menton. You can easily avoid him."

Brinna shook her head grimly. "I cannot."

"You must," Joan hissed, grabbing her hand desperately and giving it a squeeze. "Just this one last time."

"But—"

"You got me into this," Joan said accusingly, her patience snapping, and Brinna's eyes widened in amazement.

"Me?"

"Aye, you. If you hadn't let Royce drag you off to the stables for a quick tumble like some cheap—" She snapped her mouth closed on the rest of what she was going to say and sighed.

"How did you find out?" Brinna asked, her voice heavy with guilt.

"What do you think Father wished to speak to me about?" she asked grimacing, then bit her lip miserably. "The wedding is tomorrow. I have to warn—" She snapped her mouth closed again and frowned, then turned away, took two steps, then turned back. "Please? Just this one last time. You will not be discovered. I promise. Truly, you know as well as I that 'twill be chaotic today."

"Not at Mass it won't be."

Sensing that she was weakening, Joan pounced. "You shall leave late for Mass. That way, Father will be seated at the front with Lord and Lady Menton, and you and Lord Thurleah will be at the back of the chapel. Just don't let Thurleah dawdle once Mass is over and it should be all right."

Brinna blew her breath out on a sigh, then nodded and continued to undress, wondering as she did why she had even hesitated. She wanted to do this. She was eager to spend any little moment of time with Royce that she could while she could.

"Oh, good," Joan said.

Brinna whirled from closing the bedroom door to stare at Joan in amazement as she rushed toward her. Truly, she had not expected the other girl to be there yet. She had thought Joan would spend every last moment of freedom she had as far from this room as possible. Actually, she had rather hoped that Joan would. After the day she had had, Brinna could have used a few moments of peace and quiet.

As per Joan's instructions, Brinna had kept Royce waiting that morning, leaving him cooling his heels in the hall as she and Joan had paced nervously inside the room until Joan had determined that enough time had passed so that Brinna and Royce would be late for Mass and end up seated far from Lord Laythem and the possibility of his noticing something amiss. And the girl had been right. Mass was already started when they reached the chapel. Royce ushered her to the nearest seat, as far from her "father" as Brinna could have wished, and they had sat silently through the Mass.

Royce would have waited then to return to the great hall with the other Menton guests, but Brinna had exited the moment it was over, forcing him to follow or leave her without an escort. She had apologized prettily once they were out of the chapel, claiming a need for air with a suggestive smile that had made his eyes glow with the memory of the last time she had proclaimed a desire for air. Moments later Brinna had found herself locked in his arms in a handy alcove, being kissed silly. And so the day had gone, with Brinna spending half her time dodging Joan's father and the other half locked in Royce's arms in some handy secluded spot. The only chance she had had to relax was during the feast itself. She, along with everyone else, had cheered the crowning of the kitchen lad who usually manned the spit as the Lord of Misrule, then had helped Lord and Lady Menton and most of their younger guests in serving the servants while Joan's father and another guest had taken on the role of minstrels and attempted to provide music for the celebrants.

Once it was over, however, Brinna had again found herself dodging Lord Laythem and spending more and more time in dim corners and dark alcoves, her head growing increasingly fuzzy with a combination of drink and lust. Royce had not gone unaffected by the revelry and their passion himself. The last time she had dragged him off to avoid Lord Laythem, he had nearly taken her in the

shadows at the head of the stairs before recalling himself
and putting an end to their embrace. Then he had suggested a little breathlessly that mayhap they should end
that evening early so that their wedding day would come
that much quicker. Which was why Brinna was now back
in Joan's room before the usual time.

"I am glad you are here," Joan went on, clasping her
hands with a smile. "I was afraid I would not have the opportunity to thank you and say good-bye ere I left."

"Left?" Brinna echoed faintly.

"Aye. I am leaving. Phillip and I are running away to
be married."

"Phillip?" Brinna stared at her blankly, sure the drink
had affected her more than she had realized.

"Phillip of Radfurn. Lord Thurleah's cousin?" Joan
prompted with amusement. "When he visited Laythem
we—" She shrugged. "We fell in love. He followed me to
court, then on here, and has been staying in the village so
that we could see each other."

"But he told Royce that you were a spoiled brat,"
Brinna reminded her in confusion.

"Aye. He was hoping to convince him to break the
contract. He wanted me for himself, you see."

"I see," Brinna murmured, but shook her head. She
didn't really see at all. "Did you say you were running
away?"

"Aye. To be married. Phillip is fetching the horses now."

"But you can't. You are supposed to marry Royce tomorrow morning."

"Well, obviously I will not be there."

"But you cannot do this. He's—"

"I know, I know," Joan rolled her eyes as she moved to
the window to peer down into the darkness of the courtyard below. "He is a nice man. Well, if you like him so

much, why do you not marry him? He will be looking for a wife now that I am out of the picture anyway. As for me, Phillip is more my sort. We understand each other. And we will not spend our days moldering out on some old estate. He adores court as much as I do."

"What of your father?"

Joan grimaced. "He will be furious. He may even withhold my dower. But Phillip does not care. He loves me and will take me with or without—" She paused suddenly, then smiled. "There he is. He has the horses. Well, I'm off."

Whirling away from the window, she pulled the hood of her mantle over her head and hurried to the door. Pausing there, she glanced back. "I left the rest of the coins I promised you in the chest. Thank you for everything, Brinna."

She was gone before Brinna could think of a thing to say to stop her. Sighing as the door snapped closed, Brinna sank down on the edge of the bed in dismay.

What a mess. It was all a mess. Joan was rushing off with Lord Radfurn. Royce's plans would be ruined. His hopes for his people crushed. And she was at fault, she realized with horror. She had ruined everything for him. If she had not masqueraded as Joan, Joan would have been forced to remain here and spend time with him and—

Oh, dear Lord, how could she have done this to him?

"Joan!" Sabrina rushed into the room, slamming the door behind her with a sigh. "It is madness out there. Everyone is drunk and I thought I saw Brinna slipping out of the keep—" She paused as she drew close enough to see the color of Brinna's eyes and the miserable expression on her face. "Brinna?"

She nodded solemnly.

"Then that was Joan I saw slipping out of the keep?"

"Aye," Brinna sighed "She is running off with Phillip of Radfurn."

"What?" Sabrina shrieked. "Oh, I knew that man was trouble."

Brinna's eyes widened in surprise. "Phillip of Radfurn?"

"Aye. He was all over her at Laythem. Trailing after her like a puppy dog. Going on and on about how grand Henry's court is. As if Joan's head wasn't already stuffed with the thought herself." She shook her head in disgust and dropped to sit on the bed beside Brinna. "He must have followed us here."

"Aye, he did."

"Then she has probably been slipping out to see him every day. No wonder she wanted me to accompany you. That way she could flit about unchaperoned. Lord knows what they have been getting up to. They—oh, my God!" Sabrina turned on her in horror as if just understanding the significance of Joan's running away. "What are we going to do? Lord Laythem will be furious when he finds out."

"No doubt," Brinna agreed, thinking that the man would also be mightily confused after coming across someone he thought was Joan messing about with Royce in the stables just last night. He would be furious to think that after that, she had then run off with Radfurn. Royce would be just as confused and angry.

"Oh, dear Lord." Sabrina stood abruptly and moved toward the door. "I am getting out of here."

"Out of here?" Brinna stood up anxiously. "What do you mean out of here?"

"My father sent men with Uncle Edmund to escort me home to be married. I had insisted that we wait until after the wedding to go, but now . . ." Pausing at the door, she turned back to shake her head. "I will insist we leave first thing on the morrow. I do not want to be here when Uncle Edmund discovers this. He will skin me alive for my involvement. And I would rather be far and away from here before he finds out."

"But should we not tell them? They will worry and—"

"Worry? Girl, what are you thinking of? Forget their worry and think of yourself."

Brinna blinked in surprise. "I have nothing to worry about. I am just a servant."

"Who has been parading as a noble for the past nearly two weeks," Sabrina pointed out, then bit her lip. "Oh, dear Lord, I knew I should have told you this sooner."

"What?" Brinna asked warily.

Sabrina shook her head "I was talking to Christina that first night at table. The night Joan stayed up here to train you to be a lady," she explained. "She happened to mention that a neighbor's smithy got caught impersonating Lord Menton this last summer. It seems the lord had commissioned a new suit of mail. The smithy finished it earlier than expected, but rather than take it at once to his lord, he donned it and paraded about, masquerading as him. He was caught, and they buried him alive with the mail saying that since he coveted it so much he could spend eternity with it."

Brinna paled and winced at the story, then shook her head. "Aye, but that was different. Lady Joan insisted I masquerade as her. She said she would say 'twas all a jest and all would be well. She—"

"She is not here to tell anyone that, is she? And as it turns out, 'tis not much of a jest. At least I don't think Lord Laythem or Lord Thurleah will see it as one." Sabrina nodded as Brinna's eyes widened in dawning horror.

"Mark my words. Dirty your face and hair with soot, re-don your kerchief and clothes, then get you on that pallet by the door and feign sleep until the morrow. When they come looking for Joan, claim she did not return last night and you know not where she is, then just get out of the way. As for me, I am going to speak to my father's man and see if 'tis too late to leave tonight."

Brinna leapt into action the moment the door was closed, rushing to the chest to begin digging through it for her ratty old gown and the strip of cloth to cover her hair. She had just sunk to her knees by the chest in horror as she recalled that Joan had been wearing her clothes when she left, when the door to the room opened again.

"Ah, yer here already," the old crone who entered murmured with disappointment as she spotted Brinna by the chest. "I was hoping to beat ye here and see yer bed turned down ere ye arrived."

Brinna made a choking sound and the old woman smiled benignly. "Now, now. I know ye insisted I rest a bit longer to be sure I'm recovered, but really, I am well now and ready to take on my duties again. 'Sides, I wouldn't leave ye in the hands of some inexperienced little kitchen maid on the eve of yer wedding."

Brinna held her breath in horror as the woman, who could only be Joan's maid, approached. At any moment the woman would cry out in horror once she saw Brinna up close and realized that her eye color was all wrong and her features just a touch off—but it never happened. Instead, Brinna's eyes were the ones to widen in realization as she saw the clouds that obscured the woman's eyes leaving her nearly blind. Brinna was safe for now, so long as she kept her mouth shut. But she had to figure a way out of this mess by morning, else she might find herself spending the day watching them dig a grave to bury her alive in.

Brinna stood silently between Royce and Lord Laythem, her head bowed to hide the color of her eyes and her shaking knees. She couldn't be sure whether they shook from her fear of discovery, or the fact that she had been standing with her knees slightly bent all throughout the priest's short morning Mass in an effort to appear an inch or so shorter so as not to give herself away to Joan's father.

It was fate that had brought her here. Fickle fate, blocking her at every turn, making escape impossible. First her clothes had left the room on Joan's back; then Joan's maid had arrived to usher her to bed before settling herself on the pallet before the door, ensuring that no one entered . . . and that Brinna couldn't leave. She had spent the night wide awake, tossing and turning, as she tried to find a way out of this cauldron of trouble. The only thing she had been able to come up with was to simply slip away at her first opportunity, find Aggie, get her to find her something more appropriate for a servant to wear, then do as Sabrina had suggested.

Fate had stepped in to remove that opportunity as well. She simply had not been given the chance. Joan's maid had barely risen in the morning and begun to fuss around Brinna before the door had burst open to allow Lady Menton and a bevy of servants to enter. Aggie had been among them, and Brinna had waited stiffly for her to say something, but the woman who had raised her from birth seemed not to recognize her as Brinna was bathed, dressed, and primped. It wasn't until just before Royce arrived that Brinna had realized that the woman had known who she was all along. The bath had been removed and Lady Menton and the rest of the servants had left with it when

Aggie had suddenly stepped up to her and placed a silver chain about her neck.

"Yer necklace, m'lady. Ye can't be getting married without this," she had murmured. "'Twas yer mother's."

Brinna had lifted the amulet that hung from the chain in her hand and peered down at it, her eyes widening as she recognized it as the one that Aggie had worn for as long as she had known her.

"All will be well," the old woman had whispered gently, and Brinna had gasped.

"You know!"

Giving her a sharp look of warning, Aggie had gestured to Joan's maid, who was busy digging through the chest, then chided Brinna gently. "I've known from the beginning. Did ye think I wouldn't when I met that other girl in here?"

"But what do I do?"

"You love him, don't you?"

Brinna's answer had been in her eyes, and Aggie had smiled. "Then marry him."

"But—"

"Here we are." Joan's maid had approached then with a veil for her to wear, and Aggie had merely offered Brinna a reassuring smile and slipped from the room. Then Joan's maid had veiled her, Royce had arrived, and she had found herself making the walk she had made every day since taking on this foolish masquerade. Only this morning she had known she was walking to her death.

Mass this morning had been delayed and shortened due to the wedding, but now the priest had finished it and moved on to the ceremony while Brinna struggled with what to do. She knew what she *should* do. Throw off the veil that half-hid her features and proclaim who she really was before this went any further. Unfortunately, fear was riding her just now. While Brinna loved Royce, she certainly did not think that she could not live without him. She was quite attached to living actually. In fact, the more she considered how some poor smithy had been killed for daring to misrepresent himself as his lord, the more she loved life.

"Do you, Joan Jean Laythem, take Royce to be your . . ."

A rushing in her ears drowned out the priest's voice briefly, and Brinna felt the sweat break out on her forehead as she swallowed some of the bile rising up in her throat.

"Love, honor, and obey . . ."

Love, she thought faintly. Aye, she loved him. And she thought he might actually love her, too. But how long would that last once he realized how she had tricked him? Good Lord, he would loathe her. How could he not when she was taking the choice away from him. Tricking him into marriage with a scullery maid.

"My lady?"

Blinking, she peered at the priest, suddenly aware of the silence that surrounded her. They were waiting for her answer. Her gaze slid to Royce, taking in the expression on his face. It was two parts loving admiration, and one part concern as he awaited her response. Swallowing, she tried to get the words out. I do, she thought. I do. I do. "I don't."

"What?"

Brinna hardly heard Lord Laythem's indignant roar as she watched the shock and alarm fill Royce's face. Shaking her head, she gave up her slouching and stood up straight and tall, wondering even as she did what madness had overcome her. "I cannot do it."

"Joan?" The confusion and pain on Royce's face tore at her.

"You need the dower for your people. If that were not so . . . But it is, and I cannot do this to you. You would never forgive me. And you shouldn't forgive a woman who could do that to you."

Royce shook his head in confusion. "What are you saying?"

"I am not Joan."

There was silence for a moment, then Royce gave an incredulous laugh. "You jest!"

"Nay. I am not Joan Laythem!" Brinna insisted, and her heart thundering in her chest, she ripped the veil from her head. As those there to witness the occasion leaned forward in confusion, wondering what they were suppose to be seeing, she whirled to face Lord Laythem. "I am naught but a scullery maid. I—your daughter—I was sent to tend to Lady Laythem when she arrived because her lady's maid was ill. When she realized how similar we were in looks, she insisted I take her place for Lord Royce to woo," she ended lamely, despair and resignation on her face.

"Joan." Lord Laythem turned her to face him, then paused in surprise as he noted the extra inches she suddenly sported. Frowning, he shook his head and looked her grimly in the eye. "Joan, I—green," he declared with dismay.

Royce frowned, his stomach clenching in concern at the expression on the man's face. "My lord?" he asked warily.

"Her eyes are green," Lord Laythem said faintly.

"Nay, my lord." Royce frowned at him, his own eyes moving to the lovely gray orbs now filling with tears of fear and loss. "Her eyes are as gray as your own."

"Aye, but my daughter's are green."

Royce blinked at that, then shook his head with horror. "Are you saying this is not your daughter?"

"Aye," he murmured, his gaze now moving slowly over her features, taking in the tiniest differences, the smallest variations with amazement, before he recalled the problem before them and asked. "Girl—what is your name?"

"Brinna," she breathed miserably.

"Well, Brinna, are you saying that since my daughter has arrived here, you have been Joan?"

"Aye," she confessed, shamefaced.

"Even in the stables?"

Her face suffusing with color, Brinna nodded, wincing as Royce cursed harshly.

"And where is my daughter now?" Lord Laythem asked, ignoring the younger man.

"She ran off to marry Phillip of Radfurn last night," Brinna murmured, turning to peer at Royce as she said the words and wincing at the way he blanched. Knowing that all his hopes for his people were now ashes at his feet, she turned away in shame, flinching when he grasped her arm and jerked her back around.

"You knew her plan all along? You helped her?" he said accusingly with bewildered hurt, and Brinna bit her lip as she shook her head.

"I helped her, aye, but I didn't know of her plan. Well, I mean, I knew she did not want to marry you and that she was looking for a way to avoid it, but I did not know how she planned to do so. And . . . and had I—I didn't know you when I agreed to help her, I just—she offered me more coins than I had ever hoped to see and I thought I could use them to make Aggie comfortable and—" Recognizing the contempt on his face and the fact that nothing she was saying was helping any, Brinna unconsciously clutched her mother's amulet and whispered, "I'm sorry."

"Look, girl," Lord Laythem began impatiently, only to pause as his gaze landed on the amulet she was clutching so desperately. Stilling, he reached a trembling hand to snatch at the charm. "Where did you get this?" he asked shakily, and Brinna swallowed nervously, afraid of next being accused of being a thief.

"It is my mother's," she murmured, recalling what Aggie had said as she placed it around her neck. Brinna had always known that Aggie was not the woman who had birthed her, but since Aggie had always avoided speaking of it, Brinna had never questioned her on the subject.

"Your mother's?" Paling, Lord Laythem stared at her blankly for a moment. Then, "What is her name?"

"I don't know."

"Of course you know, you must know." He gave her an impatient little shake. "What is her name?"

"She doesn't know."

They all turned at those words to see Aggie framed in the chapel door. Mouth tight with anger, she moved her wretched old body slowly through the parting crowd toward them. "She's telling the truth. She doesn't know. I never told her. What good would it have done?"

"Aggie?" Brinna stepped to the old woman's side, uncertainty on her face.

"I am sorry, child. There was no sense in yer knowing until now. I feared ye would grow bitter and angry. But now ye must know." Turning, she glared at Lord Laythem grimly. "Her mother was a fine lady. A real and true lady in every sense of the word. She arrived in the village twenty-one years ago, young and as beautiful as Brinna herself. The only difference between the two was that her eyes were green."

Her gaze moved from Brinna's gray eyes to Lord Laythem's own eyes of the same gray-blue shade before she continued. "I was the first person she met when she arrived. She told me she was looking to buy a cottage and perhaps set up shop. My husband had just passed on and we had no children. We used to run an alehouse from our cottage, but it was too much for a woman alone to handle, so I sold her our cottage. When she asked me to stay on and work with her, I agreed.

"As time passed, we became friends and she told me a tale, of a pretty young girl, the older of two daughters born to a fine lord and lady in the south. The girl was sent to foster with another fine lord and lady in the north, where she stayed until her eighteenth year, when the son of this lord and lady got married. The son returned from earning his knight's spurs three months before the wedding."

She glanced at Lord Menton meaningfully, nodding when his eyes widened at the realization that she spoke of him. Then her gaze slid to Lord Laythem again. "He brought with him a friend—and it was this friend who changed our girl's life. She fell in love with him. And he claimed to love her, and to want to marry her. Young as she was, she believed him," Aggie spat bitterly, making Lord Laythem wince despite his confusion.

"They became lovers, and then just before his friend's marriage, her lover was called home. His father had died and he had to take up his role as lord of the manor. He left, but not before once again vowing his undying love and giving our girl *that*." She pointed to the amulet that hung around Brinna's neck and grimaced. "He swore to return for her. Two weeks later a messenger arrived to collect our girl and take her home. She returned reluctantly only to learn that her parents had arranged a marriage for her. She refused, of course, for she loved another. But her

parents would hear none of it. Marriage was about position, not love. Then she found out she was pregnant. She
thought surely her parents would cancel the marriage and
send for her lover then, but they merely pushed up the
date of the marriage, hoping that the intended groom
would think the babe his own. Our girl collected all the
jewels she had and took part of the coins meant for her
dower and fled for here, where she knew her 'love' would
eventually return for her as he had promised.

"She came to the village because she knew that if she
approached Lady Menton . . . your mother, my lord"—
she explained, with a glance at Robert—"she would have
sent her home. She thought that if she hid in the village,
she would hear news of when her lover returned, yet not
be noticed by the people in the castle. So, she waited and
worked, and grew daily with child.

"Time passed, and I began to doubt her lover, but she
never did. 'Oh, Aggie,' she'd laugh lightly. 'Do not be silly.
He loves me. He will come.'" She was glaring so fiercely at
Lord Laythem as she said that, that Brinna was getting the
uncomfortable feeling that she knew how this was going
to end.

"He didn't, of course, but she kept her faith right up until the day she died. The day Brinna was born. She had
walked to the village market as she did every day for news,
and she returned pale and sobbing, desperately clutching
her stomach. She was in labor. A month early and angry
at the upset that had brought about her birth, the babe
came hard and fast. She was barely a handful when she
was out. So wee I didn't think she'd survive the night."

Aggie smiled affectionately at the tall strong girl beside
her as she spoke. "But you did. It was your mother who
didn't. She was bleeding inside and nothing I did could
stop it. She held you in her arms and named you Brinna,

telling you and me both that it meant of nobility. Then as her life bled out of her, she told me what had upset her and brought about her early labor. She had heard in the village that her lover had returned. He was here visiting the young Lord Menton. He had arrived early that morning. . . . With his new bride, our girl's own younger sister." Aggie's hard eyes fixed on Edmund Laythem. "Brinna's mother was Sarah Margaret Atherton, whose sister was Louise May Atherton Laythem."

Brinna gasped and turned accusing eyes on the older man standing beside Royce. She was blind at first to the tears coursing down his face.

"They told me she was dead," he whispered brokenly, then met Brinna's gaze beseechingly. "Robert knew of my love for your mother and sent word to me that she had been called home. I moved as quickly as I could, but winter struck before I got affairs in order and could leave. As soon as the spring thaw set in I hied my way south to Atherton, but when I arrived, it was only to be told that she was dead. Her parents offered me her younger sister, Louise, in her place. I was the lord now and expected to produce heirs as quickly as possible to ensure the line, and she looked so like Sarah I thought I could pretend . . ." His voice trailed away in misery. "It didn't work, of course. In the end I simply made her miserable. She wasn't my Sarah. Sarah was full of laughter and joy, she had a love for life. Louise was more sullen in nature and shy, and all her presence managed to do was remind me of what I had lost. In the end I couldn't bear to be around her, to even see her. I avoided Laythem to avoid the pain of that reminder."

Taking Brinna's hands, he met her pained gaze firmly. "I loved your mother with all of my heart. She was the one bright light in my life. I would give anything to be able to change the way things worked out in the past, but I can only work with the now. I am pleased to claim you as my daughter." Pausing, he glanced at Royce, then squeezed her hands and asked. "You love him?"

"Aye," Brinna whispered, lowering her eyes unhappily.

Nodding, he then turned to Royce. "Am I right in assuming that you love my daughter?"

Royce hesitated, then said grimly, "I don't know who your daughter is. I thought she"—he gestured toward Brinna unhappily—"I thought this was your daughter, Joan. Now, it seems she is a scullery maid who is your illegitimate daughter and that she was pretending to be Joan so that the real Joan could run off with my own cousin. I won't be married, I won't get the dowry my people need, I—" He paused in his angry tirade as Brinna gave a despairing sob and turned to hurry out of the church.

Lord Laythem watched his daughter flee, then turning determinedly on Royce, he straightened his shoulders. "Leave your anger at her deception aside and search your heart. Do you love Brinna?"

Royce didn't have to think long at all before saying, "Aye, I love the girl, whether she is Joan or Brinna, lady or scullery maid. I love her. But it matters not one whit. My people depend upon me. I have a duty to them. I have to marry a woman with a large dower." He heaved a sigh, then straightened grimly. "Now if you will excuse me, I shall leave and see if I cannot accomplish that duty and at least—"

"You have the dower." At Royce's startled look, Laythem nodded. "We had a contract. Joan has broken it. Her dower is forfeit. Now you need not marry for a dower. You may marry as you wish. If you love Brinna, I would still be proud to have you for a son-in-law."

Royce blinked once as that knowledge sank in, then

whirled to the priest and grabbed him by the lower arms. "Wait here, Father. We'll be right back," he assured him, then whirled to chase after Brinna.

Lord Laythem watched him go with a sigh, then smiled at his friend Lord Menton as he and his wife stepped forward to join him.

"I didn't know," Robert murmured, and Lady Menton stepped forward to squeeze Edmund's hand. "Had I realized that Sarah was in the village, I would have sent a messenger to you at once. And had I known she had a daughter here—"

"I know," Edmund interrupted quietly, then arched an eyebrow at his friend's daughter, Christina, as she stared after the absent Royce, shaking her head with slight bemusement. "What is it?" he asked her.

"Oh nothing really," she murmured, giving a small laugh. "I was just thinking that if Brinna is your daughter, she too is half-Norman and they really were three French hens after all." When he and her parents stared at her blankly, she opened her mouth to explain about the day she had found Sabrina, Brinna, and Joan in a huddle, and the comment she had made about "three French hens," then shook her head and murmured, "Never mind. 'Twas nothing."

Royce rushed out of the chapel just in time to see Brinna disappear into the stables. Following, he found her kneeling in the straw where they had made love, sobbing miserably. Swallowing, he moved silently up behind her and knelt at her side. "J-Brinna?"

Her sobs dying an abrupt death, she straightened and turned, her eyes growing wide as she peered at him. Then she scrambled to her feet, turning away to face the wall as she wiped the tears from her face. "Is there something you wished, my lord? A pot you need scrubbed or a—" Her voice died in her throat as he turned her to face him.

"I need you," he told her gently. "If you will have me."

Her face crumpled like an empty gown, and she shook her head miserably as tears welled in her eyes. "'Tis cruel of you to jest so, my lord."

"I am not jesting."

"Aye, you are. You must marry someone with a dower. Your people need that to survive the winter and I—" Pausing suddenly, she bent to dig under her skirt until she found the small sack she had fastened at her waist. The sack jingled with the coins Joan had given her as she held them out to him. "I have this. It is not much, and I know it won't make up for what you lost with Joan, but mayhap it will help until you find a bride with a dower large enough—"

"I have the dower." He pushed the hand holding the sack away and drew her closer. "Now I need the bride."

"I-I don't understand," Brinna stuttered as his arms closed around her.

"Joan broke the contract. The dower is mine even though we won't marry. My responsibility to my people is fulfilled. Now I can marry whom I wish," he whispered into her ear before dropping a kiss on the lobe of that shell-like appendage.

"You can?" she asked huskily.

"Aye, and I wish to marry you."

"Oh, Royce," she half-sobbed, pressing her face into his neck. "You don't know. . . . I hoped, I dreamed, I prayed that if God would just let me have this one gift, I would never ask for anything ever again."

"This gift?" Royce asked uncertainly, leaning back to peer down at her.

"You," Brinna explained. "You came to me on Christmas Day, my lord. And you were the most wonderful

Christmas gift I could ever have hoped for." She laughed suddenly, happiness glowing in her face. "And I even get to keep you."

"That you do, my love. That you do."

LEIGH GREENWOOD

Father Christmas

For Brandon, who never got to celebrate Christmas.

CHAPTER ONE

"I've got to be a fool to come here. I should be headed for California, where nobody would ever find me."

Joe Ryan glanced over at his dog, Samson. The big, yellow, short-haired mongrel was sniffing among some rocks, a growl in his throat, the hair on his back standing up.

"Stop looking for coyotes and listen to me."

The dog looked up but almost immediately turned back to the tangle of boulders and desert broom.

"You keep poking your nose into every pile of rocks you pass, and you're going to find a wolf one of these days. Maybe you can talk to him," Joe said to his horse, General Burnside. "He never listens to me."

Joe rode through the Arizona desert with care. He kept away from the flat valley floor, where a man could be seen for miles. Rather than stop for water at the cottonwood-lined San Pedro River, he looked for springs and seeps. He had shaken the posse before he left Colorado, but the law would soon figure out where he was. He planned to be gone by then.

"I can't imagine why Pete wanted a ranch in this country," Joe said aloud. "Even a coyote would have a hard time making a living."

He had fallen into the habit of talking to his dog and horse just to hear the sound of a human voice. He'd seen few people since he broke out of a Colorado jail a month earlier.

Sometime after midday, Joe pulled up just short of the crest of a small ridge. He paused to light a cigarette and let his gaze wander over every part of the landscape. When he was satisfied that there was no movement, he started forward. Using the cover of juniper thickets, scattered mesquite, and greasewood, he crossed the ridge and rode into a basin.

Pete Wilson's ranch lay below.

Joe studied the land closely as he rode in. It was good land. It would be hot in summer, but there was plenty of food for cattle. A small creek passed close to the house. He was surprised Pete had had enough sense to choose such a good spot. His former partner hadn't struck him as a far-sighted man. Impatient and bad-tempered was a better description. But then, a shrewish wife could ruin any man. And from what Pete had said, Mary Wilson was a thoroughgoing harridan.

Well, it didn't matter to Joe. He meant to find the gold, clear his name, and be on his way. It wasn't cold for December, but he was looking forward to the warm breezes of California.

"Come on, Samson. Let's get it over with."

Pressing his heels into the flanks of his lanky, mouse-gray gelding, Joe started toward the ranch.

Mary Wilson struggled to sit up. The room spun violently before her eyes. She closed them and concentrated hard. She had to get up. She was too weak to stay here any longer.

"Get the horse," she said to the blond child who watched her with anxious eyes. "Don't try to saddle him. Just put a halter on him and bring him to the porch."

"He won't come to me," Sarah Wilson said.

"Offer him some oats. I'll be outside in a moment."

The child left reluctantly. Mary didn't like forcing Sarah to fetch the animal, but she had no choice. She wasn't even sure she was strong enough to make the twenty-two-mile trip into town. She didn't know how she could be so weak without being ill. She had felt fine until two days ago. Then her strength had just vanished. Taking a firm grip on the bedpost, she pulled herself to her feet. The room spun more rapidly than ever. Gasping from the effort, Mary refused to let go of the bedpost. She *would* stand up. She *would* make it to town. She had thought she had more time. The baby wasn't due for another month.

She attempted to take a step, but her swollen stomach unbalanced her. She used a chair to steady herself. No sooner had she regained her equilibrium than she heard Sarah scream. Fear gave Mary the strength she lacked. She stumbled across the room to the rifle she kept on the wall next to the door. She took it down and managed to open the door about a foot. Leaning against the door jamb, she pushed herself forward until she could see into the ranch yard.

Sarah came flying up the steps. She almost knocked Mary down as she buried herself in Mary's skirts. Mary's gaze found and locked on the rider who had reached the corral. What she saw frightened her.

A stranger dressed in buckskin and denim, astride a huge gray horse and accompanied by a large dog, was riding into the yard. A big man with very broad shoulders, he wore a gun belt and carried a rifle. His hat was tilted too low to allow her to see much of his face, but his chin and cheeks were covered by several weeks' growth of dark blond beard. He rode right up to the porch.

Sarah tightened her grip on Mary's skirts. Mary's grip on the doorway began to give way. She leaned her shoulder against the wood to keep from falling.

The man came to a stop at the steps. He didn't dismount, just pushed his hat back from his forehead and stared hard at Mary. Mary found herself looking into the coldest blue eyes she'd ever seen.

"This Pete Wilson's place?" the man asked.

His voice was deep and rough. It didn't sound threatening, but it sounded far away. The ringing in Mary's ears distracted her. She felt her muscles begin to relax, and she tightened her grip on the rifle. "Yes," Mary said.

"You his wife?"

"I'm his widow. What can I do for you?"

The man's face seemed to go out of focus for a moment. Then it started to spin very slowly. One moment he was right side up, the next upside down. Mary fought to still the revolving image, but it only moved faster.

Then she saw nothing at all.

Joe wasn't surprised when Mary Wilson met him at the door with a rifle. He *was* surprised to see she was pregnant. He was even more surprised when she fainted. Damn! Now he'd have to take care of her. He knew absolutely nothing about the care and handling of extremely pregnant women.

Still, he was out of the saddle and up the front steps almost before her body had settled on the floor. He scooped up the unconscious woman. Despite her condition, she weighed very little. She looked white, totally drained of color. That wasn't good.

He kicked open the door and entered the small stone cabin. Looking around, he saw a rope bed in the corner. He carried her to the bed and eased her down. She rolled on her side. He put his hand on her forehead. She didn't feel hot. If anything, she seemed too cool. She looked more exhausted than anything else. Thin in the face. Almost gaunt. Maybe the baby was taking everything she ate. She looked big enough to be carrying a colt.

He pulled the blanket over her. Pete had lied. She was a pretty woman. There was nothing harsh or shrewish about her face. He'd never seen any female who could look that pretty without painting herself and putting on a fancy dress. She reminded him of some kind of fragile bird—but one with the heart of an eagle—standing guard over her chick.

She lay there, helpless. He wanted to touch her again—her skin had felt so soft under his hand—but the sight of the child cowering in the corner behind the bed caused him to back away.

"Is she sick?" he asked.

The child just stared at him, her eyes wide with fear. She pressed close to Mary but well out of his reach.

"Speak up, girl. I'm not going to hurt you. I want to know if she's sick or if she faints all the time."

The child cringed and practically buried herself in the crack between the bed and the wall. He noticed that her eyes kept going toward the doorway. He turned. Samson had followed him inside and flopped down a few feet from the door.

"Outside," Joe ordered, with a wave of his hand. "You're scaring the kid."

The dog whined in protest.

"Maybe later, but right now you're not welcome. Out."

With a protesting woof, the dog got up and ambled outside. He lay down directly in front of the open door, where Joe would have to step over him to get out.

Joe closed the door on Samson. "Nosy brute. I guess I

spoiled him. I don't suppose you have a name," he said to the girl, "something I can call you?"

The child continued to stare.

"I didn't think so. You got anything to eat around here? I'm hungry. I haven't had a decent meal since I went to jail."

Still no answer. Joe was confused about the child. Pete had talked about his wife a lot—that was how he'd conned Joe into teaming up with him—but he hadn't said a word about a daughter. Was this kid Pete's or Mary's?

"What does your ma like to eat?"

No answer.

"How about you?"

It was clear that the child wasn't going to say anything, so Joe decided to look around for himself. He found a little coffee, sugar, salt, some tea, beans, bacon, and flour. Some canned goods lined a shelf against the wall. He glanced back at Mary. She looked as if she needed something sustaining. "Do you have any milk?" Joe asked the child.

She continued to stare.

"Look, I'm not going to hurt you. I'm going to fix something to eat, but I need a little help here. Your ma's looking right run down. You want her to get better, don't you?"

The child nodded, and Joe felt a little of the tension inside him relax. It wasn't much progress, but it was a beginning.

"Do you have any milk?"

The child shook her head.

Hell, he thought, every ranch or farm kept a milk cow. What was she going to feed the baby if her milk ran dry? "How about eggs?" Come to think of it, he hadn't seen any chickens when he rode up. What kind of place was this, anyhow?

The child didn't say anything, but she cautiously left

her corner, approached the door, and opened it a crack. With a sharp intake of breath, she jumped back.

Joe crossed the room in a few strides. "Dammit, Samson, I told you to get out of here." The dog got up and moved off the porch. "Go on. Find me a rabbit or something for supper."

Samson disappeared behind the house. After peeping around the corner to make sure the dog wasn't waiting to attack her, the kid headed toward a shed that seemed to serve as a barn and chicken coop. Joe figured he'd better stay outside just in case Samson came back. He stuck his head inside, but Mary hadn't moved. When he turned back, the child was out of sight.

Hell! He was on the run from the law, and he had a pregnant woman and a child who wouldn't talk on his hands. He hadn't been around a respectable woman in years and didn't know what to do with one.

The kid emerged from the shed, cast a worried look around for Samson, and ran across the yard toward the house. She slowed and came reluctantly up the steps. Looking up, she held out her hands. She had an egg in each.

If it hadn't been for the long hair, Joe wouldn't have been able to tell if she was a boy or a girl. She wore a red-checked flannel shirt and black pants. Her shoes looked more like boots several sizes too large. There was nothing feminine or appealing about the child.

"Put them on the table," Joe said. "I've got to get a few things from my saddlebags." He should unsaddle General Burnside and give him a good rubdown, but that would have to wait. He unstrapped his saddlebags. He had started back up the steps before he turned back for his rifle. He didn't think there was anybody within twenty miles of this place, but he'd feel better if he had his rifle with him.

The kid had retreated to her position behind the bed. Joe placed his rifle against the wall and tossed his saddle-bags on the table. For now he'd have to use his own supplies. He had plenty of beef jerky. He didn't know anything like it for building up a person who was weak.

"Water," he called out to the child. "I need water." When he heard nothing, he turned around. She was pointing to a bucket. He looked inside. It was half full. It was also tepid.

"Fresh water." Joe held out the bucket.

Reluctantly the child came forward, took the bucket, and headed outside again.

Joe hadn't had time to pay attention to his surroundings. Only now did he notice the dozens of drawings covering the walls, all of them black ink on white paper. There were drawings of a town somewhere in the East, of the ranch and surrounding countryside, of the child, of Pete. Even of the stone cabin.

The winter scenes were the most incredible. Even in black and white, they had the power to evoke memories of winters back home in the foothills of North Carolina. The snow weighing heavily on pine boughs, icicles hanging from the roof of a wood frame house, a woman leaning over the porch rail, barnyards made pristine by a blanket of snow.

Joe pushed the recollections aside. Not even a mantle of snow could turn his past into a happy memory.

He moved along the wall, studying each picture in detail, until he stumbled over a bunch of twigs. "What the hell!" he muttered. He had knocked over a bundle of hackberry branches tied together. A few red berries showed among the dense green foliage. Each branch ended in a sharp, strong thorn.

A muffled cry from the doorway caused him to turn. The kid dropped the bucket and threw herself at the bundle of twigs. The water spilled out and quickly disappeared down the cracks between the floor boards. Joe watched, unbelieving, as the kid set the bundle of twigs back in the corner.

"That's Sarah's Christmas tree," Mary informed him in a weak, hesitant voice.

Joe hadn't realized Mary was conscious. He drew close to the bed, scrutinizing her. She seemed okay, but he intended to make sure she stayed in bed.

"That's a bunch of hackberry branches, for God's sake," he said, unable to understand why the kid continued to fuss over them, pulling and twisting the branches until she had arranged them to her satisfaction. "They ought to be tossed on the fire. She could kill herself on those thorns."

"Sarah is determined to have a Christmas tree, and that's the best she could do."

"Why didn't she look for a Jojoba? At least it doesn't have thorns."

"She wanted the red berries. Her mother used to tell her about decorating for Christmas with holly."

"You should have stopped her."

"Who are you?" Mary Wilson asked, changing the subject. "What are you doing here?"

"I'm Pete's old partner."

She started to throw back the covers.

"Lie still."

Joe's peremptory order stilled Mary's hand in midair. He pushed her arm down to her side and jerked the blanket back in place.

For a moment she seemed on the verge of defying him. Probably learning he was Pete's partner wasn't enough to make her trust him. But if she was afraid, she didn't show it. More likely she'd show her talons.

"I'm about to fix me something to eat. I need that water," Joe reminded the kid. She reluctantly left her tree to pick up the bucket and go back outside.

"Does the kid talk?" he asked.

"Yes."

"She got a name?"

"Sarah."

"Who is she?"

"Pete's daughter. Her mother died. I was his second wife."

Sarah entered the cabin with the fresh water. Joe took the bucket over to the work table. "Make sure your ma doesn't get up," he said over his shoulder. "Maybe if you sing to her, she'll go back to sleep."

"I can't . . . You shouldn't . . ." Mary began.

"Probably, but I'm doing it anyway," Joe said. "Sing!" he commanded the child.

Turning away from the two females watching him in open-mouthed bewilderment, Joe opened his saddlebags and began to lay out their contents. He was surprised when he heard a very soft voice begin to sing. He knew just enough to know the kid was singing in French.

He wondered what had made Pete Wilson leave such a family—a daughter who was petrified of dogs, wouldn't talk, and sang lullabies in French; a beautiful young wife who was so weak she couldn't stand up and was going to have a baby any minute if he could judge from the size of her.

Memories he thought he'd forgotten came rushing back. Damn! He hadn't thought of Flora in five years. He didn't know why he should now. The two women had nothing in common.

Flora had been vibrantly, noisily alive. She laughed, sang, cried, shouted, always at the top of her voice. He had been wildly in love with her, but she hadn't been willing to settle down. She had liked flash, excitement, money, action—all the things Joe had learned to avoid.

Mary was nothing like that. She was fair, thin, faded, and extremely pregnant. Despite that, she had a feminine allure. Soft skin, thick eyebrows and lashes, generous lips, the curve of her cheek, the expanse of her brow—all combined to give her an appearance of lushness completely at variance with her condition.

This woman would never want flash or excitement. She would work hard to build the kind of home that nurtured a man, that he would shed his blood to defend.

She'd be the kind of woman his grandmother almost was.

After Joe's father disappeared and his grandfather died, his grandmother had raised him. Sometimes when she spoke of her husband there was a light in her eye, a softening in her voice and touch, that spoke of a time when she had been happy and content. But most often she was harsh and demanding, the kind of woman she had become to survive on her own, to hide her grief over the kind of woman her daughter had become.

Joe was sure Mary would never be like that. She had the kind of strength, the kind of staying power, that it took to endure ill fortune.

Pete Wilson was a fool.

The sound of soft singing gently drew Mary out of the darkness that clutched at her. She opened her eyes. She must have fainted again. Sarah knelt by the bed, her hand gripping Mary's, as she softly sang one of the French lullabies her mother had taught her.

A noise caught Mary's attention, and she remembered the man. Pete's partner. He was at the stove. Then she realized that the cabin was warm. She hadn't been able to cut wood for a week. She had done her last cooking with twigs Sarah had gathered.

It was tempting to lie back and let him take care of everything. She was so tired. She couldn't tell what he was doing at the stove, but he moved with quiet confidence. Then she caught the delicious aroma of coffee.

He was cooking!

Her stomach immediately cramped, and saliva flooded her mouth. It had been almost two days since she had eaten a full meal.

"You never did tell me your name," she said.

The man turned. "Joe Ryan. Stay put," he ordered when she attempted to sit up. "The cornbread's not ready yet."

"I can't lie here while you fix supper."

"Why not? You couldn't do anything if you did get up."

Mary had never seen a man cook. She'd never even seen one in the kitchen except to eat. A good woman didn't get sick. There was no time. She remembered that. She'd heard it all her life, especially after her mother died and she'd had to take over managing the household.

"You don't have to take care of me."

Joe looked at her as if she were talking nonsense. "I considered leaving you lying in the doorway, but I figured I'd get tired of stepping over you."

"What did you fix?" Mary asked.

"Beef and cornbread. It's not fancy, but it's good."

"I appreciate your feeding Sarah. It's been a while since I've been able to fix her a decent meal."

"Or eaten one yourself," Joe said as he began to ladle the stew into two plates. "I don't suppose you have any butter?"

"No. I haven't been able to catch the cow."

"I guess the kid will have to drink water. Do you like molasses?"

"We both do," Mary answered. "I always did have a sweet tooth."

Joe opened the oven and took out a pan of cornbread. "I made it soft. That's the way my grandma used to make it."

He hadn't had cornbread this way in years.

He scooped cornbread out of the pan and put some on each plate. He covered each portion with a generous helping of molasses. "Get your water if you want it," he said to Sarah. He moved a chair next to the bed.

"I can get up," Mary said.

"I told you to stay put."

"I'm not an invalid."

"Then why did you faint twice today?"

"I'm sorry."

"I don't mind that," Joe said. "I just mind you acting like you're well. It's not sensible. I don't like it when people don't act sensible."

"Then what is the *sensible* thing to do?" Mary asked, slightly put out.

"Lie back and let me feed you. Then go to sleep until supper. You're worn down. I'm surprised you didn't faint before you reached the door."

She would have if it hadn't been for Sarah's scream. Only fear for the child had gotten her that far. She had passed out the minute she realized Joe didn't mean them any harm. She watched as he picked up the table and moved it next to the chair. Then he placed both plates on the table. He placed a spoon beside one. He pulled up a second chair, and Sarah slid into it.

"Eat," he said to Sarah.

"Go on," Mary said when the child hesitated. "I'm sure it's as good as anything I could make."

"I'm a good cook," Joe said. "You sure you can sit up?"

"Of course." Mary managed to pull herself into a sitting position. She hoped he didn't know how close she was to fainting again.

"Lean forward."

She couldn't. He lifted her up and placed the pillows behind her.

"You're weak as a damned kitten."

"I was on my way to town when you got here."

"You wouldn't have made it out of the damned yard."

She would have loved to disagree with him, but she doubted she would have made it out of the house. "I would appreciate it if you would watch your language in front of Sarah."

"She's heard worse if Pete's her pa."

"Not since I've been here."

"You stopped Pete's cussing?"

"No, but he did make an effort to curb his tongue."

He looked as if he was considering her in a new light. Mary wasn't at all certain it was a flattering one.

"Open up. Your dinner's getting cold."

Mary half hoped she'd be able to tell him how truly awful it was, but the first taste confirmed his opinion of himself. He was a fine cook. It was all she could do to wait until he brought a second spoonful to her mouth.

"Eat a little cornbread. I put two eggs in it. As soon as I can find that cow, we'll have some butter. Beef's good for building a body up, but nothing works like eggs and butter."

Sarah looked up at Joe, glanced at Mary, then back at Joe. Mary was delighted to see her plate already empty.

"Get yourself some more if you want, kid," Joe said.

Sarah filled half her plate with stew, the rest with corn-bread.

"For a little thing, she sure can eat." Joe put a spoonful of stew into Mary's mouth. "For a woman who was about to meet her maker, you sure talk frisky."

"I'm afraid any frisk I had disappeared long ago," Mary said, feeling a little as if she'd been chastised, "but I do have a sharp tongue. That's been a problem all my life." She swallowed another spoonful of stew. Her stomach didn't hurt anymore. Much to her surprise, she was beginning to feel full. She leaned back on the pillows.

"You haven't told me a thing about yourself," she said. "I don't even know why you're here."

"That can wait. All you have to do now is eat and sleep. It would help, though, if you could convince the kid to talk to me."

"The *kid* is named Sarah."

"Maybe, but she doesn't answer to that either."

"Talk to the gentleman, Sarah. It would be rude to re-main silent, especially after he's been kind enough to cook our dinner."

"I'm not kind, and I'm not a gentleman," Joe said. "At least, no one ever thought so before."

"Maybe you never gave them reason, but you have me. Thank you."

"The only thanks I want is to see you eat up every bit of this food."

"I'm feeling rather full."

"That's because your stomach has shrunk to nothing. Eat a little more. Then we'll let you rest until supper."

By the time Mary managed to eat everything on the plate, she was exhausted. She was also hardly able to keep her eyes open. The hot food, the warmth in the cabin, and the knowledge that she was safe combined to overcome her desire to stay awake and question this un-usual man.

"You must tell me what you're doing here," she said as she slipped back down in the bed. Joe adjusted the pillows under her head and pulled the covers up to her chin.

"Later. I'm going outside now so you can get some rest." He picked up his saddlebags and headed toward the door. He turned back. "Tell the kid she doesn't have to be afraid of Samson. He never did more than growl at a kid in his life."

"I'll explain it to *Sarah*," Mary replied.

Joe disappeared through the door. A moment later she heard him start to whistle.

Mary nestled down in the bed, but she couldn't sleep. She had never met a man in the least like Joe Ryan. She couldn't imagine him being Pete's partner.

Mary had disliked her husband. She was ashamed to admit it, but now that he was dead, it seemed pointless to continue pretending. He'd been mean, thoughtless, fre-quently brutal. She had never been able to imagine why her uncle had thought his stepson would make her a good husband. Not even her uncle's affection for his wife could blind him to the fact that her son was a cruel, selfish man. Her father should have protected her, but he was eager to get her out of the house. One less mouth to feed. Mary had been relieved when Pete left to prospect for gold in Colorado. Not even learning she was pregnant had made her wish for his return.

"Look out the window and see what he's doing," Mary said to Sarah.

"He's just looking," Sarah told her.

"At what?"

"Everything."

"The horse?"

"Yes."

"What's he doing now?"

"Looking in the shed."

"Anything else?"

"He's digging a hole next to the shed."

That made Mary uneasy. Any partner of Pete's was likely to be of poor character. Stealing horses from a helpless woman would probably be a small thing to him.

"Bring me the pistol," she said to Sarah. The child got the pistol from its place in the dresser drawer and brought it to Mary.

Mary checked to see that it was loaded. "Tell Mr. Ryan I would like to see him."

CHAPTER TWO

Joe rubbed the last of the dried sweat off General Burnside with a handful of straw. "I shouldn't have left you standing this long," he apologized to his mount, "but I had to dig a few holes first. No gold buried next to the shed."

He tossed the straw aside. They both contemplated the corral. "I suppose you might stay in that if you'd been ridden so hard you were wobbly in the knees." He pushed on a rotten rail. It broke into two pieces and fell to the ground. "I guess I'll have to hobble you."

Samson trotted up from his round of inspection. "Did you find any likely places to bury gold?" he asked the dog as he put hobbles on General Burnside. "I hope you didn't eat any of those chickens. Apparently the coyotes consider them their own personal property." He shook his head at the gaping holes in the chicken fence.

He walked to the shed, a large structure open in the front and the back. In between was a room entered through a door from the house side. Much to his surprise, Joe found wire for the chicken yard and a large number of rails for the corral. From the dust on them, they had been there a long time. Apparently Pete hadn't lacked the money or the materials to keep up the ranch, only the will to use them. Joe looked around, but saw no likely place to hide a strongbox. He'd look under the floorboards, but he doubted he'd find anything. Too obvious.

"I don't know why Pete thought panning for gold was easier than fixing a few fences now and then," Joe said. All the tools anybody would ever need were scattered around the shed. "It's a hell of a lot harder to build a sluice box and defend it from some rascal who'd rather shoot you than build his own."

He walked back out into the December sun, pulling his hat lower over his eyes. He glanced toward the house. The gold had to be there, but was it inside or out? He'd have to make a thorough search.

He could see the kid watching him through the window. Funny little kid. Odd she should be afraid of dogs. It was almost as if she was afraid of him, too. Her mother wasn't. In fact, she'd sent the kid to tell him she wanted to see him. He'd obey the summons once he'd finished in the yard.

"Don't know why Pete left a woman like that," Joe said to Samson, who followed at his heels. "She's got a bit of an edge to her, but she's got standards. A woman ought to have standards. Gives a man something to live up to." He tested the poles in the chicken yard. They needed bracing. "I can't believe Pete was such a lazy skunk."

The broken fence irritated him. It was such a little job, so easy. But it wasn't his responsibility. He looked up into the hills beyond the ranch house. If the gold was up there, he'd probably never find it.

He didn't think Pete had told his wife about it. The place didn't look like five dollars had been spent on it, certainly not twenty thousand. No, Pete had buried it here because he didn't have time to bury it anyplace else before he was killed in a card game over a pot worth less than two hundred dollars. Only a fool like Pete would do something like that when he had twenty thousand buried.

His irritation made it even harder to ignore the broken

fence. "Oh hell, I might as well fix it. Why should the coyotes have all those chickens?"

He was silent while he braced the corner poles and replaced others that looked ready to break. Then he cut out the broken sections of wire, leaving clean sections to be replaced. "Can't say I look forward to catching all these chickens," he said to Samson as he wired a new piece of fence into place. "But she'll need eggs to get back on her feet. After the baby comes, she won't have time to be chasing them down."

He finished one section of wire and began cutting a piece to fit the next gap.

"Can't figure why a woman like that would marry Pete, the lazy son-of-a-bitch. She wasn't brought up out here. You can tell that from her voice. It's soft, sort of gives the words a little squeeze before she says them. You know, leaves off a few letters here and there. Virginia or Carolina. After bringing her all this way, why did Pete run off and leave her, especially with a baby coming? It's a terrible thing for a woman to be alone."

He finished the last piece of wire, tested his work, and found it strong enough to withstand coyotes and wolves.

"A lot of good work was done on this place some time ago, Samson. The man who built that cabin knew what he was doing. This shed, too. But everything is in bad need of work now."

Joe hadn't been on a farm since he was sixteen. He'd thought he hated it. But as he had grown older, he'd come to treasure his memories of the years he'd spent with his grandmother. But that kind of life needed a family, and he'd had none since she died. He'd never found a woman who made him want to stop drifting. He'd never found the right kind of place. Despite the sagging corral, the missing shingles in the roof, loose hinges, broken windows, this place seemed the right kind, Mary the right kind of woman.

No use letting those thoughts take root in his mind. He'd be gone in a few days. This place needed a man here day after day, a man who loved it as much as the man who built it. Maybe Mary Wilson could find her a better husband this time. She sure was pretty enough. Dainty and feminine. She was the kind of woman to mess up a man's thinking, start him to doing things he didn't want to do.

Like fixing a chicken yard.

Joe went into the shed and started tossing out fence posts and corral rails until he got down to the floorboards. They came up easily. The ground didn't look as if it had ever been disturbed, but he took a shovel to it anyway. Half an hour later, he knew Pete hadn't buried the gold under the shed. He replaced the floorboards, but balked at dragging all those posts and rails back inside.

"Hell! As long as I've got everything out, I may as well fix the corral. I'm going to need someplace to put that damned cow once I find her."

Joe picked up the poles and started for the first gap in the rails. He wasn't able to get thoughts of Mary out of his mind. Nor of the farm he hadn't seen in seventeen years. In his mind they just naturally seemed to go together.

Mary woke up feeling better than she had in days. She was strongly tempted to get up and have some more of the stew. But she resisted. She was going to tell him to leave. She couldn't have a stranger of unknown character hanging about the place.

"He's coming!" Fear sounded in Sarah's voice and showed in her eyes. She bolted from the window into the corner between the bed and the wall.

Mary felt tension mount within her. It was a lot easier

to plan to tell Joe to leave than actually do it. The sound of his footsteps on the porch made her flinch. The grating sound of the door frayed her nerves.

He entered with a plucked chicken in his hand.

"I figured the coyotes could do without this cockerel," he said as he walked over to the table and laid the chicken down. He poured part of the water into a pot, the rest into a basin.

"More water," he said to Sarah, holding out the bucket.

Sarah glanced at Mary. Mary nodded her head, and Sarah inched forward to take the bucket. However, she froze when she opened the door.

"Your dog," Mary said.

"We've got to do something about that."

Joe sent his dog to keep his horse company. At least that was what he told him to do. Mary doubted the animal would actually obey.

"Do you want this chicken cooked any special way?" Joe asked, going back to the table and beginning to prepare the chicken for cooking.

"No." She had meant to tell him to go at once, but he had taken the wind out of her sails. She was acutely aware of his overpowering male presence. Just watching him move about the cabin in those tight pants caused something inside her to warm and soften. The feeling unnerved her. She found Mr. Ryan very attractive. Stranger or not.

"You never did tell me how you and Pete came to be partners, or why you decided to come here now."

She shouldn't be asking questions. It would just postpone the inevitable. She decided to sit up. It was impossible to talk to this man lying down. She felt at such a disadvantage. Unlike her attempt earlier, Mary was able to sit up and position the pillows behind her

"It was more an accident than anything else." Joe spoke

without facing her as he worked over the chicken. "We had claims next to each other. A mining camp is a dangerous place. Men who find color sometimes disappear or turn up dead. I watched Joe's back, and he watched mine. When our claims played out, it made sense to take what gold we'd found and hire on to guard a shipment of gold to Denver."

He started cutting up the chicken and dropping the pieces into the pot.

"I don't remember anything after the first mile."

Joe had paused before the last sentence. He went back to work, cutting through the joints with short, powerful thrusts of the knife.

"I woke up in my bedroll with the sheriff standing over me and the empty gold sacks on the ground next to me. I was convicted and sent to jail."

He finished cutting up the chicken, wiped his hands, and set the pot on the stove. He looked straight at Mary. "Pete set me up. He stole that gold. When I found out he was dead and the gold never found, I broke out and came here. This must be where he hid it."

Mary was too stunned to speak. He couldn't possibly expect her to believe that. She had never thought much of her husband's honesty, but she couldn't believe Pete was a common thief.

She started but discarded several responses. "That's absurd," she finally said. "Pete didn't steal any gold. He didn't hide anything here."

"He did both. I mean to find it and clear my name. Besides, part of that gold is mine. Some is yours."

Mary wondered how much gold was hers. She needed to hire someone to help with the ranch. There was so much she couldn't do, especially with a baby. Of course, he might not be telling the truth. She wasn't going to get excited about the money until she saw it.

Joe started a fire under the chicken. When he was satisfied that it was well caught, he opened the window and tossed out the dirty water.

Sarah entered with the fresh water. Joe placed the bucket on the table, and Sarah retreated to her place in the corner.

"You don't have to hide from me," he said.

Mary thought he sounded as if his feelings were hurt.

"Why don't you rummage around on those shelves and see if you can find some canned fruit or vegetables," he told Sarah. He took out some coffee beans and put them in a pan to roast on the stove. Next he measured out rice and set it on the edge of the stove. Then he cleaned the table and set out plates.

Mary didn't know what to do. Her hands closed over the gun under the covers. She had to tell him to leave. It was out of the question to let him stay. He had to go now. It would soon be night.

"I find it hard to believe Pete did what you said. But if he did, I'm truly sorry." She didn't know how to say there were times she had come close to hating her husband. "It was very kind of you to fix us something to eat, but you needn't stay any longer. I'm much stronger now. I'm sure you'll want to make it to town in time to get a room in the hotel."

Joe looked at her. She felt a flush burn her cheeks. She would swear he was laughing at her. Inside, of course. His expression didn't change.

"If you're trying to get rid of me, you're wasting your time. As soon as I find the gold, I'll head out for California, but not one day before. As for a hotel, I don't dare go near town. Somebody might recognize me."

"There's no gold here. Pete was home only one night

after he came back from Colorado. He went off again the next day and got himself shot."

"Don't worry, I don't mean to stay any longer than I have to. And if you're worried about your reputation, your condition is protection enough." He directed a frankly amused look at her. "I wish you'd put that pistol back where it belongs. It's not a good idea to sleep with a loaded gun."

Mary didn't know why she brought the pistol out from under the covers. Maybe it was the fact that he seemed to be able to read her mind. Maybe she felt she ought to do something and nothing else had worked. Whatever the reason, she found herself pointing the pistol at Joe.

"If you're going to shoot me, get on your feet first. I'd hate to have it known I was killed by a woman so weak she couldn't stand up."

"I can stand up," Mary insisted. To prove her point, she threw back the covers and started to get to her feet. Immediately she felt faint.

Joe caught her before she fell.

"I never met such a foolish woman in my life. Stay in that bed, or I'll tie you down. You can shoot me when you feel better. Meantime, you'd better give me this." He took the pistol from her slackened grasp. "Next thing you know, you'll drop it and put a hole through the chicken pot. I'm not chasing down another rooster."

Mary started to laugh. The whole situation was too absurd. Nothing like this happened to ordinary people. She was ordinary, so it shouldn't be happening to her.

She certainly shouldn't be experiencing this odd feeling. It almost felt as if she wanted to cry. But she didn't feel at all sad. She felt bemused and bewildered. Her brain was numb. Here she was, completely helpless, and she had tried to shoot the only human who had come along to help her.

She must be losing her mind. This man, this stranger, had taken the gun from her hands, put her to bed, then gone back to fixing her supper. And he planned to stay until he found the gold he insisted Pete had hidden here.

He was always ahead of her. That was a new experience for Mary. She had never known a man to act intelligently. She wasn't even sure she thought men could be intelligent, but Joe was. He was kind, too, despite his gruff manner.

"The kid has found some peaches," Joe announced. "I hope that's all right with you."

"I like peaches," Mary said. The aroma of roasting coffee beans permeated the cabin. The smell made her mouth water.

"Supper will be ready in less than an hour. Time for a nap. You can dream of ways to spend your share of the gold when I find it."

Again he had read her mind. The first thing she intended to buy was a dress for Sarah.

"Dinner was delicious. You could make a living as a cook."

"Don't much like cooking."

"But you're so good at it."

"If I have to eat it, I want it to taste good. Just put those dishes in the sink, kid. If you cover them with water, most of the stuff will soak off by itself."

"Why won't you call Sarah by her name?"

"Why won't she speak to me?"

"I don't know."

"Neither do I."

"I thought a man like you would have an answer for everything."

"Hell, there's more I don't know than I'll ever be able to figure out."

"That doesn't bother you?"

"I know what I need. The rest would just clutter up my head."

The clatter of plates caught his attention. "Well, I think I'll see about fixing up a bed for myself."

Mary figured she must have looked startled.

"Don't worry about me crowding in here. Samson and I will bed down outside. I don't like being closed in, in case somebody comes looking for me."

He stood and stretched. "I've had me a full day. I imagine I'll sleep tight. Leave the chicken and coffee right where they are, kid. All they need is a little heat, and they'll be just as good tomorrow. Don't worry about locking the door. With Samson around, nothing's going to come near the house."

Mary wondered how he knew she was planning to lock herself in.

Joe backed into Sarah's tree and knocked it over. Uttering a sharp oath, he bent to set it up. Sarah was there before him. She cast him a glance that was at once fearful and accusatory.

"I asked you to watch your language," Mary reminded him.

"I did," Joe said, looking aggrieved. "I could have said much worse." He rubbed a spot on his leg. "That damned tree stuck me."

"I appreciate your restraint."

"No, you don't. You're like every other woman God ever made. You smile and mumble about restraint, but you keep after a man until you get exactly what you want. I had a grandmother just like you. Sorry about your tree, kid."

"She has a name."

"And I'll use it when she talks to me. 'Night, ma'am."

When the door closed behind him, Mary felt the strength go out of her body just like water from a sink when the plug was pulled. The man energized everything around him. Now that he had gone, she felt exhausted. Being full of hot food didn't help.

"Leave the dishes in the water, Sarah. I ought to be able to get up tomorrow. We can do them then."

"I'll do them now," the child replied. "He wouldn't leave them."

No, he wasn't the kind of man to leave things undone. He seemed methodical, capable, dependable, yet he was drifting through life, able to do any job required of him, but never stopping to put down roots.

Mary had decided not to marry again. Her father and Pete had taught her that a bad husband could destroy all the love and comfort around him. But if she ever changed her mind, she meant to find a man she could depend on to stay in one place year after year. That wasn't Joe. Yet somehow she kept thinking about him.

"Is he really going to sleep in the shed?" Sarah asked.

"That's what he said."

"Is he going to be here tomorrow?"

"Why do you ask?"

"I like him. He's nice."

"Then why don't you speak to him?"

"Pa never liked it when I talked. He said girls ought to keep quiet because they have nothing to say."

"Your father didn't think much of women. It seems to be quite the opposite with Mr. Ryan. I've never in my life seen a man pay so much attention to a woman's comfort."

"Do you think he'll stay?"

"He said he would stay until I was stronger."

"I mean all the time."

That warm feeling flooded through Mary. "He means to go to California. He's only staying out of politeness."

"I wish his dog would go to California."

"I'm sure he won't hurt you."

"He so big."

"So is Mr. Ryan, but you're not afraid of him, are you?"

"I don't think so."

Mary felt a silent chuckle inside. "I don't think I am either. Now it's time to go to sleep. I have a feeling Mr. Ryan will be up early in the morning."

"That's one beautiful woman," Joe said to Samson. He took a last puff on his cigarette and rubbed it out. "A man like me ought not stay around here too long. I should head for California as soon as she can get out of bed without falling over."

The night had turned cold. Millions of stars glimmered in a cloudless sky. The saguaro cactus cast black shadows against the horizon. The spidery arms of an ocotillo contrasted with the broom-like arms of the paloverde, the more dense ironwood and mesquite. An owl hooted. Some field mouse wouldn't be around to see the dawn.

This place made him uneasy. It was like a home, the kind that folded itself around a man and made him want to stay put. It made him think of his mother and the time he saw her last. He was just sixteen when she threw him out for the man she was living with. Five months later she was dead.

"There are two kinds of women," Joe said to Samson as they walked across the ranch yard. "There's the kind that's hot to get married but doesn't like men the way they are. They pretend they do, but as soon as the preacher says a few words over them, they set about changing their husbands into something they like better than what they got.

Stay away from them. They'll either drive you to drink or drive you out of the house."

Joe untied his bedroll. He climbed into the loft and spread it over the straw. Samson looked up as if he were waiting for Joe to invite him in, but Joe didn't.

"Then there's the other kind, the kind that use men and let men use them. They destroy themselves. Like Flora. Nothing was ever enough. She always had to have more. Until one day she just burned herself out."

Samson sat down on his haunches. Joe leaned back on the straw and smiled. It sure beat his rock-and-sand bed from last night.

"Of course Mary is different from either one of them. She's pretty enough to make a man forget his responsibilities. She's so delicate and fragile, you want to protect her. You saw me. I couldn't wait to cook her dinner and fix up her chicken yard.

"But she's strong. She's got staying power. Once she picks out a man, she won't throw him out no matter how much work he needs. She'd even have made something of Pete if the fool had stayed."

Joe told himself he should have been looking for gold instead of mending fences and chasing chickens. This woman was going to get him into trouble yet. He turned over, didn't like his position, turned back again.

"Of course she tried to be brave, to pretend she wasn't scared to death. She could hardly hold the gun. I doubt she'd have had the strength to pull the trigger if a wolf had been coming through the door. Makes you want to hold her close and tell her nothing's ever going to hurt her again."

Joe sat up and glared at Samson.

"And that's how they get you," he said. "You got to keep alert. Because if that's not enough, they throw in babies and little girls. That Mary Wilson has got a quiver full of arrows. The first man who sets foot on this place won't have a chance. He'll be Mr. Wilson before the dust settles."

Joe flopped back down. He was the first man on the place.

"That's why I'm heading out to California the minute I find the gold."

Some time in the night Joe awoke to the sound of a crescendo of growls. Then he heard a yip cut off in mid-cry.

"Samson, I sure wish you could smell gold as quick as you can coyotes," he commented before he turned over and went back to sleep.

CHAPTER THREE

Joe wondered if Mary and the kid always slept this soundly. Mary had locked the door, but it had been a simple matter to enter through the window. He'd searched almost every corner of the cabin, and neither of them had awakened. He would have liked to think this trusting slumber was due to his presence, but if it was, it would vanish the minute they found out what he had done.

Joe didn't like going through Mary's things. It made him feel like a sneak, but he had to search every part of the cabin. It was stupid to let scruples stop him now. Still, he was uncomfortable when he opened a drawer to find it filled with undergarments. He almost closed it again. It hardly looked big enough to hide one bag of gold. He closed his eyes and ran his hands under the neat piles of garments to the bottom and back of the drawer.

Nothing.

He felt his body relax. He hadn't realized he was so edgy. Nor did he know why. Mary was a virtual stranger. Searching her home shouldn't bother him at all. But seeing and touching her clothes produced a feeling of intimacy he didn't welcome. It made him acutely aware of her physical presence. His body's response embarrassed him. He was a decent man. He shouldn't feel this way about a pregnant woman.

He quickly finished the wardrobe and turned his attention to the trunk. It wasn't locked. The top shelf needed no search to see there was nothing there. He had his hands deep among the dresses and blankets underneath when he heard a pistol click. He turned to see Mary sitting up in the bed, the cocked pistol aimed at him.

"What do you think you're doing?" she asked.

"Searching for the gold." He didn't think she would shoot him, but he couldn't be sure. He boldly finished running his hand along the bottom of the trunk.

"I told you I knew nothing of the gold," Mary said.

"I had to make sure for myself."

"I ought to shoot you."

"You'd have trouble getting rid of the body. And if you didn't kill me, you'd have to take care of me."

The kid woke up. She was frightened to find Joe in the house, Mary holding a pistol on him.

"I ought to turn you in to the sheriff."

"I'd be gone before he could get here. And I'd come back."

Mary kept the pistol pointed at Joe a moment longer, then slowly lowered it. He felt the tension in his muscles ease.

"You really think Pete stole that gold and buried it here, don't you?"

Joe began to put Mary's things back in order. "There's no other explanation for what happened. He came here right after the trial. It hasn't turned up anywhere else, and it wasn't on him when he was killed."

"He certainly didn't give it to me."

Joe closed the trunk and got to his feet. "I can see that, unless you're the kind who can sit on a fortune for six months and not spend a penny."

Mary looked him in the eye. "I could sit on it for a lifetime. I won't touch stolen money."

He believed her. There was a quality about her that said she would have nothing to do with a dishonest man.

Joe went to the woodbox and started picking up pieces of wood to start a fire in the stove. "Well, it's not inside the cabin, so you don't have to worry about me going through your things again."

"Despite your actions, I think you're honest."

Joe laid the fire carefully. Her response was unexpected. At best, he'd supposed she would only tolerate him. What else could she do? She was alone, down in bed, twenty-two miles from town, with no one to help her but a six-year-old kid. But to decide he was honorable! She must be up to something.

"No need to go flattering me. I know what I am. I never pretended to be anything else."

"And just what are you, Mr. Ryan?"

Joe lighted the coal oil-soaked stick he had placed at the center of the wood. A pale yellow flame illuminated the inside of the stove, casting flickering shadows on its sooty walls.

He had avoided that question for years. He wanted to think he was like everybody else—worthy of dreams, worthy of success. But Flora said he was nothing but a two-bit drifter, a poor and overly serious one at that.

"Nothing much, ma'am. I guess you could say I'm drifting along looking for a reason to stay put. Kid, I need some eggs for breakfast. See what you can find." He poured water into the coffeepot and put it on to heat.

"Where is your dog?" Mary asked. "You know she's afraid of it."

He went to the door and looked outside. "He's gone," he said to Sarah. "Scram."

The child stuck her head out the door, looked around, then darted outside.

"Don't you want to be something else?" Mary asked after Sarah had gone.

He poured out a handful of coffee beans and dumped them into a grinder.

"I want my name cleared," he said over the noise of the grinder. "Once a man is branded a thief, it doesn't matter what else he is. People can't see anything else."

"Isn't there anybody who can speak for you?"

"It won't do any good. I broke jail. As long as the gold is missing, nothing else matters." He poured the freshly ground coffee into a pot.

"Then I hope you find it."

"Enough to help?" He unwrapped the bacon and began to cut thick slices from it.

"I don't know anything."

"You can try to remember everything he did while he was here, every movement, every word he spoke. Even his expression, his mood." He pulled the curtain across the alcove where Mary slept. "You'd better get dressed. Breakfast will be ready in half an hour."

"What was that noise last night?" Mary asked.

She was seated at the table, a cup of coffee in front of her, waiting for Joe to finish filling her plate. He had tried to keep her in bed, but she had been determined to get up. He had insisted on helping her walk. She didn't need his help, but it was nice of him to offer. The least she could do was lean on him.

"It was Samson," Joe said, setting down a plate with

bacon, one egg, and a thick slice of bread in front of Sarah
and another in front of Mary. "You won't be troubled by
coyotes any more. Give him a month, and there won't be
one within ten miles."

"It's a shame you can't leave him here when you go to
California. We could sure use him."

"Can't do that. If Samson stays, so do I."

The statement had been made in jest—at least Mary
thought so—but the effect on each of them was electric.
Mary realized that she had practically issued Joe an invita-
tion to remain at the ranch indefinitely. Judging from his
expression, he had considered accepting it. What shocked
Mary even more was the realization that she wanted him
to stay. She didn't know what kind of arrangement they
might be able to work out, but the idea of having Joe Ryan
around all the time was a pleasant one.

"Eat your breakfast," Joe said. "There's nothing much
worse than cold eggs." He glanced over at Sarah. "We're
going to have to do something about that cow. A kid like
you should be drinking milk. You're nothing but skin and
bones."

"Sarah has always been thin," Mary said.

"Thin is okay. Skinny as a stick isn't," Joe said. "You
know where that cow got to?"

Sarah nodded.

"As soon as we clean up, you show me. I refuse to let an
old cow turn her nose up at me."

Mary watched him clear away the breakfast things,
talking to a mute Sarah as if they were old friends. He
didn't act like any man she'd ever known. In some ways
he was just as dictatorial, just as unconcerned with her
feelings as Pete had been. In other ways, he was the kind-
est, most thoughtful man she'd ever met. He was certainly the most helpful.

He must be up to something.

After Pete was killed, Mary had realized that she had never been able to trust men or depend on them. She had looked toward this Christmas as the beginning of her new life—just her, Sarah, and the baby.

Then Joe had showed up and she had started to question her decision. She found herself thinking *if all men were like Joe,* or *if I could find a husband like Joe....* The fact that he was an escaped criminal, a man on the run, didn't seem to weigh with her emotions. It didn't even weigh much with her mind.

She tried to tell herself to be sensible, but she couldn't. Maybe it was the baby. Her mother used to say pregnant women were prone to being emotional and sentimental. Her mother also said love nourished life. Nobody had ever nourished Mary like Joe. Whatever the reason, she liked him. She didn't want him to go away.

Joe had reached the conclusion that six months in jail had made him crazy. There was no other way to explain why he was leading a milk cow and talking to a six-year-old girl who wouldn't say a word to him. He ought to be turning the place inside out. Failing that, he ought to be on his way to California. Some U.S. marshal was sure to be on his trail by now.

But here he was, walking through the desert with a cow and a kid as if he didn't have a care in the world. Yep, he was crazy.

"You got to be firm with a cow," he said as they reached the yard. "They're real stubborn, especially if you're little. My grandma had an old black-and-yellow cow who used to chase me until I beat her with a stick. Never had any trouble after that. Get me that bucket I left on the porch."

"You got to tie the cow's head close to the post," he

said when Sarah returned with the bucket he had washed and set out on the porch earlier. "That way they can't turn around. Won't fight so much if they can't see. Now fetch me the stool."

Joe felt silly sitting on the tiny stool, but he had to show the kid what to do. After that, she could do all the sitting.

"You got to watch her at first," Joe said. "She's been on her own and won't like being milked." The cow kicked at Joe when he started to wash her teats. Joe slapped her on the hip. "Let her know you won't put up with any nonsense." He pushed on the cow's hip, but she wouldn't move her leg back. "Keep pushing on her until she moves that leg," he told Sarah. "It's easier to milk her that way."

Joe pulled on a teat. A stream of warm milk hit the bucket. He jerked the pail out of the way just as the cow kicked at him. He smacked her on the hip again.

"She'll do that a few more times before she figures out you mean business. Cows are stubborn, but they're not dumb. Has she got a name?"

The kid shook her head.

"She's got to have a name. How will she know when you're talking to her?" Joe thought a moment. "How about Queen Charlotte? She acts like a queen, and she's just as ugly as the real one."

Sarah nodded her agreement.

"Good. Now it's your turn."

Sarah looked reluctant.

"You can't let her know you're afraid, kid, or she'll keep on kicking until you give up. Come on, sit down."

Sarah sat. She reached out a tentative hand.

"Don't be timid. You're the boss."

Sarah squeezed the teat three times before the cow kicked the bucket over.

Joe smacked Queen Charlotte on the hip and moved

her back into milking position. "Now try again." Seconds later the cow kicked again. Sarah stood up.

"Here, let me show you," Joe said, taking his place on the stool. "I haven't done this in nearly fifteen years, but it's something you don't forget. Move over, Queen Charlotte," he said to the cow. "You're about to get the milking of your life. You kick this bucket one more time, and I'll feed you to Samson piece by piece."

Sarah giggled.

Through the window, Mary watched, bemused, as Joe milked the cow, talking to Sarah and the cow equally. When Samson wandered up, Joe included him in his conversation, introducing him to Sarah just as if he was an equal.

The man fascinated Mary. The more she saw of him, the more she wanted to know about him. She was drawn to him in a way that defied her notions about the feelings that could exist between a man and a woman. He touched a part of her that had lain silent all these years, the loving and longing part that Pete had nearly killed. She wanted to reach out and touch him, as though physical contact would recapture the youthful dreams she'd nearly forgotten.

She found herself looking at his body, admiring the shape of his thighs, the curve of his backside, the power of his shoulders. She had never felt this way about Pete. She had never looked forward to their nights in bed, nor did she miss them after he had gone. But Joe touched something deeper in her, far beyond anything Pete had touched. She found herself blushing, wondering what it would be like to sleep with Joe.

Samson tried to lick Sarah's face. The child was still frightened of the huge dog, but Joe made her hold out her hand for Samson to smell. Then she had to pat him on the head. Sarah was still wary, but Joe had broken the back of her fear.

Joe laughed, and the sound sent a frisson of pleasure racing through Mary. It was a deep, rolling sound, a sound that promised something very special to the person who could find the source and tap into it.

She picked up her pad and began to draw. In a few moments, she had preserved forever some of the magic of this morning.

Joe looked over Mary's shoulder as she drew a picture of Queen Charlotte and General Burnside staked out in the meadow beyond the barn, mountains in the distance.

"It's incredible," Joe marveled. "I don't see how you do it. You put a few squiggly lines here, a few more there, and you have a picture. All I'd have would be a bunch of squiggly lines."

Mary laughed, pleased with the compliment. Pete had never liked her drawings. He had considered them a waste of time. "It's not very hard. You just have to practice."

"Hell, I could—Sorry, I can't seem to control my tongue. It doesn't hardly know how to talk without cussing."

"That will come with practice, too."

"Maybe. What do you do with all those pictures?"

"What should I do with them?"

Joe looked at the drawing again. "Sell them. I know hundreds of miners who'd pay plenty to have something like that to brighten up their walls. You could make more money than you can running cows on this place."

"I'm perfectly content to stay here running cows. Besides, I like to do drawings for people I know. I ought to be doing some for Sarah. She wants to decorate the house for Christmas."

"If that pathetic tree is any example," he said, indicating Sarah's bundle of thorns, "she ought to give up the idea."

"If you understood about her mother, you'd understand why it's so important to her."

"Then tell me. I won't figure it out otherwise."

"Sarah's mother died when Sarah was four. I don't know why Pete married her. He seems to have hated everything about her. He got rid of everything that belonged to her or reminded him of her. According to Sarah, her mother loved Christmas and would spend weeks getting ready for it. She used to spend hours singing to Sarah, telling her stories about *Père Noel*. Last Christmas was Sarah's first since her mother's death. Pete wouldn't let her decorate, have a tree, or do anything for Christmas. To Sarah, that was like taking away the last link with her mother. She likes me, but she adored her mother. Christmas is all she has left of her. It's terribly important to her."

"Pete was a real bastard," Joe said. "Why in hell did you marry him?"

Mary ignored the curses. "Pete's stepfather was my uncle. He thought Pete would make a good husband for me. My father was anxious to get me out of the house. One less mouth to feed; one less female to contend with. I guess I was tired of waiting for a man who didn't exist."

Joe gave her the strangest look. Mary badly wanted to know what he was thinking. She wondered if he'd ever been in love, if he'd found his perfect woman. He seemed light-hearted, but beneath that she detected a cynical streak. He didn't believe in goodness. That was odd, considering he had so much of it in him.

"If she's hoping that ratty old tree will attract her *Père Noel*, she's looking down an empty chute."

"Please don't tell her that." Mary looked to where

Sarah sat churning cream for butter. "She thinks if she believes hard enough, *Père Noel* will find her."

Joe shrugged and headed toward the door. "I don't know anything about *Père Noel*, but I do know about horses and cows. I'd better do some work on that corral."

"You don't have to do that."

"If I don't, you won't have any milk after I leave. It'll never hold Queen Charlotte the way it is now."

Still amused by his habit of bestowing fanciful names on his animals, Mary asked, "When are you leaving?" She was stunned to realize that she had known this man less than twenty-four hours, but she no longer thought in terms of his leaving.

The baby kicked, and her hand went to her swollen stomach.

She liked him. He might be a criminal, but she liked him.

No. He was an escaped convict, but she couldn't believe he was a criminal. He'd fixed three meals for them, perfect strangers he owed nothing, especially if Pete had set him up. He had spent hours helping Sarah, even though the child wouldn't speak to him. He had even praised Mary's drawings.

He was rugged, curt, and given to cursing, but underneath all that roughness he had a generous nature. He showed a wonderful understanding of her and Sarah. On top of that, he took better care of her than any man she'd ever known, including her father. Why shouldn't she fall in love with him? He was exactly the kind of man she'd always hoped to find.

No, she had to be mistaken.

She couldn't love him. She was letting his kindness go to her head. Maybe it was being pregnant. Her mother had warned her that pregnancy could do strange things to a woman.

Mary redirected her attention to her drawing pad. She needed more Christmas pictures for Sarah. Drawing would give her something to do and keep her mind off Joe and the foolish notion that she might be falling in love with him.

That evening after dinner, Mary tacked up the drawings she had done during the day. She wondered if they would mean anything to Sarah. The child had never known anything but the desert. To Mary, nothing about the desert spoke of Christmas. She had done a few drawings of the surrounding hills and mountains, but she had been in Arizona only eleven months. Christmas to her was the snow-covered pines and oaks of her native Virginia, magnolia, and bright holly berries.

It sounded strange to hear rain on the roof—it had been raining since late afternoon. Even more strange to Mary, everything would look the same tomorrow. In this land, rain didn't bring the green she longed for.

"It's a shame you don't have any paints," Joe said, inspecting a drawing before he handed it to her to put on the wall. "It just doesn't look like Christmas without color."

"Pete would never buy me any. No paper either. This is my last pad."

Pete used to get angry when she drew. But when she was drawing, she could pretend he didn't exist. Joe was a part of her drawings. He was already in several.

He liked to watch her. He said it pleased him to see the lines come to life, capturing a living scene. Her pleasure increased because of his. He would laugh and point to a cactus or a ridge that had just come into being. For a few minutes, it would seem he almost forgot the gold and the sentence hanging over his head.

At times like that, it was terribly hard to remember he'd soon be gone.

"Would you mind heating some water so Sarah can have a bath?" she asked.

Joe gave Sarah an appraising glance. "The kid *is* rather dirty."

Taking a bath was not a simple operation. A fire had to be lighted in the stove and water brought in from outside and heated in every available pot and pail. The tub had to be cleaned out and brought in from the shed. Last of all, the water had to be poured into the tub. Mary hadn't been able to do this for months. Cloth baths just weren't the same as soaking in a tub of hot water.

"What about you?" Joe asked.

"I'll take cloth baths until after the baby comes," Mary said. "I hate to ask you, but you'll have to go outside until Sarah is finished."

"I do all the work, then I'm the one who gets to sit shivering on the front porch?"

"I'm sorry, but it wouldn't seem right to—"

"Never mind. I need to dig a few more holes anyway."

The door opened with a protesting squeak. Joe reminded himself to put some bacon grease on it in the morning.

"You can take the bathtub out now," Mary said.

She was framed in the doorway, golden light behind her. Joe thought he'd never seen anyone so beautiful. Her thick, dark hair—very sensibly done up at the back of her head with a few curls loose to soften the look—seemed jet black in the dark, her skin nearly white by comparison. Her eyes glistened luminous and wide in a face that seemed too delicate for a land known to be hard on women.

Joe got up off the porch steps. His joints felt stiff. It had stopped raining, and the stars had come out, but the night was too cold for sitting on stone steps. He was surprised to see the kid still in pants. "Why isn't she wearing a dress? Girls ought to be clean and sweet smelling, all curls and ruffles and bows. She still looks like a boy."

"She doesn't have any dresses," Mary said.

"Why not?" Joe asked. He'd never heard of a girl having no dresses. It didn't seem right.

"Pete wouldn't buy her any. He said she'd only tear them up and have to wear pants anyway."

"I wish I'd known. I'd have beaten the hell out of Pete when I had the chance." He caught Mary's stern look. "I'm sorry, but it's enough to make a man cuss to see a little girl as pretty as the kid have to look like a boy because her bobcat-mean pa wouldn't buy her a dress."

Mary brushed Sarah's long auburn hair to help it dry faster. "I mean to do something about it as soon as I'm able."

Joe decided they ought to do something about it now. "You got some ribbon?"

"Yes."

"How about some good-smelling powder?"

Mary smiled. "Yes. What do you want it for?"

"I want you to put the powder on the kid, the ribbon in her hair."

"Open the trunk and hand me the round box on the top. And a piece of red ribbon if I have any."

Joe found the box easily. The ribbon was another matter. He found a tangle of red, but it was too narrow for Sarah's hair. He chose a yellow ribbon instead. "You can use the red to make bows for the tree," he said. His grandmother used to do that when he was a little boy. He handed the yellow ribbon to Mary, then turned to the tree. It was a pathetic mess. He couldn't put bows on that. His grandmother would rise out of the grave and come after him.

"We've got to have a better tree than that," he said aloud. "That's a disgrace. Are there any pines or junipers nearby?" he asked Mary.

"There're some up in the hills."

"After breakfast tomorrow I'll see what I can find." He turned to see Sarah, staring at him, eyes wide. The yellow ribbon was just the right shade to set off her hair. "See, I knew you were a pretty little thing. Pretty enough to have little boys giving each other black eyes over you." He squatted in front of her. "Would you like a real tree?"

Sarah nodded her head vigorously.

Mary had dusted Sarah's shoulders with white powder. Joe bent over and took a sniff.

"Pretty as a picture, and you smell good, too. I know your mama would be proud as a peacock to see you. Now all you need is—"

Sarah threw her arms around Joe and hugged him until he thought she was going to cut off his air. Slowly he let his arms slide around her. Her body seemed much too slight for such intense feeling. He didn't know how to re-act. In his whole life, he'd never had a child hug him.

For a while he thought she wasn't ever going to let go. Then, quite as suddenly, she unclasped him and hid her-self behind Mary.

"I was going to say all you need is a dress," he said, "but you're pretty enough without it." He stood up. His mus-cles felt as strange as his voice. "I guess it's time I get my-self over to the shed. Samson doesn't like to go hunting unless he knows I'm tucked up tight."

Joe needed some time alone. He was feeling at sixes and sevens. He was strongly attracted to Mary. That he understood, that he knew how to combat. But this business with the kid hugging him until she nearly choked him had caught him off guard. Mary had weakened him, and the kid had closed in for the kill.

Not kill exactly, but he was down and sinking fast.

He no longer thought Mary had anything to do with Pete's thievery. If she found the gold, he was certain she would hand it over to him. She hadn't even been interested enough to ask how much of it was hers.

Despite the way he'd forced himself into her life, she had been gracious. She hadn't been pleased when she found him going through her things, but she seemed to understand why he'd had to do it. That was a hell of a lot more than he'd expected. Flora would have screamed like a wildcat. His mother would have hit him up beside the head. Mary had accepted his explanation and put her gun away.

No woman had ever taken his word for anything. Except his grandmother.

Mary had every reason to throw him out, but she greeted him with a smile sweeter than a spring sunrise. She talked to him about little things, things you talked about with people you felt comfortable around.

But now the kid had hugged him and his comfort had fled. There was something about a kid hugging you that was unlike anything else in the world. There must be a special soft spot in every man reserved for little girls. He had seen men who wouldn't hesitate to commit almost any evil reduced to tears by the plight of a child, but he'd never suspected that he was similarly susceptible. But he was, and the kid had scored a bull's eye on her first throw. He wanted to march right back in there, give her a hug, and promise her that Christmas was going to be just as wonderful as she hoped.

But he couldn't. He had to find the gold and be gone before then. The longer he stayed, the greater the danger that the law would find him. He was foolishly letting Mary and the kid distract him from his goal. He'd spent no more than an hour looking for the gold today.

He dropped to his bed in the straw and pulled his bedroll around him. He'd start checking beneath all the stones in the yard tomorrow. After he and the kid found a decent Christmas tree. He couldn't stand the thought of her pinning all her hopes on that bundle of twigs.

And Mary and her baby?

That was a tough one.

CHAPTER FOUR

The kid was helping Joe fix the chimney when he heard Mary mutter something under her breath. He looked around the corner of the cabin to where she sat on the porch.

"The preacher and his sister are coming," she said, "Brother Samuel and Sister Rachel Hawkins."

Joe hadn't intended to fix the chimney this morning, or any other morning. He had been inspecting the cabin to see if any stones showed signs of having been removed recently. A few stones in the chimney were loose.

Once he realized that there was nothing behind them but more stones, his excitement had died down, to be replaced by a dull fear that he would never find the gold. Then he decided to reset the stones properly rather than just shove them back into place.

He had almost finished the job when Brother Samuel and Sister Rachel drove into the yard. Joe could tell at a glance that he wasn't going to like them.

From the look of things, they weren't going to like him any better. Brother Samuel frowned as though he'd just come upon a condemned sinner and didn't like the smell. Sister Rachel looked as if she'd never had any fun in her life and was determined that nobody else would have any either. They were both dressed in black.

Joe didn't like black. It depressed him. Seemed it had depressed Brother and Sister Hawkins, too.

Samson had been lying next to Mary's chair. When the Hawkinses got down from their buggy, he rose to his feet, a growl deep in his throat.

"Good morning," Mary said, greeting the pair without getting up. She patted Samson until the growls stopped. "It's awfully kind of you to drive so far to see me."

"It didn't seem so far," Brother Samuel said. "The morning is brisk, the sun heartening."

"I've been expecting to see you in town," Sister Rachel said. "You know my brother can't think of you out here alone without becoming distressed." Brother Samuel helped his sister mount the porch steps. She walked around Samson to take the chair Mary offered her. Brother Samuel chose to stand.

"I know I look as big as a cow, but I've got another month," Mary told her. "Besides, if all goes well, I mean to have the baby here."

"Surely you don't mean to have it by yourself."

"Oh, no. I'll hire someone to stay with me."

"I'd feel so much better if you would move to town now," Brother Samuel said. "I'm most concerned about you."

"I can't afford the cost of putting Sarah and myself up in a hotel for a month."

"I'm sure the ladies of Pine Flat would be glad to offer you and Sarah places to stay."

Joe wondered why neither brother nor sister offered to take Sarah and Mary into their own home.

"I couldn't be separated from Sarah," Mary replied, "not after her losing both her mother and her father. Neither could I settle myself on anyone. I won't have a friend in the world if I start doing that."

"You'll have a friend in us no matter what you do."

"We'd offer to keep you with us," Sister Rachel said, "but we're away from home nearly all the time."

"Nonetheless, you can stay with us if it will convince you to come to town."

Joe noticed that Sister Rachel didn't look quite so enthusiastic as her brother. He guessed Brother Samuel was in the habit of offering haven to people and leaving Sister Rachel to do all the work.

"I didn't know you had hired a man to work for you," Brother Samuel said, eying Joe.

"Oh, he's not a hired hand. He's Pete's old partner. . . ." Mary's lips formed Joe's name, but she didn't say it.

Brother Samuel didn't come down the steps to shake hands with Joe. The inclination of his head was the only acknowledgment he made of their introduction.

"Pete's been dead six months. What's he doing here now?" Sister Rachel asked.

"He's here to . . ." Mary's voice trailed off.

". . . to settle a partnership," Joe said, leaving his work and coming around the corner.

"Then why are you fixing the chimney?" Sister Rachel demanded.

"It needed fixing."

"It's not suitable!"

"I'm not a stone mason, but I think it'll hold up for a while."

"My sister means it's not suitable for you to be staying with a single woman without proper chaperonage."

"I should think her belly and the kid are chaperons enough."

Joe's answer was mild enough, but he felt anger boiling up inside him. Who the hell was this man to come in here and stick his nose in their business? Joe had read the

Bible, and he didn't remember anything giving preachers permission to interfere in other people's affairs. Sister Rachel's shocked response to his answer amused him. The old biddie would probably fall down dead if a man so much as kissed her.

"In that case, I don't imagine you'll be staying long," Brother Samuel said. He didn't appear to be quite as shocked as his sister. He seemed angry. Joe suddenly wondered if the Reverend Brother had designs on Mary for himself. She was certainly pretty enough to tempt a man, even a cold fish like the Reverend Brother.

"I probably won't be here longer than a couple more days," Joe said. "Mary was a little run-down when I arrived. I'd like to be sure she's back on her feet before I leave."

"Why didn't you tell us you were unwell?" Sister Rachel asked. "I'd have come right away. In fact, I'll stay with you now. Samuel will just have to do without me for a few days."

"That's not necessary," Mary hastened to assure them. "I'm feeling much like my old self. I know your brother depends quite heavily on you, especially during the Christmas season. No, I'm fine now."

"If you're sure."

Joe would have sworn Sister Rachel was disappointed. Maybe she would have appreciated some relief from the heavy duties of the season.

"Will you be stopping by town when you leave?" Brother Samuel inquired of Joe.

"Probably," Joe replied. "I imagine I'll need to pick up a few things."

"We have other calls to make, so we'd better be on our way," Brother Samuel said to Mary as he helped his sister down the steps. "I'll be looking for you in town in a day or two," he said to Joe. "I know you wouldn't do anything that might damage Mrs. Wilson's reputation, but you can't be too careful. People will talk."

"They'd better not within my hearing," Joe answered.

Brother Samuel looked as though he hadn't expected that answer. His smile was uncertain.

"We'll be expecting you and Sarah in town to stay right after the New Year," Sister Rachel said to Mary. "If not, I'm coming to stay until after the baby arrives."

"I'll let you know," Mary said. She got to her feet, but didn't go down the steps.

Joe went back to his work. But he kept watch until Brother Samuel and Sister Rachel had disappeared over the ridge. "I wonder where Sister Rachel left her broomstick?" he said to no one in particular. "Bound to be faster than that old buggy."

Mary laughed, then tried to pretend she hadn't.

Mary eased down on the bed and leaned against the mound of pillows. She had to do some serious thinking. She couldn't have Brother Samuel thinking she would become his wife. He had never asked her, but she couldn't fail to notice the look in his eye.

She had been given no opportunity to dispel his illusions, but she would never marry him. She felt lucky to have survived her marriage to Pete, and she had no intention of putting herself in that trap again. She wanted a quiet, stable life, not one manipulated by a man.

Yet she didn't want Joe to leave. She had felt her heart lurch when he said he'd see Brother Samuel in town in a couple of days. Already she had come to depend on him, to look forward to his company.

It was impossible not to compare the two men. Brother Samuel was an ardent man, even a passionate one, but his passion had nothing to do with the flesh. Being around

Joe had made Mary very aware of her physical nature. It was impossible to look at him and not feel the magnetism of his presence. He was simply the kind of man who made a woman achingly aware of her femininity. Even pregnant, he made her feel desirable.

Mary decided that was a dangerous situation. It would undoubtedly be safer if Joe did meet Brother Samuel in town and then continued on to California. But she knew her life would be very empty if he left.

Her mother had warned her she wouldn't always be able to find love where she wanted it. Was she looking for it with Joe?

Joe was jealous. There was no point in denying it. From the moment that man drove into the yard, he had felt it gnawing at his insides. He hadn't recognized it at first, but he did now.

He was jealous of the Reverend Brother Samuel Hawkins.

He looked around. There was nothing that could remotely be considered a Christmas tree. Sarah rode behind him, the little pinto struggling to keep up with his big gelding. Samson loped ahead on the lookout for coyotes. The low hills were covered with a scattering of vegetation—mesquite, catclaw, and ironwood all looking much alike; ocotillo and prickly pear cactus; spiky agave with their tall blooming stalks; assorted grasses and bushes.

But no pines or junipers.

They would have to go higher if they were to find a Christmas tree.

Could he be falling in love? He couldn't allow that to happen. But wasn't that what being jealous meant? He'd only loved two women, and both of them had sent him away. Mary had tried—even held a gun on him. He didn't know if she had changed her mind, but he knew he wasn't the kind of man she wanted or the kind who would be good for her. She'd send him away in the end.

"What do you think of that tree?" he asked Sarah. It was a pitiful excuse for a tree, but it was a pine.

She shook her head.

"Look, if I'm going to traipse all over this mountain looking for a tree, you're going to have to talk to me."

The kid watched him out of silent eyes.

"You ought to know by now I won't hurt you. Even Samson likes you."

She still didn't speak.

"Okay, let's go back."

Before he could turn General Burnside around, she said, "It's not pretty," just as if she'd been talking all along. "Let's go higher."

As they wound their way up the mountainside, Joe decided that women got the hang of being female at an early age. Boys didn't figure out what it meant to be a man until much later. By the time they started courting, the girls had a ten-year head start. It was like shooting fish in a pond.

He headed General Burnside up a slope toward a patch of green about a mile away. Samson disappeared down a canyon.

He was letting himself get distracted. A dangerous thing. It was time he went back to looking for the gold and got out of here. He was getting too settled. He was starting to like where he was.

He'd forgotten what being on a farm was like. For years he'd thought only of his mother and the man she threw him out for. But being here reminded him of the things he had liked about the farm. It seemed strange to him now, but he liked the way he was living. He didn't even mind the chores. He was beginning to get ideas about how to improve things, ideas about what Mary ought to do come spring. He'd enjoyed teaching Sarah how to milk Queen Charlotte. Hell, he'd sworn he'd never milk another cow after he left the farm. But there was something solid and comfortable about their big brown bodies. And it sure as hell was nice to have butter to put on his biscuits.

"Do you like that man?" Sarah asked.

"What man?"

"The one who came to the house this morning."

"No reason to dislike him."

"I don't like him. He makes Mary sad."

"How's that?"

"She gets all jumpy whenever he comes. She mumbles a lot after he's gone. I think she's afraid of that woman."

"I think your ma is just afraid they'll try to take too much care of her."

"Mary doesn't need anybody to take care of her. She has me."

Joe thought it was a nice thing for a little girl to say, but Sarah had no idea just how much a woman needed someone to take care of her. He didn't see how Mary was going to make out by herself.

"Do you always call your ma Mary?"

"Mary says she loves me like a mama, but she knows I have a real mama who's gone to Heaven and is waiting for me there."

That would teach him to stick his nose in where it didn't belong.

"I bet she'd like it though. She won't think you're forgetting your real ma, but women like to be called Ma. It's just not the same when you call her Mary."

"If you were married to her, would you want me to call you Pa?"

That nearly knocked him out of his saddle. No messing around. The kid had cut to the heart of the matter.

Joe wanted to marry Mary. He had fallen in love with her when she fainted pointing a rifle at him. He'd just been dancing around the issue since then, trying to fool himself and everybody else.

"Yes. If I were married to Mary, I'd want you to call me Pa. I'd like having a little girl like you. I know Pete's your real pa, but I'd want you to call me Pa because that's how I'd feel about you."

Joe realized that he'd stayed away from women because he didn't believe in love. He'd never felt it. His mother and Flora talked about it all the time, but he didn't want any part of the destructive emotion they felt.

Mary and Sarah loved each other in an entirely different way. Wasn't it possible they could love him as well?

Don't be a fool. You're on the run. You can't stay here or anywhere else.

"Let's look up there," Sarah said, pointing to a clump of green even more distant than the one he had picked out.

Samson climbed out of the canyon and came to join them.

"Why is Christmas so important to you?" Joe asked.

"Mama told me she was going to die," Sarah began. She looked up at Joe. "But she said she wouldn't really be gone. She said she was going to stay with *Père Noel*, far away where I couldn't see her. She said *Père Noel* brought things from mommies to their little girls so they would know they hadn't forgotten them. She said she would send me something every Christmas."

Sarah looked away.

"Last year Papa said we couldn't have Christmas. He

said it was foolish. He said *Père Noel* was a lie and Mama was just telling me a story so I wouldn't cry. He said she was gone away and I'd never hear from her again. He wouldn't even let me put a ribbon on the door so *Père Noel* could find our house."

She looked up at Joe once more.

"He didn't come. I put out my shoes, but there was nothing in them. Do you think Papa was right?"

Joe decided that if anybody'd ever deserved to die by slow torture, it was Pete Wilson. "No. *Père Noel* probably couldn't find you among all these cactus. I'm sure he's got all your presents saved up. He's going to look extra special hard this year to make sure he doesn't miss you again. We'll put an extra big bow on the door. We can leave a light in the window, too. We're a long way from town, you know."

"You really think he'll come?"

"I'm sure of it. Now we'd better find that tree and get back home, or we'll never get it decorated."

They had climbed several thousand feet. There were pines and junipers all around to choose from.

Sarah stopped and pointed to a ledge fifty feet above their heads. "There, that's the tree I want."

Mary saw them when they topped the ridge a mile away. Joe on his big gelding, a big man silhouetted against the landscape; Sarah on the pinto, a little girl who looked even smaller next to Joe; Samson sniffing rocks in his never-ending quest for coyotes. And the tree. It was tied to Sarah's pony. It almost enveloped the child.

The baby turned over. Mary put her hand on her stomach. She was feeling funny today. The baby seemed to have moved lower in her body. It caused her to waddle like a duck. Just the thing to make a man like Joe look on her with approval.

She had given up pretending she didn't like him. Watching him riding patiently with Sarah conjured up even warmer emotions.

She loved Joe Ryan.

She still found it hard to believe a man like him existed. All the other men in her life had ended up being pretty much alike—rotten. She had given up hoping to find anybody different. Then, just when she felt she could carry on alone, Joe Ryan had come into her life and upset everything. He was exactly the kind of man she wanted.

But she couldn't have him.

If she were a sensible woman, she would marry Brother Samuel. He wasn't a warm man, but he was a kind one. He would prove to be stubborn in many ways, but a clever woman could probably handle him quite easily. And she was a clever woman.

But she didn't want Brother Samuel, even if he hadn't been a preacher, even if Sister Rachel hadn't been his sister. She wanted an escaped convict who was on the run. That made her real clever.

They stopped. Apparently Joe had to readjust the tree. She wondered where they'd found it. They had been gone for most of the day. It was nearly eight o'clock. The sun had dipped beyond the western hills, leaving streaks of orange, mauve, and a deep purply-black across the sky. She had become worried about them. She had been sitting on the porch for nearly two hours.

The fire in the stove would have gone out. Dinner would be cold. But that didn't matter now. Joe would be home in a little while. She could warm everything up.

Yes, Joe was coming home. This was where he belonged, where she felt he wanted to be, where she wanted him to be. But the world outside wouldn't let him stay.

She picked up her pen and began, with swift, sure

strokes, to create a picture of Sarah and Joe silhouetted against the evening sky.

While she waited, she had tried to think of what she might do to help him. She had racked her brain for any possible clue to where Pete had hidden the gold. She had even thought of hiding Joe. There were miles of hills in which a man could lose himself. But she knew Joe wouldn't agree to that. He had come here to clear his name. He would never consider marrying her until he had.

And she wanted to marry Joe. She wanted him to be her husband, her lover, the father of the child she carried, the other children she hoped to have. She didn't know what she could do, but she made up her mind not to give up hope. She'd never thought a man like Joe existed, but he did. There had to be a way to keep him.

She flipped the page and began a second picture as Joe and Sarah rode into the yard.

Sarah seemed hardly able to contain her excitement. She flitted around the cabin, talking enough to make up for several months of silence.

"I bet it's the biggest Christmas tree in Arizona," she said.

Joe leaned the tree against the wall, then made a stand for it. It almost reached the ceiling. The branches spread out three feet on either side of the trunk.

"I'm sure it is," Mary agreed.

"We found dozens of other trees," Joe told her, "but she wouldn't be satisfied with any of them. She had to have the one growing on the highest ledge."

"It was the prettiest."

"You should have seen me clambering up the rocks like a mountain goat," Joe said. "Nearly broke my neck."

"It's beautiful," Mary said, "but a smaller one would have been nice. There's hardly enough room left for us."

"You can put lots of pictures on it," Sarah said, "lots more than that other old tree."

That other old tree had been shoved into the stove, its existence forgotten and unlamented.

"Joe said we could put ribbons all over it," Sarah told Mary. "I can't reach the top. Will you lift me, Joe?"

"If you don't stop dancing about, he's liable to hang you from the ceiling," Mary said.

"No, he won't. He said he'd like having a little girl like me. He said if he was married to you, he'd want me to call him Papa."

The escalation of tension was tangible. Joe kept his eyes on his work. He laid the tree on its side and measured the stand to make sure it fit. "Any marrying man would like a kid like Sarah," he said as he drove a nail through the stand into the bottom of the tree. "She rides like she was born to it." He drove in a second nail. "She'll probably learn to rope cows before she's ten."

"Will you teach me?"

The tension increased another notch.

Joe nailed one of the braces, turned the tree over, and nailed the second. "It's like Brother Samuel said, it's not proper to have a man like me hanging around." He nailed another brace. "I should have left by now." He nailed the last brace. He stood the tree up before he dared glance at Mary. "Some men just aren't born to settle down."

Joe set the tree in the corner.

Sarah's face broke into an ear-to-ear grin, and she jumped up and down, clapping her hands in her excitement. "It will be the most beautiful tree in Arizona. I know it will."

"We'll certainly do our best," Mary said, coming out of her trance. "I'll make the bows. You and Joe can tie them on."

"Give me one. Give me one," Sarah begged, too excited to be silent.

Mary quickly made a bow and handed it to the child.

"Lift me up," Sarah said to Joe. "Lift me high."

Mary's fingers flew, cutting ribbon and making bows as fast as she could, but nearly every other fiber of her being was focused on Joe. Time and time again he lifted Sarah as if she weighed nothing, good-naturedly joining in her excitement, talking to her as though she was the most important person in his life.

The child blossomed under his attention. It was hard to remember the scared, silent, hollow-eyed child she'd found when she became Pete's wife. Joe might think he wasn't meant to settle down, but he had the key to Sarah's heart.

And her own. She watched those powerful arms lift the child and longed to feel them wrapped around her. She saw his smile, felt the warmth of his caring. His presence transformed everything around him—her, Sarah, the cramped and cold cabin. Mary felt warm and protected. She felt happy and content. She felt a longing so intense that it blocked out the pain in her back.

"That's all the ribbon," she said. "It's time for the pictures. Make sure you tie them on the tips of the branches so they'll hang right."

"You can do that," Joe said.

"I think I'll watch."

Sarah took her hand and pulled. "Please, you help, too."

Mary started to get up, but the pain in her back grew worse.

"I'd better sit down. I think I did too much today."

"I told you I'd fix dinner when I got home," Joe said, worry clouding his eyes.

"You've done that often enough. Besides, I thought you'd like something warm after a long, cold ride. Only then I let it get cold."

"We came home too late."

Home! He'd said it. He couldn't be as untouched as he acted. He might not think he was a family man, but that was probably because things hadn't worked out for him in the past. That didn't mean he couldn't be a family man now.

The ugly fact of his uncompleted prison term reared its head, but Mary pushed it aside. Given time, they could find an answer to that. The real problem was how Joe felt.

She shifted position to ease the pain in her back. She wished the baby hadn't settled so low. It made it easier for her to breathe, but it put extra pressure on her spine.

Almost instinctively she reached for her drawing pad. Of all the scenes she had rendered with her pen, this was the most important. She regretted having no colors. Without them, there was no way to capture the golden quality of the light that illuminated the cabin. It was impossible to show the drab, ordinary nature of Joe's clothes in contrast to the vibrant love of life that glowed in his eyes. It was impossible to show the transformation that had taken place in Sarah.

Most important of all, it was impossible to show the difference he had made in her life. Black and white had been all she needed before. That was how she'd viewed the world. But Joe had changed all that. He had brought spirit and passion into her life. He had brought love.

It was impossible to show that without color.

She looked down at her drawing. She hadn't missed anything—the cabin, the tree, Sarah, even herself in the corner. But Joe was at the heart of the picture. Without him, this would have been just one more in a long string of dismal evenings.

"Your mother is drawing again," Joe said to Sarah. "Let's see what she's doing this time."

Mary turned the page over quickly. "I'm trying to get you two and the Christmas tree in the same picture. That one didn't turn out the way I expected. Stop trying to look over my shoulder. I can't concentrate when you do that."

"I can't help it," Joe said. "I can't get over the way you make a picture appear—like magic."

Nothing like the magic you've wrought, Mary thought.

But as Mary turned her attention to her drawing, she realized that there was something missing.

There were no presents under the tree.

Joe thought about the presents, too. He imagined Mary had something hidden away for Sarah, but it couldn't be much. She hadn't been able to get to town, and Christmas was only three days off.

He paused on his walk to the barn. The night was radiant. The full moon flooded the landscape with light. It wasn't the warm light of the day, and it was too weak to vanquish the shadows, but it was beautiful nonetheless. There was a ghostly stillness that was comforting, as though all the trouble of the world were held at a safe distance by some almighty hand. Countless stars winked in the dark canopy of the sky, their tiny lights friendly and cheerful.

Samson trotted up. "Are you taking the night off?" Samson licked Joe's hand. "Don't come oiling up to me. I know you like Mary better than me. I can't say I blame you, but I'm not going to forgive you either. I know she's prettier than I am, but we've been together for six years. I even rescued you from that drunken old squatter. I was planning on taking you to California, and look at the thanks I get."

The dog gamboled around him, wagging his tail and barking playfully. "Don't think you're going to talk me into letting you share my bed. You'll just get me up in an hour to let you out."

Fifteen minutes later, settled into his bedroll with Samson nestled beside him, Joe thought about the presents that weren't under that tree. He knew Sarah didn't expect much, but that wasn't the point. Presents would mean that *Père Noel* had come. Presents would mean her mother still remembered her, still loved her.

Either he was going to have to be Father Christmas, or Sarah would be disappointed again.

Then there was Mary. She probably didn't want anything. She certainly didn't expect anything, but for her, Christmas would be a new beginning. Especially with the baby. He wanted to give her something to celebrate that new beginning, but he couldn't think what. He certainly didn't have anything in his saddlebags. Even if he could find her share of the gold, that wouldn't be it either. What he wanted to give her couldn't be found under any tree, but he didn't allow himself to dwell on that.

He would go into town tomorrow and hope no one recognized him.

"Are you sure you have to go?" Mary asked next morning when he told her he was going into town.

"I've got a few things I need to buy before I leave. And I told Brother Samuel I'd see him in a couple of days. He's liable to come out here again if I don't show up."

She didn't care about Brother Samuel. She could put

up with a hundred of his visits as long as Joe was here. She was afraid he meant to ride out and never come back. She was afraid that going to town was only a ruse to cover his leaving forever.

"You've got to hurry back," Sarah said. "You don't want to miss Christmas."

"That's not for two days," Joe said. "That's enough time to go to Tucson and back."

"I don't want you to go to Tucson," Sarah said.

"I won't. Now be sure to milk Queen Charlotte, gather the eggs, and take care of your ma. She's not feeling too well."

Joe had noticed the moment he walked in the door. He always noticed.

"I'll leave Samson here to take care of you. Now I've got to be on my way. If I don't leave soon, I won't get back before midnight."

Mary felt some of the anxiety leave her. He wouldn't go off and leave his dog. He had to be coming back. But she didn't feel entirely reassured. She wouldn't be until she saw him riding back over the ridge.

CHAPTER FIVE

Pine Flat wasn't much of a town. There weren't any pines in it either. The town had been thrown up on a flat piece of desert between mountains. A dry wash ran along the base of the near ridge. The unpainted, weathered wood of the buildings stood out in stark contrast to the backdrop of orange-grey rock, pale-green cactus, and sapphire-blue sky.

Joe pulled the brim of his hat low over his face. He rode down the single street quietly and slowly. He didn't want to attract attention. It was after twelve o'clock. He'd timed it that way, hoping most people would be eating their midday meal. The fewer who saw him, the less chance there was of anyone recognizing him.

He stopped in front of Jones Emporium because it was the largest store in town. He wasn't sure what he wanted to buy. He didn't have much money. He had plenty in a bank in Denver, but he couldn't touch that. He wouldn't have any now if he hadn't been in the habit of keeping a little gold dust back every time he made a shipment. After breaking out of jail, he'd made a quick trip to his claim to dig up the gold before heading south.

He hoped the law still thought he was hiding somewhere in the Colorado mountains.

"Wish me luck," he said to General Burnside as he dismounted, "and keep your eyes open. If you see the law, go to bucking and whinnying for all you're worth. If they catch me now, they'll be auctioning you off before the month's out. No telling what kind of sidewinder might buy you."

Inside the store, four oil lamps suspended from the ceiling couldn't dispel a gloom made worse by dark wood and no windows. "Do you have any dresses for a six-year-old girl?" Joe asked a young female clerk.

"How big is she?"

Joe held his hand barely above his waist. "About this high."

"Over here," the young woman said, leading him to a table covered with dresses. She showed him three of the correct size, a blue serge, a yellow party frock, and a dark blue dress with a white pinafore.

Joe bought all three.

"You got anything to make a house look like Christmas?" he asked. "Red ribbon and stuff like that?"

"Not much," the girl said.

Joe bought ribbon, colored paper, and streamers of colored crepe paper to wrap around the tree.

That was when he found the set of paints.

"This all you got?" he asked. He opened the box. Inside were sixteen little compartments containing a rainbow of colors.

"It's the last one," the salesgirl said.

"I need some drawing paper."

He was in luck. They had several pads. He bought them all. He also bought a baby's rattle, a white dress the girl said could be used for a christening, and a thick blanket. His grandmother used to say all babies caught cold in the winter. He didn't want Mary's baby catching anything.

He also bought some canned fruit, a jar of jelly, a ham,

a side of bacon, and a sack of flour. He bought Sarah a box of bath powder and a mirror; he bought Mary a box of scented soap and a small cameo pin.

He also bought himself a coat. It would be a long, cold trip to California.

"You got quite a haul there," the man behind the counter said when Joe had added stick candy and a small box of chocolates to his pile.

"I don't get home much," Joe said. "Almost missed Christmas."

"They'll sure be glad to see you this time," the man said as he sorted Joe's purchases and added up the prices. "You'll want this wrapped up?"

"Good and tight," Joe said. "I'm on horseback."

"Better be a strong horse," the clerk said as he gave Joe the total.

Joe took out a small bag of gold dust. "Got some scales?"

"I'll have to get Mr. Jones," the clerk said.

Joe fidgeted while the clerk found the proprietor. He forced himself to remain outwardly calm while Hiram Jones peppered him with questions as he weighed out the proper amount of gold.

Joe was anxious to get out of town. He had drawn too much attention to himself by the amount of his purchases and paying in gold. He wanted to be gone before Mr. Jones and his clerks had a chance to spread the story.

He cussed aloud when, just as he had loaded his purchases and mounted up, Brother Samuel Hawkins came striding down the boardwalk. The man eyed Joe's bundles with suspicion.

"That seems like a lot to be carrying all the way to California," Brother Samuel observed.

"It's mostly Christmas presents for Mary and the kid," Joe said, damning Brother Samuel for his nosiness. "I decided I couldn't leave just now. Nobody likes to be alone at Christmas. Besides, with the baby coming, Mary hasn't been able to get to town to buy anything for the kid."

"*Mrs. Wilson* needed only to ask my sister or myself. We would have been more than happy to make any purchases for her."

Joe gathered up the reins and started General Burnside walking down the street. If the Reverend Brother Samuel wanted to talk to him, he was going to have to keep up.

"She probably didn't want to bother anybody. She'll most likely be mad enough to chew splinters when she sees what I've done. But I couldn't do anything else. Sort of in Pete's memory, you know."

The Reverend Brother looked as though he didn't like the answer but didn't know quite how to punch a hole in it. "My sister and I were planning to visit on Christmas."

"You come right ahead. I'm sure she'll be glad to see you. Now I gotta be going. General Burnside here is getting impatient to be home before dark."

"I believe my sister and I will come out this afternoon."

Joe pulled General Burnside to a halt and leveled a stony glance at Brother Samuel. "Now why would you be wanting to do a thing like that? You were just out there."

Brother Samuel didn't look quite so self-assured now. "I tried to explain how important it is to be scrupulous with Mrs. Wilson's reputation."

Joe could feel cold anger start to build in him. "There's nobody I know of doubting Mary except you."

"I don't doubt Mrs. Wilson!" Brother Samuel exclaimed.

"Sounds like it to me. I thought preachers were supposed to have faith in good people."

"Not everybody is so high-minded."

"Then I wouldn't care a whit about what they thought."

"I have to care," Brother Samuel announced. "I intend to ask Mrs. Wilson to marry me. My wife's reputation must be above reproach."

Joe glared at the preacher. He was a little beetle of a man, an insect dressed in black. How dared he think of touching Mary, much less marrying her. She was too good for him. He would be too stupid to know what he had found. He'd try to hedge her in with restrictions and rules and protocol and everything else he could think of to squeeze the life and soul out of her.

Joe didn't want Brother Samuel to marry Mary because he wanted to marry her himself.

"Mary's reputation is good enough for you or anybody else," Joe said, his anger rising. "I'll break the neck of any man who says otherwise."

"I said nothing like that! I merely said—"

"You've said too much. You'd better go home to your midday meal. Hunger is making you sound out of temper."

Joe turned his horse and nearly rode into the sheriff.

"Howdy," the sheriff said. "You're new in town, aren't you?"

It took Joe a moment to calm his anger enough to answer in an even voice. "Just passing through."

"You've got quite a load for a traveling man."

"Christmas," Joe said. "For friends."

Brother Samuel started to introduce the two men. The sheriff's name was Howells. "I just realized I don't know your name," Brother Samuel said to Joe.

"Hank Frazier," Joe said. "I used to be Pete Wilson's partner. Just stopped off to give my respects to his widow on my way to California."

"It's a sad thing to happen to a new bride," Sheriff Howells commented. "She hardly got here before her husband was killed. Then to find herself expecting a baby."

"The Reverend here seems to think he's the one to lend her a helping hand," Joe said.

"She could do worse," Sheriff Howells said. "Much worse."

"Well that's none of my concern," Joe said. "Nice to meet you, Sheriff, but I got to be on my way."

Joe pulled his hat a little lower on his head and walked General Burnside out of town. He couldn't decide which worried him more, the possibility that Mary might marry Brother Samuel or the chance that the sheriff had recognized him.

"This is what comes from getting hooked up with a woman," he told General Burnside. "Normally I wouldn't care who a pregnant woman married. Never cared two hoots about kids, especially little girls. Now look at me. I've spent nearly half my money, I still haven't found the gold, and I'm running around town talking to a sheriff who probably has my picture on his wall. Worst of all, I'm jealous of some beak-nosed fool who calls himself Brother Samuel Hawkins."

Joe rode for a few miles in silence.

"I can't marry her. Everything was against it from the start. It's done nothing but get worse since. Besides, who's to say she would have me? Any sensible woman would choose the Reverend Brother Samuel over me. Now that's a lowering thought. Samson would be laughing out of both sides of his mouth."

Of course women preferred almost any kind of man to an ex-convict. You couldn't get much lower than that without killing a man. And if Joe could have gotten his hands on Pete right after the conviction, he might have done that.

Joe was late getting back. Mary had expected him by mid-afternoon. It was dusk now, and there was still no sign of him. She knew she shouldn't try to milk the cow, but she needed to keep busy. It helped keep her mind off Joe's absence. And she needed to be outside, away from all the Christmas decorations.

"You sure he's coming back?" Sarah asked for the dozenth time. She was more worried about Joe than Mary was.

"Absolutely," Mary said. "Now help me down these steps. Queen Charlotte is probably in a fret to be milked by now."

Mary paused on her way across the yard to let a pain in her back pass. The pains had been getting worse all day. She had started to worry that something was wrong with the baby. It wasn't supposed to come for another month. Between worry about Joe and the baby and trying to reassure Sarah that Joe would be back, she was nearly frantic.

"He wouldn't leave Samson," she said to Sarah. "Now stop fretting and fetch the cow."

But when Mary reached the shed, she turned to the room where Joe slept. She stepped into the shadowy interior. She could see his bedroll spread out over the deep straw. She felt even closer to him here.

Without warning, a pain wrapped itself around her and squeezed until she was sure she would faint. Clutching her belly, she fell to her knees. The pain let up long enough for her to call for Sarah before it struck again. It was blinding in its intensity. She couldn't move. She couldn't think. She could only sink to the straw.

The baby was coming!

"Joe will be home soon," she told Sarah as the frightened child hovered over her. "Everything will be all right then."

By the time the cabin came into view, Joe had made up his mind to leave the next day. He had given up any hope of finding the gold. Maybe he could come back, but for now, his time had run out. Sooner or later people would forget him.

Even Mary.

He was surprised not to see a light in the cabin. It was only dusk, but it would be dark inside. It seemed unlikely that both Mary and Sarah would be taking a nap at this time of day.

He urged General Burnside into a trot. The packages bounced noisily, but he didn't slow down. He urged his horse into a canter when he saw the cow standing in front of the shed, lowing in distress.

Something was wrong. He was headed toward the house when he saw Sarah emerge from the shed.

"Where's Mary?" he called as he slid from the saddle.

"In the shed," Sarah said. The child looked badly frightened.

"What's wrong?" Joe said, heading toward the barn at a run.

"She fell down and can't get up again," Sarah said. "She said the baby's coming."

Inside the shed, Joe dropped to his knees next to Mary. He could hardly see her in the dim interior. "What are you doing here?"

"I can't move."

"I've got to get you inside. You can't have this child in a cow shed." Joe slid his arms under her. "Brother Samuel would have apoplexy."

Mary groaned when he picked her up. She groaned even louder when a pain struck.

"You had no business leaving the house," Joe said as he carried her across the yard. "Open the door, Sarah. And turn back the bed covers."

Mary moaned, but she seemed relieved to be inside.

"How long have you been in pain?"

"The really bad ones started this afternoon, but my back has been hurting ever since last night."

"You mean you were getting ready to have this baby this morning and you didn't tell me?"

"I didn't know. It's not due for another month. I thought I had a backache."

"How long is having a baby supposed to take?"

"It depends. Maybe five or six hours."

"You mean I don't have time to go back to town for Sister Rachel?"

"No," Mary said. The word was changed into a howl by the pain. "You're going to have to help."

"Me!"

"You and Sarah."

"But I don't know anything about having babies."

Mary tried to smile. "It pretty much happens by itself. All you have to do is keep telling me it will soon be over and that it'll all be worth it because I'll have a beautiful baby to show for it."

"Shouldn't I get hot water and things like that?"

"You won't need water until time to clean up."

Joe decided the baby had *better* come pretty much by itself. He was too dumbfounded to do anything but stand around wringing his hands. Mary was equally helpless as one pain after another gripped her in its coils.

"You're going to have to catch the baby," Mary managed to tell him between gasping breaths.

"In what?"

"Your hands."

Joe looked down at his hands as if he'd never seen them before and didn't know what they were for.

"Sarah will help you."

But Sarah was even more upset than he was. The poor

child didn't know what was happening. He couldn't help her. He didn't know what was happening, either.

Instinctively he reached out to take Mary's hand. She took hold of him as if he were a lifeline and she a drowning sailor. He had no idea a woman could be so strong. When the pain hit her and she squeezed his fingers, he expected to come away with a collection of broken bones.

He directed Sarah to gather towels, put water on to heat, and find the extra blankets. But each time the pain hit Mary, Sarah would stop, her gaze shifting between Joe and Mary. Only when the pain had passed and Mary's face was once again reasonably calm would she move.

Joe had never felt more helpless in his life. It was even worse than watching himself be convicted for a crime he hadn't committed. Then he had had his anger to sustain him, his plans for what he would do to Pete Wilson when he got out. Now he easily understood why men got drunk and left birthing babies to the women. Joe wasn't a drinking man, but he wished he had a drink right now. As Mary's pains got worse, he found himself wanting a whole bottle.

"Help me sit up a little," Mary said. "I need a pillow under my back."

Just as Joe slid his arms around Mary, she screamed in pain.

"What!" he said, jumping back. Sarah was hitting and kicking and scratching him for all she was worth.

Joe decided they had both gone mad.

"No!" Mary managed to say as the pain started to recede. "He's not hurting me."

Sarah didn't stop until Joe took her by the shoulder and pushed her away from him. Even then she would have bitten him if he hadn't jerked his hand back when he saw her go for him with bared teeth.

"It's all right," Mary said, reaching out to pull the child to her. "He's not hurting me. It's the baby."

"You mean she thinks I did that?" Joe asked.

"Her father used to hit her mother. I saw him hit Sarah once. I told him if he ever hit her again, or me, I'd kill him."

Joe looked at Sarah and felt anger surge through him. He wasn't proud of a lot of things he'd done, but he'd never hurt a child. "Why the hell did you think I'd hurt Mary?" he demanded.

"She doesn't," Mary assured him. "She's just frightened. She doesn't know what to think."

"Do I look like I'm beating her?" Joe demanded, his own worry finding release in anger.

Sarah stared up at him, frightened.

"I'm trying to help her have this baby," Joe said, "and I don't know what the hell I'm doing. I can't figure it out if I've got you biting and scratching like a bobcat."

"She won't," Mary said, hugging the child to her. "You won't, Sarah. I'm going to scream a lot more. Joe's helping. You've got to help too."

As though to prove her words, Mary went rigid and cried out. Joe jumped to her side, holding her hand, supporting her until the pain released its grip.

"The baby is almost here," Mary said. "See if its head is showing."

"Huh?" Joe said, stunned.

"See if it's showing. If it is, you've got to get ready for it."

"Can't Sarah do it?"

"No."

Joe had never been shy around women, but this was different. He felt that in some way he was violating Mary, and that went against his grain.

"What am I supposed to look for?"

"The muscles have to relax to allow the baby to pass. If you can see the top of its head, you know it will be born soon."

It was easy for Joe to clear his head of coherent thoughts. He didn't have any. To pretend he wasn't doing what he *was* doing was more difficult.

"I see it," he said, so excited he forgot his embarrassment. "I can see almost the whole top."

"Good," Mary said. "Then I might not die before it's born."

Another excruciating pain caused her to cry out.

"Hold her hand," Joe told Sarah. "I think it's getting ready to come."

It seemed to Joe that the pains came one right after another, giving Mary no time to rest or recover in between. Then it was all over, and he held a baby girl in his hands. He stared down at the child, unable to believe he had just witnessed the birth of another human being, the beginning of a brand-new life. He had looked like this once. So had Mary, Pete, and Sarah. Someday this baby would be a grown woman and have her own children.

It was amazing, incredible, unbelievable.

The baby's cry brought Joe out of his daze. "It's a girl," he said, handing the infant to her mother. "And she looks like you."

Mary was exhausted, but she managed a smile. "She doesn't look like anybody yet. But she's beautiful just the same."

"She's all messed up," Sarah said.

Mary laughed. "Yes, she is. Why don't you help Joe clean her up."

"Me!" Joe was counting himself lucky to have done nothing wrong so far. "I'll bring the water to you," he said. "I don't know a thing about washing babies."

"It's simple."

"Maybe, when I'm not shaking so much." He held his hand up in front of him. It was quivering.

Mary managed a weak smile. "Maybe you'd better let Sarah bring me the water."

Joe turned away from the bed and came up short. Samson sat by the door, his gaze following every movement. Outside, General Burnside and the cow stood with their noses to the window, their breath fogging the panes. They looked as if they had been watching the entire proceedings. "I forgot all about them," he said, turning to Mary. "The presents are still tied to the saddle, and Queen Charlotte hasn't been milked."

"Then you'd better take care of them," Mary said. "Sarah and I will try to have everything cleaned up by the time you get back."

Joe stumbled out the door, too dazed by the events of the last few hours to be aware of the cold or that Samson had followed him. Like a man in a trance, he caught up General Burnside's reins. Queen Charlotte followed on her own.

"Did you see what just happened?" he asked the animals. "Mary had a baby. It's a tiny little thing, so tiny you can hardly imagine it growing up into a real person."

He began to untie the ropes that held the packages to General Burnside's back.

"One minute there were just three of us. Next minute, there were four. A brand new person, just like that." He snapped his fingers.

Samson was sniffing the packages with particular attention to the ones containing the ham and bacon.

"She's got little tufts of black hair all over her head. She's all wrinkled up from being squeezed inside Mary. Can't be too much room inside a little woman like that, even for a tiny baby. Leave that alone," Joe spoke sharply to Samson. "That's Christmas dinner."

He put all the packages inside the shed and closed the door on Samson. He unsaddled General Burnside and turned him into the corral.

"Okay, it's your turn, Queen Charlotte." He patted her side as he settled himself on the milking stool. He looked again, then ran his hand carefully along her side. "Looks like you'll be having a little one come spring," he said, the streams of milk beginning to hit the pail with rhythmic smoothness. As the milk filled the pail, the high ping thickened until it more closely resembled a rip in a piece of fabric.

"You get busy on those coyotes," he said to Samson. "We can't leave any hanging around. We don't want Queen Charlotte here to lose another calf. And no telling what they might do to a baby girl. No, sir, you get up off your haunches and get going."

Almost on cue, a coyote yip-yipped somewhere in the hills close by. A second answered.

"See, I told you there was work to be done." But Samson had already disappeared into the night on silent feet, a growl deep in his throat.

Joe finished milking the cow and let her into the corral. He looked toward the house, at the light shining brightly through the window in the dark night, and felt a wonderful sense of peace. The horse and cow were in the corral, the chickens were safe in their pen, and it was warm and secure inside the house where Mary, Sarah, and the baby awaited his return. Everything he'd ever wanted was right here.

Only he had to leave.

But he couldn't, not until he was sure Mary and the baby were all right. He was worried about her. She looked so worn out. Sister Rachel was coming on Christmas. He couldn't leave until then.

Tomorrow was Christmas Eve. He had to help Sarah make a bow for the front door. And he wanted to see her open her presents on Christmas morning. He wanted her to have some pretty dresses, but the biggest reason for staying was to see the expression on her face when she unwrapped them.

He wanted her to know her mother still remembered her.

He'd stay until Christmas. Then he'd go.

CHAPTER SIX

Mary had never felt so happy or content. She held her daughter in her arms, the infant nursing contentedly. Sarah bustled about helping Joe fix breakfast for all three of them. Nothing more was needed to make Mary's life complete. It was all here in this small cabin.

She loved Joe. She was comfortable with that now. It would never change. But she knew he couldn't stay. It would mean capture and return to prison with very little chance that he would get out for a long time.

"Have you been thinking of a name for her?" Joe asked.

"I had several in mind."

"Like what?"

"Elizabeth. Anne. Ruth."

"They're such sober names. Don't you think a greedy little puss like her ought to have a different kind of name?"

The baby nursed with noisy, slurping sounds. "What did you have in mind?"

"I haven't known many good women, but I think Holly's okay."

"Holly," Mary said half to herself. "It is a nice name. It makes her sound strong, bright-eyed, and ready to fight if she needs to."

"Like right now."

Mary was changing Holly to the other side, and the infant screamed her anger at having her meal interrupted.

"I think Holly is a fine name," Mary said. "I'll always think of you when I call her name."

The silence that fell made them both painfully aware that their time together was drawing to a close.

"You haven't found the gold."

"No."

"What are you going to do?"

"Go to California. Somewhere else if I have to. Maybe after a while I can come back and look for it again."

She knew he wouldn't. If he didn't find it now, he would never come back.

"When do you have to go?" She didn't want to know the answer, but she had to ask.

"Christmas. I got a few presents in town."

Her eyes filled with tears. Her husband had caused him to be sent to jail. She had caused him to risk being caught. Still he had taken the time to buy presents for them. How could anybody believe he'd stolen that gold? "You didn't have to do that."

"It's not much, just some little things."

The baby finished eating. She rewarded Mary with an enormous burp. "That's what you get for eating too fast," Mary said, but her smile and tone turned her censure into words of love. "Here, why don't you hold her while I eat?"

"Me?" Joe said.

Mary smiled. He always seemed to be saying that, like there were things he'd never considered he could do. "She's a lot nicer to hold now than she was last night."

"I don't—"

"All you have to do is put her in the crook of your arm. Come here, and I'll show you."

Joe approached reluctantly.

"Put your arm across your chest," Mary said.

He did, and she placed the baby in his arm. He

immediately clamped her against his chest with his other arm. He was certain he would drop her before he made it to the chair so he could sit down. Holly looked up at him with the biggest black eyes he'd ever seen.

Joe walked to the chair with small, stiff-legged steps. He felt as if he'd never walked before, as if his legs had forgotten how. He practically fell into the chair. Holly continued to look at him with her big eyes.

"She ought to go to sleep in a few minutes," Mary said as she prepared to get up.

"Stay in that bed." Joe's order was so sharp that Holly started to cry. He held her a little closer and, miraculously, she stopped. "You're too weak to get up," he said in a hushed voice. "Sarah can bring your breakfast to you."

"I feel fine. I—"

"You can get up this afternoon. For now, you stay where you are."

Satisfied that Mary would remain in bed, Joe turned his attention back to Holly. Mary had dressed her in a soft flannel gown that was twice her size. She looked too small to be real. He rubbed her cheek with his callused finger. It was incredibly soft. She opened her mouth wide and yawned. She took hold of his finger with her hand. It looked absurdly small, too small to encircle his finger.

She closed her eyes but continued to hold on to his finger. He thought her pug nose was cute. He supposed it would grow to look like her mother's, but it was just the right kind of nose for a baby. He compared her fingers to his own. She had the same number of joints, the same wrinkles at the knuckles, fingernails—everything he had, only so much smaller.

She was asleep in his arms. It almost made him want to cry, and she wasn't even his kid.

Something turned over inside Joe. This was what he wanted—Mary, Sarah, and Holly. He wouldn't ask anything more of life if he could have that much. He understood love now. He could trust his feeling for Mary and hers for him. Holly had made him understand that he could love and be loved.

"You better give her to me," Mary said. "You need to find that gold."

Joe's gaze locked with hers. "If I do?"

"Then you won't have to leave."

Joe couldn't speak for a few minutes. "Are you sure? I've never had a family. I might not be good at it. I'll always be an ex-con."

"I don't care. I never met a man like you, Joe. I didn't think there was one. I don't know why you should be so different from Pete, my father, and all the other men I've known, but you are. Sarah knows it. Even Holly. Look at her sleeping. She knows she's safe as long as you're holding her."

Joe hadn't thought about it that way, but he knew there wasn't much he wouldn't do to protect this child. He managed to lever himself out of the chair without waking Holly. He handed her over to Mary.

"I'm going to make her a cradle. She ought to have a bed of her own. Then I'm going to turn this place inside out. I've still got twenty-four hours to look for the gold."

"Is Joe going to leave?" Sarah asked.

"I hope not," Mary said.

"Why can't he stay?"

Mary was reluctant to tell Sarah the truth, but she knew she would have to learn it some day. "Pete stole some gold and blamed Joe for it. They put him in jail. He broke out so he could find the gold and prove he didn't steal it. Pete buried the gold here, but Joe can't find it. He has to leave, or they will put him back in jail."

"Can't we go with him?"

Mary felt excitement leap within her. Why hadn't she thought of that? It was so simple, so obvious. "Would you want to go with him?"

"Joe's nice. I want him to be my papa. He said he would like having a little girl like me."

"I'm not sure he would let us go. Joe's a very proud man. He'd probably feel he couldn't share his name with us if he couldn't do it without fear of being put back in jail. If he could just find the gold, everything would be all right. Can you remember anything unusual Pete did when he came home?"

Sarah shook her head.

"I know you were afraid of him, but please try to remember. Anything might help Joe. Now you'd better finish cleaning up. I'm going to take a nap. I promised I'll be strong enough to help with dinner."

But Mary's thoughts weren't on dinner or getting stronger. She was trying to think of some way to convince Joe to take her and the children with him.

Joe had never built a cradle, but it wasn't a difficult task. There were tools for everything in the shed. He bet Pete had never used half of them. "We can't have Holly sleeping on Mary's bed," he said to Samson. The big dog sat watching everything he did. "She's pretty quiet now, but she won't be for long. She could roll right out of that bed."

He tested the bed. "The runner isn't smooth enough," he told Samson. "You can't expect a baby to go to sleep when you're bouncing it all to bits." He turned the cradle over and started to file down some of the ridges. "Of course she can't stay in this cradle forever. As soon as she's able to pull up, she'll have to have a crib. We don't want her falling out on her head."

Samson yawned.

"I know this isn't as exciting as hunting coyotes, but you don't have to be rude. Go talk to General Burnside if you're so bored."

But Samson just yawned again, rested his head on his paws, and continued to watch Joe.

"I think that'll do it," Joe said when the cradle finally rocked smoothly. "It doesn't look very fancy, but it'll give her a place to sleep." Joe picked up the cradle and started toward the cabin. "Well come on," he said to Samson when the dog didn't move. "I don't think Sarah's scared of you anymore. At least, she won't be if you behave yourself. Just go inside, lie down, and keep quiet."

Samson followed Joe into the house. Sarah did look a little apprehensive, but when the big dog lay down, she looked relieved.

"It didn't seem a good thing, the three of you sleeping in that bed together," Joe said as he set the cradle on the floor next to the bed. "Somebody could roll over on that baby and never know it."

Tears pooled in Mary's eyes. "That was very thoughtful of you, Joe."

"You want me to fix it for her now?"

"No, I'd rather hold her."

"Well, I'll be outside taking the place apart if you need me," Joe said as he backed out of the room. "Just give a yell if you need anything."

"Now, Samson," Joe said once they were outside, "I want you to put coyotes completely out of your mind and concentrate on gold. Unless you want to wear out your feet trotting all the way to California, we got to find it before nightfall."

The hours of the afternoon stretched longer and longer. Mary could hear Joe as he moved about the ranch, digging, sounding for hollow spaces, cursing when another idea proved to be as useless as all the previous ones. She found herself praying that he would find the gold. She knew she would never find another man like Joe. She could never love anyone else the way she loved him.

She marveled to herself. She had known him less than a week, yet it seemed they had always known each other. It was as if they were the missing halves of each other. Now that they were together, it was as though they had never been apart.

She looked down at Holly. She wanted more babies—Joe's babies.

"Did you find anything?" Mary asked Joe when he came in, a full milk pail in hand, to begin supper. She knew the answer, but she kept hoping he would say something to give her hope. She couldn't give up yet.

"No, but I got a few more places to look."

"It'll soon be dark."

"I can use a lantern."

"You're never going to find it, Joe. You know that."

"There's always a chance that—"

"If you haven't found it by now, you won't. You might as well accept it."

"I can't."

"Why?"

"Because it means I'll have to leave you."

"You could take us with you."

Joe turned sharply. "No."

"I wouldn't mind."

"I would. I couldn't have you following me all over the country, wondering if the law was going to catch up with me one day or the next."

"It would be better than never seeing you again. I love you, Joe Ryan. I never thought it would be possible to love anybody like I love you."

Joe fell down beside the bed, took Mary in his arms, and kissed her. "I love you. Too much to turn you into a vagabond."

"I won't mind."

"I know you'd try. You might even succeed, but you'd never like it. You long for stability, permanence, a feeling things will be the same tomorrow and the day after. It wouldn't be fair to Sarah and Holly, or any children we might have. I've been wandering since I was sixteen. It was hard for me even then."

"Then you've got to keep coming back until you do find the gold. Sarah and I will help look. You can't give up."

"Where is Sarah?" Joe asked.

"I don't know. I thought she was with you."

"I haven't seen her all afternoon. When did she leave?"

"While I was taking a nap."

"That was more than six hours ago."

"Did she take the pinto?"

Joe looked out the window. "He's not in the corral. I can't believe I didn't hear her leave."

"You were concentrating on finding the gold."

"I was wasting my time," Joe said. He turned to the stove. "If she isn't back by the time supper's ready, I'll go look for her. It's getting cold. Wouldn't be surprised if it freezes tonight."

Sarah returned before supper, but all she would say in response to where she'd been was, "I was looking for some branches to make a Christmas wreath."

"You have no business being gone by yourself so long," Joe said. "You nearly scared your mother out of a year's growth."

"Did I scare you out of a year's growth, too?"

Joe decided that things turning over inside him was going to be a regular occurrence as long as he was around Mary and Sarah. "You scared me out of two years," he said. "Look here," he said, pointing to the hair at his temples, "I'll bet you can see gray hairs."

Sarah looked. "No."

"Well, you will if you do anything like that again."

"I won't."

"Promise?"

"Promise."

They spent the rest of the evening decorating. Joe cut the crepe paper into thin strips and ringed the tree with them. Sarah made big bows out of the ribbon. Joe helped her tack these up on the windows. Then they made a wreath, wired several pine cones in it, tied a huge bow to the bottom, and attached it to the front door. Mary cut out scenes in colored paper, and they pasted them on the windows. By the time they finished, there was hardly a part of the cabin that didn't have some sign of Christmas.

"There's nothing left to do but put a lantern in the window, go to bed, and wait for Christmas morning," Joe said, rubbing his hands together.

"Are you sure *Père Noel* will find us?" Sarah asked anxiously.

"Sure," Joe said. "With that wreath on the door and the lantern in the window, he can't miss." Joe looked at

Mary. She was putting an extra blanket over Holly. The baby slept soundly in the cradle.

"I guess it's about time I said good night," he said.

Mary straightened up. "I don't want you to go."

"Mary, I already told you I can't—"

"I mean tonight. I don't want you to go tonight."

"But I can't sleep here. Brother Samuel would be horrified."

"The Devil take Brother Samuel."

"We can only hope," Joe murmured.

"If this is to be your last night, I want you to spend it with us."

Joe stood still. He'd been thrown out of many places in his life. People had turned their backs on him, but he'd never been invited in. He ought to go. If they came for him in the night, he'd be trapped here. Worse still, Mary's reputation would be ruined.

But he wanted to stay. More than anything in his whole life, he wanted to stay in this room with these people. If tonight was all he was to be granted, then he would take it.

"I'll put my bedroll by the door. That way—"

"I want you to sleep here," Mary said, patting the bed, "with Sarah and me."

"But you've just had . . . Sarah won't . . . Sister Rachel would fall down in a dead faint if she knew."

"I'm not asking for anything more than to be near you."

"Are you sure?"

"Absolutely."

"Okay, but I'll sleep on top of the covers."

Joe was prey to so many conflicting emotions, he hardly knew what he felt. He had never slept with a woman without touching her. He vowed he'd cut off his right hand before he touched Mary. She'd just had a baby, for God's sake. Besides, he was leaving tomorrow. He couldn't make love to her, then walk out of her life. Maybe other men could, but he couldn't.

And he knew he wouldn't be back. He would never find the gold. He accepted that now. Without the gold, he could never ask Mary to be his wife. He couldn't accept that. Something inside wouldn't let him give up. Maybe he could look again in the morning. Maybe he could come back in a few months.

Maybe.

But all he had—all he might ever have—was this night. He moved closer to Mary, reached out, and took her hand in his. He felt as if he was fighting for his share of her attention. Holly wouldn't settle down. Finally he released Mary's hand, put his arm around her, and pulled her to him. Holly settled between her breasts and went to sleep. Sarah reached up to take hold of the hand Joe had around Mary's shoulder. In moments she was asleep as well.

"This wasn't what I had in mind," Mary whispered as she clasped Joe's free hand.

"Me, either," Joe whispered back. He kissed her hair. "But I wouldn't trade it for anything in the world."

It was far more than he had expected. So much less than he wanted. He told himself to concentrate on the moment. It was warm and wonderful. It just might be enough to last him for a lifetime.

Mary woke when Holly began to stir. She fed the baby before her cries woke Joe or Sarah. Even in sleep, Sarah held tightly to Joe's hand. Mary wanted to do the same thing for the rest of her life. Joe had gone to sleep with his head on her shoulder. She felt almost crushed by the love that surrounded her.

And it all came from Joe.

Joe woke at dawn. The cabin was cold. Taking care not to wake Mary, Sarah, or the baby, he eased out of bed. Still in his stockinged feet, he opened the stove and began to lay a fire. "Shut up, Samson," he said when the dog started to whine. "I'll let you out shortly."

In a few minutes he had water on for coffee. He looked outside. The ground was covered with a light dusting of snow. It was closer to a white Christmas than he had ever had growing up. He shoved his feet into his boots, grabbed the milk bucket, and eased the door open on silent hinges he'd oiled two days ago.

The frozen ground crunched under his feet. "Queen Charlotte's just going to love getting milked this morning," he said to Samson, who frisked about, his breath making clouds in the frigid air.

The cow did mind being milked, but Joe milked her under the shed out of the wind. She showed her appreciation by kicking only once. Joe set the milk on the porch. "Let the cream rise to the top and freeze. Used to do that back in Carolina," he told Samson. "Sweetest cream you ever did taste." He fed and watered General Burnside, then got his presents from the shed.

Mary was at the stove slicing bacon when he entered the cabin, loaded with presents. She stopped, her knife suspended in midair. "What have you got there?" she asked.

"Just a few things I thought you and Sarah might like."

Mary put her knife down, went to the trunk, and opened it. She took out a handmade doll and a pair of white shoes. "I couldn't afford to buy anything but the shoes. I was going to make her a dress."

"It doesn't matter. I got her some."

Mary watched as Joe stuffed each of Sarah's shoes as full as he could get with powder, a mirror, candy, ribbons, and all the little things the girl in Jones Emporium assured him a little girl would want. "So that's why you risked going to town."

"No, it isn't. I—"

Mary put her hands on his shoulders, stood on tiptoe, and kissed him hard on the lips, her knife dangerously close to his jugular.

"Don't tell lies, not even little ones. It's Christmas."

The word worked its magic, and Sarah and Holly woke up at the same time.

Sarah's gaze went straight to the tree. She rubbed her eyes, looked, and rubbed them again. "*Père Noel* really did come," Sarah said, staring at her shoes.

"I told you he wouldn't miss the light in the window," Joe said. "Now you can't open anything until after breakfast. I'll take that while you feed the baby," Joe said, removing the knife from Mary's hand. "Sarah, you can set the table."

Joe tried not to think that this was the last time he would sit down to eat with Mary and her family. He tried to tell himself this was the high point of his stay. He would concentrate on enjoying it. He would have more than enough time to think about what he would be missing.

Joe gave Mary the rattle, dress, and blanket for Holly. Sarah emptied her shoes, exclaiming over everything she found. But when she opened the package Joe handed her with the three dresses inside, she shrieked so loudly that he thought she didn't like them. She bounded up, threw herself across the room, and hugged him until he thought he couldn't breathe.

"Every pretty little girl ought to have a dress," Joe said. "I just bought you a couple of spares. Here, put this one on," he said, handing her the party dress. "And don't forget to powder yourself real good," Joe said as Sarah retreated behind the curtain. "I like my little girls to smell good."

"You shouldn't have spent all your money on us," Mary said, her eyes filling with tears.

"I bought myself a coat. I've got plenty left."

"You're telling lies again."

"Enough, then." He reached back into the welter of brown paper and handed Mary the box of scented soaps. While she was thanking him for that, he handed her the books of drawing paper, the pens, and ink. Before she had recovered completely, he handed her the set of colored paints.

She just sat there, her hand over her mouth, tears pouring down her cheeks.

"Next Christmas, I want every one of those drawings to be in color," he said, a huskiness in his voice. He cleared his throat. "Christmas should never lack color, even in Arizona."

"Oh, Joe," Mary said, and threw her arms around him.

Joe found himself hugging Mary and Holly at the same time. Holly objected. Loudly.

"Be quiet, child."

"No, she's right," Joe said, pulling back. "No point pretending. We've got to face up to it. This is the last we'll see of each other for a time."

"Joe," Sarah said.

But Joe didn't answer her. Mary was clinging to him, and he couldn't summon the willpower to let her go. He buried his face in her hair, willing himself to remember this moment forever.

"Why won't you let us go with you? It won't be a hardship, not like it will be living here without you."

"Mary, I already explained why I can't do that."

"Joe," Sarah called.

"Just a minute," Joe said to her. He wanted to memorize the feel of Mary in his arms, the smell of her. "I'll come back, I promise. Maybe by then you can remember something that will help, but I can't take you with me while this stolen gold is hanging over my head."

"Joe."

"What is it?" Joe said, finally turning to Sarah. "Can't you see—" Joe froze. Sarah was dressed in her party dress, a ribbon in her hair, the white shoes on her feet. She was beautiful. She looked like a little angel.

But that wasn't what mesmerized him. She was holding her hands up toward him. In them was a bag of the missing gold.

"Can you stay now? Can you be my papa?"

CHAPTER SEVEN

Mary saw them long before they turned into the yard—Brother Samuel and Sister Rachel, accompanied by Sheriff Howells. She wrapped the baby in Joe's blanket, put her in her crib, and put on water for coffee. She threw a heavy woolen shawl, the last of Joe's presents, over her shoulders and met them at the door.

"You poor woman," Sister Rachel exclaimed as soon as she stepped inside, "we came the moment the sheriff told us." She threw her arms around Mary and embraced her.

"To think you've been alone with him all this time," Brother Samuel said.

"Saints preserve us!" Sister Rachel exclaimed, patting Mary's flat stomach. "What happened to the baby?"

"She's asleep in her crib," Mary said. "Apparently I miscalculated when she was due."

"But how . . . who . . . when?"

"Two days ago. Joe and Sarah helped me."

"You let that strange man, that *criminal*, help you!" Brother Samuel exclaimed.

"I didn't have much choice. He found me in the shed unable to get up."

"Poor woman. And all the time you didn't know what he was."

"I know exactly what he is," Mary said, proud, calm, and happy. "He's the man I'm going to marry."

Sister Rachel and Brother Samuel practically threw Mary down in a chair. "Having the child so unexpectedly must have brought on brain fever," Sister Rachel said.

"He's an escaped convict, Mrs. Wilson," Sheriff Howells added.

"Suppose he didn't steal that gold?" Mary asked. "Would you have to take him back?"

"Well, I don't know. He did break jail."

"But he broke out so he could find the gold and prove he didn't steal it. Wouldn't that be reason enough not to send him back?"

"If he can come up with the gold, the transport company would drop the charges. They'd probably give him a reward, too."

"That's a perfectly absurd question," Brother Samuel said. "Of course he has to go back to jail."

"I never trusted him, not from the first," Sister Rachel said.

But Mary wasn't to be sidetracked by Brother Samuel or Sister Rachel.

"So if he can return the gold and prove he didn't steal it, do you promise not to send him back to Colorado?"

"Yes, ma'am, but I can't promise Colorado won't still charge him with breaking jail."

"But why should he be punished for that when he shouldn't have been in jail in the first place?"

"You got a point there, ma'am. I think we could work things out. Of course, he might have to go up there a while later to talk to some people, but I don't imagine they'd hold anything against him. If he can prove he didn't steal that gold, that is."

Mary got to her feet. "How about coffee? I've made a new pot."

Joe had expected to see Brother Samuel's buggy in front of the cabin, but he wasn't surprised to see the sheriff's horse as well. He balanced the strong box across the saddle in front of him. His and Mary's gold was safely stowed in the bottom of his saddlebags.

"How did you know where to find the gold?" he asked Sarah, who rode beside him.

"Papa showed me the cave once. He threatened to put me in it if I was bad."

"Why didn't you tell me last night?"

"I wanted to surprise you."

"You sure did that."

"Are you going to be my papa now?"

"It depends on what the man riding that horse says." Joe pulled up in front of the house. The sheriff and Brother Samuel came out to meet him.

"You want to give me a hand with this box?" Joe asked.

"That the stolen shipment?" the sheriff asked as he came down the steps.

"Yes."

"Where did you find it?"

"I didn't. Sarah did."

"Papa hid it in a cave," Sarah said.

"How did you know?" The sheriff took the box from Joe. Joe dismounted and helped Sarah down.

"Last night Mama said Joe would have to go away if he couldn't find the gold. She told me to try to think of everything Papa did when he was home that time. That's when I remembered him sneaking out of the house."

Mary came down the steps. "You called me Mama."

Sarah threw her arms around Mary's neck. "Joe said you'd like it."

"I do," Mary said, hugging the little girl tight to her chest. "I like it very much."

"Pete set me up," Joe explained to Sheriff Howells. "But he was killed before he could come back and get the gold. It's all there. See for yourself."

Mary came to stand by Joe, one arm around him, the other resting on Sarah's shoulders. "The sheriff says you won't have to go back to Colorado. He said you can stay here."

"You sure about that?" Joe asked.

"I don't see why not. They've got their money back. The way I see it, they owe you something for being locked up all that time."

"You think I can get that conviction taken off my record? I don't want my kids' pa to have a record."

"Ought to be able to do that, too."

Joe turned to Brother Samuel. "I want you to marry us."

"Right now?" Sister Rachel asked. It was almost a shriek.

"Yes, right now," Mary confirmed.

Brother Samuel looked horrified. "I can't do that."

"Why not?" Joe asked. "You're a preacher, and you have two witnesses."

"You don't have a license."

"Please," Mary asked.

"I can't without a license," Brother Samuel repeated, looking belligerent.

"Mary can't travel into town for a while yet," Joe said. "And I don't intend to set one foot off this ranch until she does. Unless you want me to ruin that reputation you were so worried about, you'll marry us right now."

"It wouldn't be right. I can't—"

"Oh, shut up, Samuel, and marry them," the sheriff

said. "We can make out the license when we go into town. I'll bring it out tomorrow. I think we've caused this man enough trouble as it is."

"I still can't believe it," Mary said that evening as she snuggled down next to Joe. "I swore I'd never get married again. Wait until I tell my family."

Holly was asleep in her cradle. Over in the corner, Sarah had burrowed deep into Joe's bedroll. Samson lay next to her. Joe and Mary occupied the bed alone.

"I'm not sure Brother Samuel believes it, and he married us."

"Poor man. I thought he would choke on the words. He looked miserable."

"Not half as miserable as you'd have been if you'd married him."

"I never would."

"Let's forget about Brother Samuel and Sister Rachel. From now on, it's just you and me."

"And Sarah and Holly."

"And General Burnside and Samson."

"And Queen Charlotte and her calf-to-be."

There seemed to be no end to the love that surrounded Joe. But that was the way it ought to be. Love was what Christmas was really about.

LEIGH GREENWOOD

The freedom of the range, the bawling of the longhorns, the lonesome night watch beneath a vast, starry sky—they got into a woman's blood until she knew there was nothing better than the life of a cowgirl . . . except the love of a good man.

Born and raised on the Broken Circle Ranch, Eden never expected to fall head over heels for the heir to a British earldom. As the youngest of the Maxwell clan, she was used to riding her mustang across the plains, not a carriage through Hyde Park, and she'd sooner have coffee from a chuck wagon than tea in a society drawing room. But there was one thing London offered that was not to be found in all the Lone Star State: A man who captured her heart and thrilled her senses. Now the only challenge was convincing him to try love, Texas style.

Texas Loving

ISBN 13: 978-0-8439-5686-3

LYNSAY SANDS

The BRAT

All the knights have heard tales of Lady Murie, King Edward III's goddaughter. It is said she is stunningly beautiful. It is also said that the king dotes on the girl and spoils her rotten.

But there is more to Murie than meets the eye, and Sir Balan soon learns that he'll be lucky indeed to deserve such a bride. Yet he is not the only one to discern the truth, and the other hopeful hubby is not quite as honorable. Soon will come a reckoning, a time to show who is chivalrous, who is a cad…and who has won the love of a heart unspoiled.

ISBN 13: 978-0-8439-5501-9

Sky Brewster's heart cries out for justice,
and she will not be satisfied until she sees her
husband's murderer dead at her feet. To get the job done,
she'll leave her Sioux people to make a devil's bargain with a
man whose talent as an assassin is surpassed only by his skills
at seduction.

Max Stanhope is an infamous English bounty hunter who
always delivers—dead or alive. But now he must take a wife
to claim his birthright. When his newest client turns out to
be as delectable as she is passionate, he figures he'll mix business with pleasure.

The beautiful widow and the Limey make a deal: her hand
in marriage for his special skills. But an old Cheyenne medicine man has seen the Great Spirit's grand design, and True
Dreamer knows Sky Eyes of the Sioux is destined to love
the...

PALE MOON STALKER

ISBN 13: 978-0-8439-6112-6

DAWN MacTavish

The battle that won Robert Mack his scars was lost in the cradle, and thus the third Laird of Berwickshire wore his silver helm not for personal protection but the sake of others. While the right side of his face was untouched—handsome, even—the left lay in ruin. No man could look upon him without fear. Nor could any woman. Such a life was worse than any prison, so Robert set out for Paris and the great healer Nostradamus.

The powerful young Scot reached a land in conflict. With a boy on its throne and her people at war, all of France was shadows, intrigue and blood. All except for Violette Cherier, a blind flower girl with honey-colored hair, as beautiful and fragile as her namesake. Soon enough, what at first seemed Robert's unwise act of kindness proved sage. The fires of civil war were rising, and Violette was the only one who could free the...

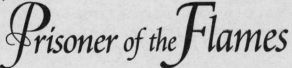

Prisoner of the Flames

ISBN 13: 978-0-8439-5982-6

Alissa Johnson

"A joyous book from a bright star." —Kathe Robin, *RT BOOKreviews*

As Luck Would Have It

A WOMAN OF THE WORLD...

After years of wild adventures overseas, Miss Sophie Everton is in no hurry to return home to the boring strictures of the ton. But she's determined to reclaim her family's fortune—even if she has to become a spy for the Prince Regent to do it.

A MAN ON A MISSION...

Before she can get her first assignment, she lands right in the lap of the dark and dashing Duke of Rockeforte. She's faced hungry tigers that didn't look nearly as predatory. Somehow the blasted man manages to foil her at every turn—and make her pulse thrum with something more than just the thrill of danger.

AND THE FICKLE FINGER OF FATE

To make a true love match, they'll have to learn to trust in each other...and, of course, a little bit of luck.

Available October 2008!   ISBN 13: 978-0-8439-6155-3

☐ **YES!**

Sign me up for the Historical Romance Book Club and send my FREE BOOKS! If I choose to stay in the club, I will pay only $8.50* each month, a savings of $6.48!

NAME: _____

ADDRESS: _____

TELEPHONE: _____

EMAIL: _____

☐ I want to pay by credit card.

☐ **VISA**   ☐ MasterCard.   ☐ DISCOVER

ACCOUNT #: _____

EXPIRATION DATE: _____

SIGNATURE: _____

Mail this page along with $2.00 shipping and handling to:
Historical Romance Book Club
PO Box 6640
Wayne, PA 19087
Or fax (must include credit card information) to:
610-995-9274

You can also sign up online at **www.dorchesterpub.com**.

*Plus $2.00 for shipping. Offer open to residents of the U.S. and Canada only. Canadian residents please call 1-800-481-9191 for pricing information.

If under 18, a parent or guardian must sign. Terms, prices and conditions subject to change. Subscription subject to acceptance. Dorchester Publishing reserves the right to reject any order or cancel any subscription.